HEALING THE DEAD

D. F. BAILEY

*For my mother and father,
and Linda and Joan*

Vinci Books

vinci-books.com

Published by Vinci Books Ltd in 2026

1

Copyright © D.F. Bailey 2013

The author has asserted their moral right to be identified as the author of this work in accordance with the Copyright, Designs and Patents Act 1988. This work is a work of fiction. Names, characters, places and incidents are the product of the author's imagination or are used fictitiously. Any resemblance to actual persons, living or dead, places and incidents is entirely coincidental.

All rights reserved. No part of this publication may be copied, reproduced, distributed, stored in any retrieval system, or transmitted in any form or by any means, including photocopying, recording, or other electronic or mechanical methods, nor used as a source for any form of machine learning including AI datasets, without the prior written permission of the publisher.

The publisher and the author have made every effort to obtain permissions for any third party material used in this book and to comply with copyright law. Any queries in this respect should be brought to the attention of the publisher and any omissions will be corrected in future editions.

A CIP catalogue record for this book is available from the British Library.

Paperback ISBN: 9781036703493

The EU GPSR authorised representative is Logos Europe, 9 rue Nicolas Poussion, 17000 La Rochelle, France
contact@logoseurope.eu

By D.F. Bailey

Standalone Thrillers

Healing the Dead
Exit From America
Fire Eyes
The Good Lie

Will Finch Mystery Thriller Series

Five Knives (Prequel)
Bone Maker
Stone Eater
Lone Hunter
Second Life
Open Chains
Run Time
White Sphere
Burnt Embers

And when He thus had spoken
He cried with a loud voice
"Lazarus come forth."
And he that was dead came forth
bound hand and foot with grave clothes.
— John II, 43-44

Chapter One

The day that Brad died Rose Sykes had been thinking about war. She sat on her bed and gazed at the rain as it danced against her window. She thought about Flanders Fields and about the millions of worms that would have been there in 1918. Miss Kirby had told her class all about Flanders Fields as part of the Regal Road School Remembrance Day ceremony but it was her sister Jayne who'd told her about the worms; that when you died the worms took over and ate you.

"But how do the worms get into the coffins?" Rose asked. She knew that worms could eat wood but surely they wouldn't gnaw through all the soldiers' coffins. Not through thousands and thousands all at once.

"They don't gnaw through the coffins," Jayne explained. "Besides, they didn't get coffins in the war. They just dumped the dead into the ground, raw."

"Come off it."

"I'm serious!" Jayne frowned and shook her head. "See,

the worms don't come from the outside. They're already living in the soldiers' stomachs."

Rose stared at her sister. For a moment she didn't follow.

"And when the soldiers die, the worms eat their way out."

Rose almost threw up. It was tricky but she choked the bile back. The vomit toyed with her stomach all day. She could feel it rising and falling but in the end she forced it down, certain that confronting the sight of her own worms would be worse than spewing up.

Rose watched the tiny rain tracks on the window, each one squiggling along the glass, squirming downwards in mindless frenzy. She shouldn't watch this, she told herself. The worms were too sneaky. They knew how to get inside her.

"Rose. David."

She turned her head. Her mother's voice calling them.

"Brad and Susan Watson are here. Come on down. You can play in the basement."

She stood up and stared at the window. Then she forced herself to bend forward and push her nose against the inside of the glass.

"Rose, come on, the Watsons are here!"

After a moment her nose felt wet and cold. She reached over and pulled the flowered curtains across the window.

Once he got down to the basement, David scanned the room for something to do. He opened the drapes to the playroom window and looked at the rain sheeting across the glass. He put on a record, Jayne's latest favorite, Elvis Presley.

David's cowboy outfit lay next to the sofa. While

everyone else was singing "You Ain't Nothing but a Hound Dog," he slipped on the cowhide vest and chaps and pulled the six-shooter from the holster and started firing at Rose and Susan. He didn't have any of the small, circular caps that fit snugly against the flat end of the plastic bullets. With the caps doubled against the bullet casings, he could make the gun blasts echo through the basement and the room fill with the acrid grey smoke that plumed from the barrel. The gun hammer snapped as he shot the girls from the sofa, the TV, the wooden box that held his erector set.

"Oh, Davy, knock it off!" Rose lifted her head into the air. She turned up the volume on the record player to drown the sound of her brother's gun.

"Not me!" he yelled, and he burst into a chant that he'd heard in the Regal Road school yard:

Shoot 'em up and shoot 'em down
the dead don't laugh and
the dead don't frown.

"David!" Rose cranked up the volume all the way. Brad and Susan started laughing and so did David. He thought Rose was going to break into tears. But instead of crying, she tugged on his cowboy hat. Her face turned flat and pale, and she grabbed the gun from her brother's hand and started shooting at him. Her long red hair danced wildly as she fired, and the gun jumped closer to his head with every shot.

"Stop it!" He covered his face and felt himself backing against the TV.

"Pow! Pow!" Her red curls shook and her face hardened.

"I said stop!" David was sure she wanted to kill him. He

didn't mean to cry, but the tears broke loose and he began to wail.

"Now what's all this?" His mother had heard the crying from the kitchen. "And please turn that awful noise off." To Catrina, "Hound Dog" was noise, not music. Fortunately, the record player came with an oversized volume knob that could shut Elvis down in one flick of the wrist. She turned off the record and glanced from child to child. "If you kids can't play together, then you should think about playing alone — in your own rooms."

Everybody frowned. Catrina's chief form of punishment was isolation. And she could make it last hours, sometimes days; however long it took the guilty to apologize.

"All right. I'm sorry." Rose looked down at the tattered fringe at the end of the rug and then over to her brother. She hated this.

"Don't tell me," her mother said shaking her head. "You owe the apology to your brother." She always worked it out this way, pushing them back together one step at a time.

"I'm sorry, David." Rose's cheeks were red. Burning. She turned her nose into the air and locked her eyes on the ceiling tiles.

"Good." Catrina thought of asking her children to kiss at this point, but she stopped herself short when Brad crossed his eyes, rolled across the sofa and moaned.

"Bananas!" he cried, but it was muffled in the cushions.

"Now, I'll go get a box of clothes and some other dressups," she said, "and you kids can pretend it's Hallowe'en."

"But Hallowe'en's still six months away, Mom." Rose glanced at Susan, then back to her mother.

"And if you're really good," she said, raising one finger in the air, "I'll give costume prizes in one hour."

"All right!"

Healing the Dead

Within minutes Catrina found the box of play clothes and carted them downstairs to the playroom, and everyone tried on old shirts and jackets, worn hats and faded ties. Then she gave Rose's camera to David and asked him to take some pictures.

David had become used to the Kodak, a Brownie Bull's-Eye, with its L-shaped flash attachment. He surprised everyone by taking candid shots of people, a talent that depended on his knack for sneaking up on them. He'd got a snapshot of his father picking his nose, a picture he wanted to show Grampy. But Jayne said that was grotesque — the sickest idea she'd heard in a century — so he burned the picture instead, fascinated by the green flare that erupted from the chemical finish.

Rose and Susan dressed in long, pleated skirts Catrina had saved since the war. David mounted the flash attachment and took pictures of the girls whirling around the room as they danced cheek to cheek like Fred Astaire and Ginger Rogers. But there wasn't much for the boys to wear.

David loaned Brad his cowboy vest that had a tin star sewn over the heart, but he didn't want to give up his chaps or hat or especially the six-shooter. Then Brad got an idea.

"I know!" He slapped his hands together. "I'll get some stuff from our place!"

"Just what do you think you'll get at our house?" Clinging to the arms of the Invisible Man, Susan flitted her eyelashes and swooped around the record player.

"Just wait and see!" With David following, Brad ran up the basement stairs to the back door and pulled on his rain jacket. David watched him run across the yard and through the hole in the bushes that separated their homes. Then he shut the door carefully and looked at his mother in the kitchen.

5

She was making pastry, and the brisk energy of her hands pressing the dough out on the counter gave him a sense of comfort. He detached the flash from the camera and took a picture of her like that, without her knowing, and went downstairs to the girls.

Twenty minutes later Brad came back with a paper bag stuffed with costumes, disguises, medals. But before he could empty it onto the floor, the lights began flickering and a roll of thunder cracked through the air and rumbled into the basement.

When the lights cut out completely, Brad had another idea. "I know, let's play Mob!" He shook the rain drops from his brush cut and pulled an old felt hat from the bag and slipped it onto his head. Raising his hands every time he described a new detail, Brad explained the rules for Mob. The four of them had to pair up, gangsters and molls, and then have a shoot-out to see who could control the basement.

"All right. But we get to choose our clothes first." Rose and Susan dug into Catrina's clothes basket and pulled out blouses, hats, garters.

Then they went into the little bathroom next to the playroom to change.

As the lights flickered and thunder burst over the house, they laughed and whimpered. David felt chills running through his stomach. He wondered if the lightning would slash out of the sky and strike right through the basement window.

But Brad was fearless. He drew David towards him and opened the bag. Inside was a knife, a German dagger in a black leather sheath. He tugged off the cowboy vest and cinched on a soldier's belt. "The Mob were knife artists," he whispered, slipping the dagger into his belt. "You should see what else I got in here."

David realized that Brad had been into his father's trunk, a wooden trunk full of war souvenirs locked in the attic above Brad's bedroom. David had never seen the trunk itself, but he had seen the padlock key that Brad had found.

"Look at these." Brad held some old medals and buttons that looked brand new, as though they'd just been awarded to a regiment out on parade. "And this," he whispered as he pulled the dagger from its sheath. It was a knife made for killing: serrated teeth ran up one edge of the blade, perfect for cutting through enemy bone, and David imagined the steel shaft sinking between two bands of ribs into a bulging heart. My heart, he thought, and his teeth bit lightly into his lip.

The lights cut out again, and the girls screamed from the toilet. There were no windows to the little bathroom that their father had built between the furnace and hot water tank, so Rose opened the door to see what she was doing.

"Everyone all right?" Catrina called from the top of the stairs.

"Sure!" Brad called back to her. "We're playing Mob!"

"Okay. If you need a flashlight, just let me know."

The girls came back into the grey light of the playroom and stood together in their moll-wear. Except for the brown felt hat pulled over his forehead, Brad was dressed as a soldier. David was a mix of cowboy and Indian.

"Okay, grab your weapons." Brad tightened the cinch on his soldier belt. "Susan and I'll make a break for the east side of town. When you're ready, come for us!" He grabbed Susan by the wrist and dragged her towards the laundry room. A flash of lightning cut against the wall as they slipped out of sight.

"Weapons?" Rose frowned a little when she realized that she was going to have to be David's moll. "What kind of weapons do we have?"

"Brad's got a German dagger." David eased his six gun in and out of its holster. "But I don't think Susan's got anything."

"Yes, she does. She's got a gun." Rose bent over the bag and peered at Brad's supplies in the half-light. "She's got your old water pistol that you always leave next to the toilet."

"Cripes." He wondered whether she'd loaded it with toilet water. The last thing he wanted was a blast in the head from the pee bowl.

"Okay! Come and get us!" Brad's voice echoed across the hall from the preserve cellar. David knew instantly where they were hiding. The small room was built like a concrete cell and his mother used it to store preserves and root vegetables.

"All right," he whispered to Rose. "Now be very quiet." Even though Rose was three years older, she knew nothing about guns or fighting or the element of surprise. But David had carefully studied the art of war. Not only could he creep through the house without making a sound, he had watched countless TV westerns and seen dozens of barefoot attacks led by the Sioux Indians.

"So what am I supposed to use?" She frowned at her brother and rummaged through Brad's bag.

"Quiet!" He yanked the bag from her quickly, dipped his hand inside and pulled out a small pistol. "Here. Just take anything," he said and scouted the way toward the preserve cellar.

"Hey, what is this?" she asked. A flash of lightning danced against the wall and David could see her holding the pistol.

"Ssshh." He could hear Brad and Susan giggling just ahead of them.

"Okay." Rose was beside him now. "I was just asking."

"Look, I'll go over to the ping-pong table and come at them from the washing machine." He whispered right into her ear so that no one else could hear a breath of it. "Then you give me the signal when you're ready and we'll have them in a crossfire." David had just learned about crossfire tactics from a new *Hopalong Cassidy* show.

"What signal?"

"Hoot owl." He cupped his hands over his mouth to show her. "Whoot-whoot, whooo."

She laid her pistol on the stairs and tried the call. David noticed how shiny the gun was. Even in the dark it seemed bright. And it was small, the size that would slip into a moll's silk purse. "Ooo-oot," she called with her hands bunched over her lips. "This is nuts. Forget it."

"How 'bout if I just say 'now' when *I'm* ready?" He drew his revolver from its holster and raised it in the air. "Okay?"

"Oh, all right." Rose was getting bored; she felt pressed into a stupidity that made her angry. She decided to play one game of Mob and then she'd quit. She fingered the pistol trigger and waited.

"Here I go!" David took a deep breath and slipped into the laundry room and hid behind one of the concrete pillars that supported the house. At the same time a series of lightning flashes pulsed through the windows. But there was no sound of thunder, just the light alone. Then he heard Susan giggling; they were in the preserve cellar all right. He inched over to the door and quietly pulled it open. More giggles. He tiptoed back to the edge of the ping-pong table and lay on the floor. If he shot them from the floor it would come as a surprise. By the time they realized his angle he could plug both of them. Lightning flickered around the room again and he realized that if he didn't make a move soon they'd spot him. He waited for a period of calm. There was no more thunder at all, just the light flashing. Flash, flash, flash. Then it stopped.

"Now!" he screamed and started blasting them with his gun. "Bang, bang, bang!"

Brad pulled a cap gun out of his pants and fired three rounds from the preserve room. Then, shooting as he ran, he stormed into the laundry room with the Nazi knife held high above his head. Susan was right behind him, laughing, squirting toilet water into the air with the water pistol.

It was just what David hoped they'd do — blunder out into the open so he could nail them in the crossfire. "Fire!" he yelled to Rose. "Now."

Rose stepped into the room with the gun pointing straight ahead. David thought it was strange, somehow cartoonish, the way she looked, like a shadow in the grey light of the basement, a robot wound up and stepping ahead metal-legged, brittle, mindless. Then the whole room exploded with the sound of her gun. And then she fired a second shot.

Later on, from the way the bullet matched the shell casing, the police said they could tell it was the second shot that hit him — banged through Brad's nose into his brain and out the back of his head.

And it was the second shot that got Rose, too. It drove her half crazy wondering why she fired twice.

Chapter Two

Jayne stood in David's bedroom and listened to the sound of the wind slipping through the hairline cracks in the windows. His room had been converted from a solarium adjacent to their parents' bedroom. Three windows filled the south wall and two others butted together on the southeast corner. She pulled the curtains half open and looked across the yard to the Watson's house. Their screen door had been left ajar, and it swung noisily as the wind played it back and forth. Although the rain had stopped ten minutes ago, she could still hear water draining through the gutters. Then she heard her own breathing and decided to look for David elsewhere.

As she passed through her parents' room Jayne lifted the bedspread and glanced under their bed, then into the footwell of her mother's vanity. Nothing. From the bedroom she walked into the hallway and opened the door which led up to the attic. "David?" She paused, closed the door and continued downstairs to the entrance hallway. "David?" she called again and looked into the dining room. Through the glass curtains she could see the wind lifting the branches of the maple trees and Judge Sutter's new Buick parked outside his garage across the street.

She glanced into the kitchen at the pastry and cookie cutters scattered across the counter. Her mother hadn't bothered to clean anything. The police, the ambulance attendants — someone had carried her mother and Rose away. Jayne let the door swing shut, crossed the hallway into the living room and leaned against the bay window. She could see David's pant leg tucked under the sofa. She knew he'd be hiding here, in the one place she'd avoided for the last half hour.

"Hi, David." Jayne crouched on her knees and pressed her chin to the carpet. "Granny and Grampy are supposed to come over to look after us." She turned her head at an angle and looked directly into his face. "So why don't you come out now and help me get ready okay?"

David didn't say anything. He'd wedged himself so far under the sofa that he believed even God couldn't see him.

Jayne flattened her body onto the floor. She bent her arm slightly and reached under the sofa and touched his head with her fingers. When he opened his eyes she smiled.

"Whatcha doing under there anyway?" Her eyebrows rose slightly then sank again.

"Hiding out," he said.

"With the camera?" She pointed to the Brownie Bull's-Eye sitting next to his holster.

"I guess so." He didn't know why, but he'd brought it upstairs after his mother started screaming in the basement. He held the camera up to his eye and looked at Jayne's face through the viewfinder. But he didn't take a picture. He'd used the last shot in the basement.

She smiled again to reassure her brother that if he

Healing the Dead

wanted to take her picture it would be all right with her. "Why don't you come out now and we'll get ready for Granny, okay?"

"Is Mom back yet?" He pushed the camera from his face and held onto her hand.

"Probably she'll be back after dinner." Her throat bobbed up and down when she spoke and for a moment David wondered if she were choking. "There's just the two of us. Until Granny and Grampy get here."

"Is Daddy still away?"

"He's in New York. Granny called him and he's going to be home tonight."

"Oh." He had forgotten where his father had gone. He was often away but David imagined he was upstairs sleeping. He always liked it when Daddy and Mummy slept in on Sunday mornings. Then he could sneak downstairs and watch TV. Just knowing they were up there together made everything safe and warm.

If she weren't careful, Jayne thought, she was going to cry. Then she decided to tell him the truth. The truth was evident; she could never invent a big enough lie to cover the truth that lay dead in their basement. "And Brad's gone, too," she whispered and squeezed his hand a little. "They took him in an ambulance up to the hospital."

"I know."

"And ... he's dead, Davy."

A tear came out of her eye and rolled along her cheek. He watched it slip over her face, leaving a wet trail against her skin. It was that solitary tear that made him start to cry too. And once he started crying, the tears poured out hard and sore, and so fast that he couldn't stop sobbing. He pressed his feet against the wall and pushed forward until he could brace his arms against the sofa frame. Then he pulled himself onto the clean blue rug that lay in the middle of the floor.

As soon as he was free, she pulled him to her chest and pressed their heads together. "Oh shit, Davy. This is just awful, I know." She rocked him in her arms, back and forth, her elbows nudging her knees and then bending away again. "Just cry — just cry it all away until there's nothing left inside."

He rocked in her arms until he stopped crying; all his energy drained from his legs and arms and he could hardly hold his head up without leaning on Jayne's shoulder. After a while she stood him up and helped him climb the stairs to his bedroom. She put the camera on his bureau and pulled his cowboy suit off and threw it onto the closet floor. Then she tucked him into bed and stared at him.

"What are you thinking?" She looked straight into his eyes. This was a trick that their mother used to drag the truth out of her whenever she suspected Jayne of lying. It worked every time, and Jayne had learned it well.

"Nothing."

"You are so," she said. "Just remember that *you* didn't do it," she told him. "Just remember that, all right?"

"Okay."

"It was Rose who had the gun, and even then it wasn't her fault. Remember that, too."

But David didn't say anything more. He wasn't sure what he wanted to remember or what he could hope to forget. A thousand prickles shivered back and forth over his scalp. Then he glanced at the camera and knew it would remember everything.

Healing the Dead

By the time Harris Sykes returned from New York, Catrina had already downed half a pint of Dewar's scotch. Rose had been hospitalized in the Toronto General and the doctors had her sedated. The police had questioned the children until they didn't know what they were saying any more. Eventually Catrina started screaming again, and Granny led her upstairs to her bedroom. "Now dear," she said, "just sit down and I'll talk to them so they understand." After the police left, Granny brought her the bottle of scotch and the two-ounce medicine glass she'd always used to drink cough syrup whenever she had a cold.

After he changed out of his suit, Harris drove to the hospital to see Rose. The fact that she wasn't speaking bothered the psychiatrist. He ordered the nurses to cut the sedatives. More than anything he wanted her to open up, to start talking about the shooting. And if the doctor couldn't pry her open, he wanted Harris to do it. But Rose hardly glanced at him. She gazed across the room, at the yellow doors, at the far end of the hall, sometimes at nothing at all. Harris didn't know what to say either; the only certainty was that he couldn't deal with Rose on his own.

Back home, he sat on the bed beside Catrina and stared at her face. "Cat, you've got to come around on this." Her skin was pasty and Harris knew that she was in trouble. "Rose needs our help *now*. And so does Davy." He pointed to the bedroom door.

Just behind it, in the darkness, David lay in bed. He listened to them, watching through the crack of the open door and wondering how they were going to fix things.

"The psychiatrist wants to see them. Both of them — maybe even all of us," Harris added when she didn't respond to him. "We need somebody who can sort this damn thing out."

Catrina's voice shook with anger. "I'm not letting a psychiatrist near them!" She pulled herself from the bed and slung her bathrobe over her shoulders. "Those children will not have anyone hurting them more than they already hurt."

Harris could see her chest shuddering. He pressed his tongue against a sore in his mouth until it hurt. "All right," he sighed, and slipped off his jacket and unbuttoned his shirt. "But you've got to do something that's going to help."

She didn't say anything. She was trying to concentrate on the gates to the Souris Inn, a small hotel on Prince Edward Island. The gates stood like strong, clean pillars, and she could see them straight ahead. Up the road just past the Souris Inn, her sister, Jean had died after a pickup truck loaded with bricks had crashed into their car. Catrina had sat with her until the end, for hours and hours she thought, bunched up on the bed in a small room off the hotel lobby where the manager had carried them both and left them together until the ambulance arrived. She'd been strong then, hadn't she? She'd come through Jeannie's death and everyone said she'd been so brave.

"Cat, come on." Harris stepped toward her. "Please."

"All *right*, I will." She splashed some scotch into the medicine glass. "But what about you?"

"What do you mean?" He stared at her in disbelief. "I'm the one who spent the night in the bloody hospital!"

She slumped onto the bed and looked at him. "Yes, and I'm the one who lifted our little girl up the stairs in my arms. And I'm the one that called the police and the hospital — " She wiped her eyes with a wrist then sipped at the glass.

"Look, I — "

"And then I called Diane Watson ... and I tried to tell

her that her son — " The scotch spilled over her hand and she threw the glass against the wall. It fell onto the carpet and rolled unbroken across the hardwood floor. Harris thought of going to her, of holding her but she began pushing her hands in the air, pushing away from her chest and crying in rolling heaves that frightened him with their intensity.

"Just don't go," she said at last. "Just don't go away, that's all I mean."

Harris finally came to her. "Of course I won't, Catty." He wrapped an arm around her and eased her head against his shoulder. "Why would you ever say that? Of course I won't go."

Chapter Three

Granny and Grampy Sykes were Harris's parents. They'd followed him to Toronto when he started to work in a branch office for the Department of External Affairs as an international economist. He was their only child and they were determined to remain as close to him as they possibly could. Harris had lived in Ottawa when he'd first married Catrina and in the following three years Granny and Grampy had seen their son for a total of eight days. "That's bound to change," Grampy announced during one of his rare visits to Upper Canada, "and change for the good." They bought a home three blocks away from their son's and moved into the little bungalow once they sold their old stone house in Charlottetown.

The day after Brad died, Catrina accepted her mother-in-law's offer to mind David and Jayne for a few days. Although she was worried about Grampy's frailty and unpredictable temper, she wanted time to settle things at home on her own. Everyone pledged to keep the killing a secret from Grampy at least until he had to be told. That way he would have a peace of sorts.

Granny and Grampy lived a block from Regal Road School and when the lunch bell sounded David met Jayne at the school gate and they walked down the street that led to their grandparents' house. Usually Granny had Francine, her cleaning lady, to help make up a big lunch. The two of them would wash and chop and cook while David and Jayne sat on chairs next to the telephone and told them about school. No matter what they said, the ladies smiled and laughed as they told the children how easy their lives were, and how when *they* went to school they had to bring a lump of coal for the stove which stood in the middle of the classroom. After their lunch Granny whipped some food in a mixer, loaded it onto a tray and walked down the hallway to Grampy's bedroom. He was usually supported in bed by three pillows and lay next to a table that was covered with ten or twelve medicine bottles. While Granny set the tray over Grampy's lap, David waited just outside the doorway until he was called.

"Send the boy in," he ordered. As he spoke he squeezed two rubber handgrips to exercise some flexibility back into his knobby, arthritic fingers. And it was just "the boy"; Jayne was never permitted to enter Grampy's bedroom.

As soon as David heard his grandfather's gravelly voice, he poked his head around the corner and smiled. "Hi Grampy."

It was impossible to predict his grandfather's mood, but David always tried to please him even if it meant suffering through his bouts of coughing or the painful routine of his finger-curling exercises.

"Hello, David." He pulled the food tray a little closer and began to spoon up some of the beef purée.

David sat on a cushioned footstool and watched him eat. Grampy liked that, his only grandson sitting there, his head lying on the bedside, and rather than talk, David watched and smiled whenever it seemed right.

"And so what did you learn at school today, hmm?"

"Well, nothing." He examined his grandfather's ears and eyes, the flaky skin of his face. Just looking at him was so much better than talking.

"Sit up when you speak, David." Grampy turned his chin slightly and nodded stiffly.

David lifted his head. "Well, we had art and number-work."

"Number-work, hmm? And so you can multiply now, can you?" He coughed a little and then repeated himself. "Hmm, can you?"

"Yes, Grampy." But David hoped he would not be asked to multiply anything, so he quickly changed the subject to the Union Jack. "And we all saluted the flag. Then we sang 'God Save the Queen.'"

This made him smile. "And did you read a psalm?"

"Yes." But David did not know what a psalm was. Sometimes, especially if it made him happier, it was smarter to lie than say no to Grampy.

"Good. That's the way we used to do it." He settled into his pillows and looked out the window. David could see a softness in his eyes, eyes that seemed huge because of the thinness of the skin that surrounded them. As he watched his grandfather daydreaming, David felt the room comforting them both. But whenever his eyes wandered to the medicine bottles and canes, the salves and rubber hand-grips, the pain of this slow, steady dying filled him. He turned his eyes back to Grampy's face and his soft skin, a softness he couldn't imagine touching.

Healing the Dead

Grampy blinked once and turned to David. "You know, we had to salute the flag."

"In the olden days?" David asked, knowing his grandfather loved to talk about the olden days.

"Yes," he said. "And we sang 'God save the *King*' in those days." His lips curled a little and a bubble of spittle popped and caked on his mouth. "That was in the Great War. And when we were there fighting, it took the life out of us just to wake up to the war every day. But still we saluted. And it was the flag that helped us survive."

"The flag helped you to survive?" Like a lot of what Grampy said, this didn't make sense to David. But the way he said it, with his breath wheezing through his teeth, meant that it was true.

"Yes, at least it worked for some of us."

David could see his grandfather's eyes opening, huge holes wide enough for an army of ghosts to fly in and out, haunting the trenches of his memory.

"You see, David, over there was the left flank ... the ground we'd lost last week." His hand loosened from the lunch tray and two thick fingers pointed to the corner of the room. From the flank David was led over the hill to the lookout, then back to the line of trees where the big guns were placed, then along the ravines of barbed wires to the dog kennels, where Grampy was stationed. He was in charge of the Doberman pinschers, and he described how he trained them to hate the Huns, and how eventually, after years of training, the discipline of war ruined the dogs and everything that was lovely in them.

As they sat there on the bed, David imagined them wandering together along the trenches that twisted back and forth like broken bones, retreating and then doubling back to the machine guns that flashed through the night, shattered stars flaking onto the damp soil. Grampy talked on and on, forgetting David, forgetting his disease. There had been so many good men. So many. But how quickly the dead outnumbered the good. It was only now, almost forty years later, that the Great War had any value to him. The horror of the war provided an escape from the immediate torture of his own lingering death.

Suddenly his story came to an end. "Stop picking your nose!" Grampy barked, rattling the dishes on the lunch tray.

David whipped the offending finger from his nostril.

"Only piggies pick their noses. Are you a piggy?" He coughed and squeezed mightily on his rubber handgrips. "Hmm, a picker piggy?"

"No Grampy."

"Well then?" He eyed his grandson suspiciously and coughed again. Then he thought a moment and wished that he had not chastised this precious child, his only link to eternity. He signaled him with his hand. "Come, come I must tell you something. Something important." David drew close to the pallid face and turned his head to one side. His grandfather's voice whispered into his ear and David thought it was an ocean thudding into a tidal cave in a deep pulse, certain and lonely.

Then Grampy's head snapped back onto the pillow. Granny was at the door with Jayne. Lunch hour was finished; it was time to return to school.

David looked at Grampy lying there and turned away. He hated the fact that his grandfather was dying and that death could take so long. He glanced at Jayne and followed her down the hall while Granny plumped the pillows. They waited for her at the door and could hear Grampy calling something in his smoky voice, his words fading before they reached the end of the hall.

Healing the Dead

"He'll sleep now," Granny said kissing the children good-bye. "He does so enjoy your visits, you know." She combed back tiny wisps of silvery hair with her open fingers. "We'll see you after school, then. At three-thirty?"

"Okay!" David sang out and ran down the driveway after his sister.

"But only for one more day," Jayne added when they were far enough away. "Mom's worried about you, you know."

"Why?"

"Because Grampy's so sick. She said she doesn't want you 'taking it on.' The only reason we're here is because it's an emergency."

"I know, but I like his stories."

They walked along slowly. There were no other children in sight. Jayne was supposed to drop David off and continue on her own to the high school. But they were early and David never knew what to do in the playground on his own.

"What was he saying anyhow?" Jayne leaned against a maple tree and looked at him with her head turned a little to one side.

"Lots of things. Mostly just stuff about the war."

"No, I mean at the end, when he was whispering in your ear."

"Oh ... that was private."

"Tell me."

"No!"

"Come on, Davy." She was insistent, and when she got that way, David knew he would give in. Besides, he loved her. She was fifteen and he was just nine; at times he felt she was his mother — better than his mother because he could tell her everything.

"All right." He pulled her ear close to his lips just the

way Grampy had done. And in a deep, sure voice that sounded as much like the ocean's as he could make it, he whispered right into her ear: "Don't grow old." Then he said it again the way Grampy had. *"Don't grow old!"*

Jayne backed away and stared at him. "He said that?" She had a look of dread that David had never seen before. It was the fear of dying — more than that — the fear of living through a long, angry death. "He said that to you?" A tear welled from her eye and she brushed it away.

"Yes." He didn't understand. Why was she crying? he wondered.

But Jayne didn't explain anything. Everyone was dying around them and she was just expected to tick through the daily schedule: breakfast, school, lunch, school, dinner, homework and bed. If she was a machine — that's what they really wanted, she thought, a tin robot mechanically clicking through the horror — then they could make her believe that death was just a minor nuisance in the routine chores of life.

Suddenly she broke free and ran past the school alone. David watched her go, her pleated skirt kicking in the wind as she ran, and he stood by himself, wondering, listening. Above his head he could hear the world rising in a huge wave that was about to swallow him whole. Then he saw some older kids walking up the sidewalk behind him. Laughing, they pointed at him and he knew he had to escape, too. He glanced back at Grampy's house and then ran in the opposite direction as fast as he could. Once he was on the school grounds he looked over his shoulder, but the great wave had vanished and only the sound of it remained — the deafening, hollow roar.

Chapter Four

When his father brought Rose home from the hospital David noticed her transformation as soon as she stepped out of the car. Her wide triangular face, which had always looked so open and trusting, was now gaunt and white. When she passed him on the staircase he could see that her red hair was greasy and unwashed, and her fingernails were bitten down to the quick.

"I didn't know about it," he stammered as she brushed by him. She stopped on the stair and glanced over his shoulder, as though he'd called from somewhere outside the house.

"That it was ... " *loaded* he meant to add, but Rose simply turned her back and climbed to the landing then up the next five stairs to the hallway. He heard her door click shut and the bedsprings squeak as she rolled onto her mattress.

Over the next two days David realized that of all the minor alterations in her — the pallor, the exhaustion, the fact that she barely ate — the worst change was that she couldn't look at him. She'd talk to him but only in phrases and never in any way that forced her to look straight into his eyes. And whenever she glanced past him he felt the horror return. If she would look at him, then he knew he could let some of the pain go. But she made him invisible, hid him away just by refusing to see him.

The first time they were alone in the girls' bedroom, Rose sat next to the window and David squatted at the door. That's where he usually sat whenever they had something private to discuss. He could always hear anyone coming upstairs and put out an alert right away. This became critical when Jayne started smoking and she had to ditch her cigarettes before her father came into the room. Fortunately for Jayne, he smoked too, and he could never tell anyone else's smoke from his own.

"You all right?" Jayne asked once she had a cigarette going. She had an idea that it was best to be direct. The truth seemed to be the only thing that offered any security and she wanted to hold it out like a branch for Rose to grab and hang on to. But she didn't know how far to go or how fast.

"Yeah." Rose twisted her head a little so she could glance through the window up the street. "Look, you'd better watch Mom doesn't catch you with that thing."

"I'm all right." Jayne flicked the cigarette ash into the garbage pail and kept staring at Rose. "Dad said they asked you a lot of questions in the hospital, huh?"

"Yeah, they did."

"Mom and Dad were pretty shattered." Jayne lay on her bed looking at the back of Rose's head. "Specially Mom."

Rose got up from the chair. Something had flashed by the window. She pressed her face to the wood frame and looked down the street. At the top of the maple tree she could see two bullets streak through the new leaves toward the sun. She watched them disappear then she sat down again.

"Mom started drinking pretty heavily." Everything Jayne said flowed very smoothly like warm butter spreading over a gentle heat. "But mostly at night when she didn't think we'd notice."

"Yeah. From the medicine cup," David added.

Rose pushed a bit of hair from her face, took one of the cigarettes from Jayne's Players pack and lay down on her bed. She didn't light it, she just toyed with it between her lips, moving it in and out, practicing the best way to hold it. "Mom said the funeral is going to be on Saturday." She paused a moment. "On my birthday."

"Just for the Watson family." Jayne took a long drag on the cigarette and watched the air turn grey as she exhaled. It *would* be on Rose's birthday, she thought. God, what a screw up.

"She also said the Watsons are moving away." Rose laid the cigarette down and stared at the ceiling. "Did you hear that?"

"I guess they're going to sell their place next door. Dad said they're going to live out at their cottage for a while." Jayne pulled herself up against the pillows. "You'll still be able to see them again. At least once a year when we get the Christmas tree out at their cottage."

"Well, I don't want to see them again!" Rose twisted her head away and started crying. "Not *ever*!"

"Shit." Jayne squeezed her cigarette against the rim of the wastepaper basket and dabbed the ember on her tongue to make sure it was out. Then she rolled it in a Kleenex and shoved it into her pocket. The time it took to tidy up the evidence of her smoking was just long enough for Rose's crying to break loose. It was the effect Jayne hoped for — enough lead time so that Rose could begin to clear all the horror out of her system.

"All right," she said, wrapping her arms around Rose's shoulders. "Just let it go let it all go," Jayne rocked back and forth with her knees curled beside her sister until Rose's crying became dry sobs that shook her whole body. "We've got to get everything back to where we started," she whispered. "Okay? Let's go back to where it was just us, and then we go from there."

Jayne dropped a hand from Rose's neck and beckoned David towards her. She wanted him to be part of this. Together they would take this suffering and absorb it somehow so that it would evaporate, vanish like death itself. But to David it was very scary. There was nowhere for him to hide any more. So he did everything with complete trust in Jayne. Whatever she did, he followed exactly and without question. First she took his hand and placed it on Rose's back and held it there. Rose was barely breathing and her body had become cold and dry. Jayne guided David's hand up and down Rose's spine until he started stroking her on his own. Then his other arm slipped around her shoulder and the three of them fell onto the bed together, with Jayne and David holding Rose's body. It took a long time — a part of forever, David thought — but finally she opened her eyes and looked at him without glancing away. As he watched her, the pain uncoiled from his chest and his arms and legs relaxed and the deep aching in his stomach slipped away from his body. The stillness in her eyes made him feel warm and safe again, and as he stared at her he imagined her in a picture with a white border framing her face and the light of the room reflecting the softness of her pale, cool skin.

Chapter Five

Two weeks later Grampy had David pinned to the wall. Occasionally Grampy came to the Sykeses' house with Granny, who cooked meals and managed the house while Catrina dealt with the coroner's inquest and the trauma that continued to consume Rose and the Watsons. Grampy couldn't do very much on his own, and Catrina said that it was David's job to keep him company until everyone got back to normal again. But with his grandfather's cloudy eyes following every move he made, David found it hard to be entertaining, especially now that Grampy had been told the truth about Brad, Rose and David.

"I told you never to point a gun at anyone," he said, his voice rumbling over the phlegm in his throat. He was sitting in the wingback chair in the living room next to the fireplace. David bent over the coals watching them flicker as the last few flames wiggled back and forth on the charred wood. He was lost in the tiny, dancing movements — the rolling shifts of light in each ember. Then, when he wasn't looking, Grampy pressed the tip of his cane onto the brick hearth and pinned his grandson in place. "Don't you ever listen when I'm talking to you?"

David rolled onto his back to look at him. His grandfather's head was white and lined with creases that ran down his face and over his neck. Grampy was waiting for him to explain something but David didn't know what to say.

"Hmm? All the talking I give you just runs out the other ear? Does it?"

"I don't know Grampy." David tried to sit up but the cane blocked him.

"You don't know? A young boy lies dead in the cellar and then you say you don't know?"

"I didn't kill him!" David grabbed the cane in one hand and stood up. At first he thought of throwing it at him, but then he realized the old man was too frail. His face was so very white, with small scales of skin flaking onto his collar. And then David thought, he knows that I gave the gun to Rose. He thinks I did it.

It's a lie, he told himself. I *didn't* shoot Brad. Jayne knows it, Rose knows, everybody does. But the idea that he was guilty, that *he* was the one who killed Brad, knotted his throat. "I didn't kill him!" He screamed it at the old man. "I *didn't* kill him!"

"David."

He looked around and saw his mother standing against the doorway. Her face was wet with tears. David didn't know what she was crying about, but then she pressed her face to his and he felt her tears on his skin.

"I *didn't* kill him," he whispered to her.

"Of course you didn't," she said, easing him onto the sofa next to the window. She pressed his head to her breast and brushed the hair along the crown of his head. She felt for the lump that was there, the small bump that had stayed after the girls had dropped him and he'd crashed down the stairs past her legs. He had just passed his first birthday when it happened. She'd watched him fall from Jayne's arms like a floppy sack of loose potatoes, right past her to the hallway floor. Every time her fingers prodded his skull for the point of impact, she thought of the concussion and Dr. Jenner telling her, his mouth very thin and serious, "It may be that there'll be some minor brain damage. Perhaps some dizziness, maybe even fainting spells. Or something so small that we'll never know about it. For David, it may just come as headaches or small, periodic flashes. You'll just have to soothe him until it passes." After a few minutes she started to talk very quietly, whispering into his ear so that Grampy couldn't overhear. "Just think of the gates, David. Look straight ahead and you can see them there any time you want."

"What gates?"

"The gates to heaven. They're always just ahead of you. You just have to look hard enough, then they'll open up to you."

With his head lying in his mother's lap, David stared at the ceiling, looking for the gates to heaven. For a moment he thought he saw something emerge from the plaster, heavy steel gates that swung open from a stone wall, like the entrance to the Lakeshore Tennis Club. But he hated tennis; even Brad had said that tennis was strictly for geeks. Besides, he wanted to know if Grampy had told his mother anything about passing the gun to Rose. "Why did he say that to me?" he asked, turning his head to look into her eyes.

She didn't reply at first. He saw the cords in her throat tighten as she swallowed, and he could tell she was gulping down more tears. There was a collection of them in her stomach, he thought, tears from weeks of crying, and all of them had dripped into a deepening pool. "He doesn't mean to hurt you," she whispered, pulling him closer. "He just hates the idea that things could go ... " she paused and wiped her face with the back of her hand, "that they could go on without any more love between us."

His mother had started to explain everything in terms of love. She repeated that she and Daddy still loved him, David, very much and Granny and Grampy loved him, and Jayne and Rose still loved him too. Even Mr. and Mrs. Watson loved him, but they wouldn't be able to visit for a long time. "Did you know that Brad's mom and I were friends?" she asked looking up at the ceiling. "I mean best friends. I was her maid of honor when she married Brad's dad. And she's your godmother, you know. Rose's and Jayne's too." She shifted slightly, and David could feel her arm easing away from him. "We did so many things together. Getting the Christmas trees every year from their cottage property, swimming in the lake every summer."

"I know, Mom."

"Well, then you should know that they still love you." She explained that they probably wouldn't be able to *say* that they loved him, even though they did, deep in their hearts. But the more she insisted how close they all were, the more her voice faltered.

Because of her trembling voice, David didn't say anything about his suspicion that Grampy knew he'd given the gun to Rose. No one knew that except Rose. And maybe she'd forgotten.

After a moment his mother pulled away and looked at him. "So why don't you go up to your room and play until dinner's ready. I'll call you when Daddy's home, okay?"

"Okay." He looked at the back of Grampy's head. The old man was sitting just as before, next to the fireplace with his cane braced against the side of the chair. He was so quiet. David thought that maybe he'd stopped breathing, and for a moment he felt like reaching over and touching the top of his grandfather's head. It looked very cold and bright. Instead, he slipped into the front hall and ran up the stairs to the landing. Then he tiptoed past the balcony door, up the last five steps to the guest room and crossed the hall to the girls' bedroom.

He pressed an ear to their door. They were whispering, but he couldn't make anything out. He looked through the keyhole, but as usual, the girls had hung their clothing from the doorknob to prevent any cigarette smoke from drifting into the hall. He stood there listening. All he could hear was his heart, his breathing, the solitary twisting of his arms in the air. The whole house was quiet, buried in a hush of whispers that murmured through the walls, out the windows and into the sky.

He realized then that they were being haunted.

He thought of the pictures. The last roll of film had just been developed, and his mother had given him the whole package without even opening it. Usually she would go over all the pictures and marvel at every shot and tell him what a fantastic photographer he was becoming. And she'd always be surprised to find two or three pictures of herself there — "sneak" pictures she had no idea he'd taken. That was because Jayne had taught him her theory of natural photography: that the trick to a good picture was capturing someone just as they were, without fakery and smiles or goofy-looking faces. So David combined her theory of natural photography with his talent for sneakery and always managed to get a collection of pictures that surprised everyone. But this last set of photographs had surprised him, too.

He inched away from the girls' door and walked into his

bedroom and leaned against the cast iron radiator. He glanced through the three south-facing windows that overlooked the hedge into the Watson's house, directly into Brad's room. David stood there for a moment and watched for any shadows moving against Brad's wall. Then he drew the curtains and walked to his bureau. In the bottom drawer, under his socks, David had hidden the pictures.

He closed his bedroom door and pulled open the sock drawer. His fingers lifted the photo envelope, and he stood up and stared at it. Then he lay on his bed and gazed at the ceiling. He didn't know what he was thinking or feeling, and for a moment he thought he saw the gates of heaven. Then he felt an urgency pressing him to look at Brad's face, to go back and *remember*.

He sat up and dumped the pictures into his lap. There were eight glossy black-and-whites with white borders around each shot. At the bottom of every border the date had been stamped in very small lettering: April '56. The first was a picture of Jayne hunched over her desk as she did her homework with the fingers of one hand poking through her hair, sticking straight into the air like five cigarettes. The second photograph showed his dad climbing into the Chevy, dressed in his suit, his briefcase dragging his arm down to his knees, and the peak of his felt hat pinched into a point in his other hand. And there were two wasted shots, fake shots, of Rose and Susan dressed up in their mother's old clothing, both of them dancing around the basement playroom on the morning of the storm. The next picture was the one of his mother standing next to the window in the kitchen as she rolled out the cookie dough. The grey metallic light of the storm made a silhouette of her head and shoulders. The picture caught her brittleness, the fragility of her arms as she pressed the dough back and forth with the rolling pin.

David couldn't remember taking the last three photographs. He didn't even remember going back to the playroom to get the camera. He felt as though his life had stopped between the moment Rose shot the gun until sometime later when Jayne found him hidden under the living room sofa cradling the camera in his hand. But here, in these three pictures, was the truth. The first shot was a little off-center: Susan backed against the cellar door with an arm covering her face so that only her mouth was showing, and Rose standing on the other side of the door, her lips open, her eyes staring into the camera lens. Next was the picture of his mother with her hands gripping her face, bending slightly forward to see what had happened.

The last shot was of Brad — Brad on the floor, the bullet hole neatly punched into the skin next to his nose, his jaw turned slightly away from the wound, and the concrete floor beneath his hair dark with blood. It was this picture that held David, fixed his eyes to Brad's face and burned the last second of his existence into David's mind. And the vapors of a ghost trapped in the three-by-three-inch Kodak finish began to haunt him more than his own memory. It was this picture that made death real.

Chapter Six

Six months after Jayne's eighteenth birthday she went to the Motor Vehicle Registry and got her driver's license. The fact that it was really only a learner's permit was a mere technicality to her. As long as a licensed driver sat beside her while she drove, then legally she could drive to the US border and back without a hitch. And she had lots of friends with their own licenses who were happy to go along for the ride.

It was her friends, her "buds," that first shocked her parents. Grant Preston, for example. Grant liked to roar up the back lane to the Sykeses' home on his motorcycle. He drove a Harley-Davidson and whenever they heard the engine rumbling in the alley, David, Rose and Jayne tore out the back door to look at him. That's what everybody really liked about Grant — the way he looked. He had a clean, soft face and dark hair slick with Brylcreem. He spent hours stroking his hair with a steel comb that stuck out of his back pocket like a knife. His lips were full, and he always held them together tightly except when something funny caught him off guard, then he'd start laughing and his mouth opened wide and showed his uneven teeth. He liked to lean on the seat of his motorcycle and flick the collar of his jacket up and down to lay the leather at just the right angle against his neck. David used to run around him twirling back and forth to see if he'd chase him. And Rose sat on the back steps curling her red hair through her fingers, watching every little shift and turn that Grant made. But Jayne didn't wait for anything. She was always right at his arm the minute he cut his engine. She never gave him a kiss, at least not in the back yard, but her mother could see that she wanted to. She overheard her daughter talking about it on the telephone to Angie White once. Grant's lips were like "two sweet pillows," she said. Eavesdropping from the telephone that sat next to the medicine glass on her night table, Catrina heard everything clearly. A week later she decided to intervene.

"Jayne, I don't want you to think that I'm choosing your friends, but Grant isn't the kind of young man you should be associating with." She watched Jayne pick up the car keys from the hall table. Her voice dropped slightly. "He hasn't even finished high school."

"That's because he's working. He's got a job." She sat on the sofa next to David and opened her purse.

"What kind of job?" Catrina walked over to the living room window and looked at the Chevrolet. It was April and eddies of wind swirled around the tires.

Jayne leafed through her wallet to ensure her learner's permit was still in place.

"I said, what does he do?" Catrina turned from the window and looked directly at her daughter. "And where do you think you're going?"

"I'm taking David down to the lake. I promised him I'd take him for his birthday."

They both glanced at David. He closed the *Look* magazine he'd been flicking through and stared at his sister. It's true, he thought, she had promised to take him out. But that was six months ago. She never said it would be today, right now.

"Jayne," Catrina bunched her hands on her hips, "who is driving with you?"

"Angie." Jayne worked her way over to the window, but to the end opposite her mother. She hated this: the daily Parental Inquisition.

"Angie?"

"What's so bad about Angie?"

Her mother made a soft spitting noise through her teeth.

"What?" Jayne demanded. "Tell me what!"

David could tell that his mother wished his dad were home. He didn't approve of Angie White, either. The trouble with Angie White was that she was black. Or "colored," as his father had said. But she wasn't all black. She had a half-tone color that made her skin look honeyed and warm. And it was this lighter shade of brown that spared them from hearing Harris call her "a darkie." But in spite of his father's opinion, David loved Angie's skin. Whenever she came by, he'd try to hover somewhere around her so he could examine the textures of her arms and the amber tones that sank from her throat down the hollow between her breasts.

Catrina realized there was nothing she could do about Angie White's skin. But there was some hope she could stop Jayne from seeing her. Still, she didn't say anything. She just looked at Jayne and read the determination in her face. After a moment she sighed and turned to David. "You'd better get your jacket on. And go to the bathroom first."

By the time he was ready, Jayne had the car idling. "Just

Healing the Dead

be careful," his mom warned. "And if the girls start doing anything improper, it doesn't mean you have to go along. Just think of what Jesus would do."

"Okay!" He grabbed the camera, ran out the door and sat in the front seat beside his sister. She had the radio on and was clicking the cigarette lighter in and out of the dashboard and singing along with "Rock Around the Clock" and saying "shit" whenever a rush of static cut out the radio. David wondered if Jesus would've liked rock 'n' roll or if He'd ever said "shit."

"When Angie gets here, you hop into the back seat, okay?"

"Sure." Whatever Jayne wanted was just fine. And when Angie turned the corner, Jayne gunned the engine and David slipped over the seat. From there, he'd have a close-up of Angie's neck and shoulders. If he was really careful he might get a couple of snapshots of her skin without her even knowing.

"Hey, Jay." Angie climbed into the car and smiled. "Brought young Dav-o with you, huh?"

"Yeah. It's his birthday present." Jayne twisted her head around to back out of the gravel driveway. This was a demanding maneuver, and she turned the radio up loud so that Bill Haley and the Comets could fix her concentration on the two tire tracks that led down the driveway to the road.

She drove carefully for the first half-hour, all the way downtown where they cruised up and down Yonge Street, stared at the people and dragged the odd car from light to light. David had the back seat to himself and whenever something funny happened — like the guys rumbling out of their Ford in the middle of the intersection and switching seats — he'd snap a picture of it for memory's sake. But the drive to the lake was much farther than he'd imagined. Jayne didn't intend to cruise down to the beach and then back home before their father came in for supper. Instead, they sped along the lakeshore for over an hour until they got to a park. David had no idea where they were. But Jayne and Angie both knew, and a growing excitement bubbled between them as they pulled off the highway.

"Here we are, Jay." Angie pointed to the left where one of the parking lots branched away from the main road.

As they turned the corner, none of them could believe what they saw. Dozens of motorcycles were lined up in a row and over a hundred bikers stood around their machines. They drank beer, smoked, kissed their girls. Just the look of them scared David — especially the ones peeing right onto the picnic table beside him. But it was the sound of the Harleys that ripped through his chest. They screamed.

"Holy shit." Jayne cut the engine and smiled. "Grant said only the Diamonds were going to show up."

The Black Diamonds were Grant Preston's motorcycle gang. They used to come around the house the odd Sunday afternoon when David's parents went to the tennis club. There were six of them, each with a black Harley-Davidson motorcycle. The bike fenders, bars and pipes were polished so cleanly that David could see his own teeth in the chrome as he dipped his face next to the heat pouring off the engines. But this crowd of bikers was different. David watched four of them guzzle their beer and then spit it onto one another in long, foamy jets.

"Hell, not just the Diamonds, Jay. I heard Satan's Choice were going to be up," Angie said. "Hey, and you want to bet the cops'll be squeezing along here pretty soon, too."

They heard a motorcycle rumbling behind the car and coming to a stop. Grant Preston slipped off his Harley and walked up to Jayne's door.

Jayne rolled down the window and stuck her head out. "Hi." Her head leaned to one side and she smiled.

" 'Lo," he said and bent his head down for a kiss. He nodded at David and then looked at Angie. His eyelids were half-open, and a lick of hair swept onto his forehead. Everything about Grant Preston seemed like a strip of newly paved highway — dark and clean and low, hugging the ground in anticipation of heavy traffic.

They kissed again and again until David couldn't watch any more.

Angie began shifting around in her seat and then she finally opened the door, got out of the car and walked away without saying a word.

"Competition's going to be starting pretty soon," Grant said after taking a long breath. "You ready?"

"Yeah." Jayne was ready for anything. She could feel her body tingling and she wanted something fabulous to happen. She hesitated a moment and glanced into the back seat at her brother. "Just get set up and I'll be over in five minutes," she said to Grant and rolled the window up and locked Angie's door. Then she twisted around and locked the two back doors.

"You feeling okay?" She looked straight into David's eyes. "You look a little pale."

He wondered what she would say if he answered no. Maybe she'd drive them home and that would be the end of the trip to the lake. But he knew that whatever she was doing was very important to her. In fact he felt his stomach rolling, and he was frightened — he knew then that somebody was going to die. Maybe it'll be the two guys next to the garbage can who were pissing on the picnic table, he thought. Maybe it'll be Jayne and Grant. Or maybe even me.

"Sure. I'm fine," he said and watched Grant park his bike next to the rest of the Black Diamonds. "But what's going to happen?"

"It's a rally!" Her eyes widened slightly and she smiled. "There's going to be all kinds of bike competitions and we're going to be in it."

"Who's going to be in it?" Did she mean he was going to be in it? Or just her?

"And I want you to promise me something, okay?"

"What?"

"Just don't tell Mom and Dad about this — *whatever* you do. All right?" She brushed a strand of hair from her face. "Okay?"

"Okay," he said, watching five or six more motorcycles line up with the others. Then he gazed at the sand dunes, long rows of them tufted with hanks of long grass. What are we doing here? he wondered.

"And I think you should stay in the car," she added, slipping a cigarette into her mouth and pressing the lighter into the dash. "All right?"

"Will I be able to see you?" he asked.

"Sure." She lit the end of her cigarette and pressed the lighter back into the dash. "I'll be right over there on the beach. We're just going to have some races, and I've got to ride with Grant in the pairs competition."

"The pairs competition?"

"Yes. And stop repeating everything I say. People'll think you don't have ears."

He looked out the window and rubbed his ears to make sure there wasn't something stuck to them. At the same time

Healing the Dead

Jayne slipped out of the car and locked the door. She glanced back at him once and then ran over to where Grant was checking his tires and gave him a kiss on the neck. Angie was talking with some boys at the other end of the parking lot. Two of them had their arms draped over her shoulders, and they were laughing, throwing their heads back as the wind caught their hair.

Holding the Brownie in his lap, David sat in the Chevy and watched everybody getting ready. The bikers started revving their engines louder and louder. After about ten minutes one of them cruised up and down past the whole line until he'd attracted six or seven other gang members who followed him back and forth across the parking lot. He had a long red scarf wrapped around his neck and black sunglasses pressed against the bridge of his nose. He didn't look at anybody else, but he knew that eventually he'd have all the motorcycles parading behind him, moving like a slow snake back and forth. And when about half the bikes were trailing him, he started cutting a figure-eight right through the parking lot and up the middle, so that the line of bikes intersected itself. At this point everyone had to be sharp not to crash into somebody else. Then gradually, after six or seven loops, he picked up speed and the bikes barely squeezed through the figure-eight intersection without hammering together. After two of them finally plowed into one another, the leader looked around, peeled out of the circle and sped onto the beach. Then the whole train followed him over the ridge of sand and out of sight.

The few bikers left in the parking lot finished tuning their engines and slipped onto the beach in small groups. Grant was almost the last to leave, and he had Jayne riding behind him, her arms strapped around his chest as they drove.

For a while nothing happened. David sat in the car and just looked around. Except for the sound of bikes ripping back and forth over the beach, it was quiet. And because he couldn't see them, he felt completely alone. He started to think about the color of the air, its grayness, and the way the clouds were building a very low wall just over the lake. They looked so cold, but he had no sense of chill in his body at all — only an emptiness that made him certain someone was dying.

"Hey!"

He twisted his head around to the rear window. Two bikers leaned on the back of the car, swayed back and forth, and poked their fingers at him.

"What're you doing in there, kid?" One of them had a belly that spilled over his belt in three rolls. David could tell right away that he was drunk — plastered — but still able to talk.

"Young punk out to see some titties," said his buddy, a tall lean man with strands of beard that fell like thread from his chin and cheeks. David thought he was Chinese. Fu Manchu.

"Yeah? Let's gob him." The fat man pushed his face forward and spat onto the rear windshield just inches from David's head.

He ducked. It was an instant reaction; the shift in his neck sent a flash of pain up his spine and across his scalp. "Ooooww!"

The bikers started laughing and spat their way around the car. When they'd looped back to David's door, the fat man tried to pry it open with his fist. It wouldn't budge so he gobbed it four or five times. Both of them gulped their beer to prime the salivary juices. Once they had it mixed to

Healing the Dead

the right consistency, they smeared the Chevy with everything they had.

"Stop it! Stop it, you assholes!" David had never called anyone an asshole before. But there was a certain magic to swearing at these two drunks who were screwing up his dad's car. "You fucking jerks!" It felt good calling them down; all Jayne's lessons in profanity were finally paying off. "You slimy green assholes!"

This got the Chinese biker upset. As far as he was concerned, until now their gobbing had been good, clean fun. But having a twelve-year-old calling them "fucking jerks" was more than he could tolerate. He started hammering the glass with his fists. This didn't have much effect and David didn't feel too threatened until the fat man joined in. Then the two of them began working on the back window together.

"Stop it!" But this time his voice was a whisper. This is real, he thought. *They're really gonna get me.* His stomach burned and twisted. He decided to run, considering it just long enough to decide which door to open. The other side, he told himself. And when you're out — lock it.

Once his feet hit the dirt he didn't look back. Harris had drilled that into him when he was training for the school track team. Just look straight ahead, he'd said. Look back and you're dead. His legs pumped hard, hard, hard. Don't look. Don't look, they screamed. *Don't look or you're dead!*

Then he tumbled down the back of a sandy ridge onto the beach and saw the bikes bunched in two groups. At one end, six motorcycles formed a line ready to start a race. A hundred yards along the shore a second group of bikers had marked off a finish gate. They revved their engines until the screaming spilled into the air. Slipping awkwardly, the bikers' girls scrambled onto the drivers' shoulders and locked their thighs around the boys' necks. In the last row of six pairs David recognized Grant and Jayne steadying their Harley. After a few tries Jayne successfully mounted Grant. She climbed above him like a young bird rising into the air and smiled as the wind flapped the blonde flag of hair from her head.

When the leader dropped his red scarf, two of the drivers lurched from the starting gate. Their girls fell to the ground and the bikes plowed into the sand. The other four got off without trouble, but within a few yards two more lost traction in the sand, and their motorcycles slid in long sloppy turns and finally stalled and then collided. Grant pulled away fast and drove his bike ahead of everyone for the first hundred feet. Then he hit a soft spot, and his rear tire fishtailed back and forth, spraying an arc of dirt into the air behind the wheel. Jayne grabbed his face to hold on, but the last bike skimmed past them and broke through to the finish.

"Shit." It felt good to be swearing all the time, and as David ran up to Jayne he didn't know what else to say.

"What are you doing here? I thought you were going to stay in the car."

"I was," he told her. "But two assholes started gobbing on the car."

"What?"

"Yeah." He felt so excited he could hardly speak. He wiped his mouth and continued. "And then they started smashing in the rear window."

Grant didn't say a word. Without another glance at David, he kicked his bike into gear and sped over the ridge toward the car. Jayne grabbed David's hand and they ran after him. Once they got over the sand dune, they stumbled backward in shock.

Healing the Dead

The back window of the Chevy had been smashed and glass had scattered over the trunk of the car. One of the drunks had slipped his hand inside and pulled open the lock. Then they'd really had a gob fest. They'd urinated over the upholstery and carpeting, and dumped several beers onto the back seat. Grant yanked both of them out and shoved the Chinese onto the ground. Three girls began yelling, and a crowd of people started circling them.

"Get the hell out of here!" Grant yelled at Jayne. He kicked the fat man in the ribs, then punched hard into his ear. "Just go!" He bumped Jayne into the driver's seat, and David ran over to the other door and jumped in when she popped the lock. "Go!" Grant yelled, and he smashed the Chinese in the belly with his heel. They could hear the motorcycle engines cruising up from the beach. Everyone was coming to join the rumble.

Jayne cranked the wheel and peeled out of the parking lot. A growing knot of people wailed angrily, and as the fight spread through the crowd, the Chevy curled out of the parking lot and up the main road to the highway.

"God, what are we going to do?" Jayne glanced into the back seat of the car. Glass had fallen all over the bench and floor, and beer, saliva and pee swirled across the upholstery as the car rolled down the highway towards home.

David couldn't say anything. He felt like crying, but he didn't want to do that. It would be very bad for Jayne if he started to cry now. He knew that they needed to figure something out fast. About two miles down the road she turned into a rest stop, and they stepped out of the car to examine the damage.

"What are we going to do?"

"I don't know." David stared down at the urine and wondered how anyone could pee in his dad's Chevy like that. Then he looked at the gobs of saliva that were congealing to the paint job. "We need to wash it."

"Yeah." Jayne wiped a tear from her cheek. "I guess we should." She walked over to a washroom and came back to the car with handfuls of wet paper towels. A stiff wind was blowing off the lake, pushing a huge ridge of clouds towards them. David began to feel a chill and a tingling in the top of his head. Jayne handed four or five towels to him and slapped the hood of the car. While he started rubbing it clean, she got into the back seat and began scrubbing the interior.

"Christ!" Her voice cut right through his stomach. "Those goddamn *animals!*"

David couldn't look at her. All he could think of was the trouble they were in and that this day would end with someone dying.

"David, just look at this!"

He walked to the back door and stared at the mess. She'd swept most of the glass onto the road and managed to rub the beer and swill around so that it was spread evenly over the upholstery. But hundreds of glass shards lay trapped in the carpet and the blue velvet upholstery had become a flat, muddy brown. At least she'd done something to get rid of the pee. But instead of simply seeing it, the thick pasty smell rose through his nose into his lungs and now he was inhaling it.

"What's the problem?" He thought that if they overlooked the urine and gobs, the car wouldn't seem like such a wreck.

"What's the problem? It's a disaster!" Her head slumped and she started to cry. "Look at us!"

David obediently walked to the roadside, then across the ditch and ten feet into the hay field to have a good view of things. There was the car and the road and the sky. The sky looked very big, huge enough to swallow the car completely. Yeah, the Chevy's a disaster, he thought, there's no question about it. Dad is going to slaughter us as soon as we pull into the driveway. He looked at the sky again and could see a storm coming up from the south. Soon it would be pouring rain.

He walked back to the car and touched her shoulder. "Look, I think we should just go home. We're dead no matter what happens. We might as well get it over with and not make Dad any madder by being late."

She nodded her head and brushed the tears from her cheeks. Then she closed the back door, got into the driver's seat, started the engine and pulled onto the highway. Ten minutes later, the rain started to fall.

"Oh God, what am I doing?" Her voice seemed hollow as she fumbled with two or three switches. Finally she got the wipers working, and they slapped softly across the windshield. "I mean what's this all about?" She turned her head to her brother, her eyes wide, her face red and wet with crying.

"I don't know." He didn't know what she was talking about. David just wanted to get home before he got sick from the smell of urine rising through his nostrils.

"Sometimes I think everything's going so bloody fine. You know? I'm just trying to live, for God's sake, and then this kind of shit has to happen."

"You swear too much," he told her. "You never talk like that around Dad and Mom, just when you're around me."

"I do not swear too much. At least it's real to swear. Everybody in our house spends so much goddamn time pretending nothing's real that I've got to swear just to keep my fucking sanity!"

David had never seen Jayne so upset. He felt his stomach roll and in a flash he imagined her losing control of the Chevy and smashing into another car. Then he knew he had to do everything in his power to keep the car flowing, keep it low and flat and slow, the way Grant Preston would do it, and save them both from the death spinning uncertainly in the wheels. *Talk to her,* he told himself. Make a little engine out of words and run it down the highway, humming beside her.

"What's sanity?" He kept his voice very even and calm.

"Sanity?" Her head twisted around to him and then back to the highway. "This is sanity!" Her hand slapped the dashboard, and she punched the accelerator with her foot. They sped down the road, spraying the asphalt with rain. "And this is sanity!" She unrolled the window and stuck her face into the drizzle. "But don't ever let anyone tell you that the morgue we're living in has anything to do with sanity."

"The morgue?"

"Yes. Exactly. The morgue." She rolled up the window and rubbed her wet face with one hand. "Just look at it. Ever since Brad died, Mom and Dad have sealed things up so tight I can't even breathe. I can't have the friends I want. I can't go out where I want. I can't do what I want. We might as well be living on the moon. All of us sealed in an airtight bubble on the moon."

Jayne seemed less frantic now that he had her talking, and he wanted to keep her going, spinning over the skim of water towards home. "At least they let you have the car," he said. And your friends and boyfriends and anything else you want, he added to himself.

She ignored this. "The simple fact is that it's all a charade. And instead of protecting us, they're slowly killing us all, one by one — especially you and Rose."

"No they're not." She had to be wrong. But still, he could feel this death coming.

"Look at you." She was calm now. Her hands steady on the wheel, she turned her head easily, checking the traffic as she passed a line of cars. "You don't have any friends to — "

"I do so."

"But you don't bring them home, do you?" She cocked her head and glanced at him, his brown hair spiky over his eyes. "You just sit there night after night with your photo magazines or TV or flicking through all your picture albums. Don't you see that?"

"See what?" He didn't know what she was talking about any more.

"That we have to break free. That we're dying."

"No we're not. And just stop saying that, all right?"

"I can say whatever I want."

She could. And David knew he could never argue with her. She was too smart. And besides, he felt too sick. He pushed his shoulders against the seat and tried to rest his head on the upholstery. It was impossible to keep the conversation alive, but her taut edge was blunt now, and his desire to talk fell away. So did his fear. Once he let go of his fear, a sleepy freedom rode through him, and he floated over the road all the way into Toronto, in the wet Sunday twilight, as they passed a few cars that drifted like small metal dreams on the slippery stream of the highway. When they got to Glenholme Avenue, he peered through the window and saw that the rain had washed away the corms of saliva from the hood of the Chevy.

"Look, all the gob's been washed off!"

Jayne's eyes brightened a moment and she looked over the dashboard. "Wow, maybe we'll get off okay after all."

She wasn't swearing any more, and for a moment he thought they'd have a chance of skinning through this alive. But even though he wanted to make her feel good about their chances of survival, he couldn't get very excited for her. He was too busy dealing with his stomach bobbing through the center of his body. Every time the wipers flicked across the windshield, the vomit choked in his throat.

"Now remember," she said driving up the gravel driveway, "don't say anything about what happened. When Mom and Dad ask you, just tell them that you swore not to say a word. That's the one thing they respect. Word of honor."

"I won't." Once the car stopped he felt a little better.

"All right. Take a deep breath." She cut the engine and rolled up the window.

Before Jayne could step out of the car their mother stood at the door. Her face was white, but David didn't know if it was anger or fear that infected her. "Where's Angie?" she demanded.

Neither of them said a word. Angie? They'd driven all the way back from the lake without Angie. Without a licensed driver sitting beside Jayne.

"I guess we forgot her." Jayne looked at her brother and frowned. She wanted to laugh but her mouth twisted in despair.

"We must've left her at the lake." David looked at his hands and shook his head. Suddenly his neck locked in place. He realized he was going to throw up and it was going to come right now. He tilted his head to see if this tiny adjustment would ease the vomit back down his throat. Then he saw his father standing at the door and noticed that his face was white, too — white and very worried looking. We're really in trouble, David thought. His whole body started shaking, and he had to hold onto the car.

"What in heaven's name happened to the car?" Their mother stepped around to the back and looked through the hole where the rear windshield had been.

Jayne started walking toward the house. "We had an accident," she said under her breath.

Catrina could barely hear her. She shifted her attention to David. All his energy was focussed on his hands gripping the hood of the car. She swung back to Jayne. "What was that?"

"I said we had a problem."

Catrina's face tightened and the color came back into her cheeks. "You get up to your room this minute young lady. And you can consider yourself grounded." But she didn't scream it out. Her voice was very controlled. Although none of the neighbors could hear a word, it was a blood threat.

From the driveway they walked in line towards the house without looking at one another. Jayne David and then Catrina. As David walked past his father he could see that his face was ashy and very pained.

Once David was inside all he could think about was the toilet. "The toilet, the toilet," he whispered. Just make it to the bloody toilet. Every step up the stairway was part of the chant. He turned the corner on the landing, walked up the last five steps past the girls' room and into the bathroom. And when he finally got there he realized it was perfect timing. Amazing timing. He stepped over to the toilet, kneeled on the floor and hurled. Right onto the seat cover.

"You're supposed to lift the lid before you do that."

He glanced around and saw Rose leaning against the door frame. Then he slumped onto the linoleum tile and stared at her.

She cocked her head slightly and gazed at him. She was

measuring something in him, waiting for the right moment to test his capacity for suffering. Did he know anything about the worms crawling through their stomachs? She would have to tell him sooner or later. Later, she decided.

"Grampy's dead," she said as his neck bent to the floor. "He died while you and Jayne were out — having your fun," she added. Nothing in her face moved. Her eyes were two blue stones.

Chapter Seven

"Except for the concussion you had as a baby when the girls dropped you down the stairs," Catrina said as she sponged David's head with a facecloth, "you never had a sick day in your life."

David didn't remember the concussion. From time to time he could feel the rush of a thousand pinpricks racing across his scalp and he knew it was the aftermath of the fall: the invisible tattoo needling into his skull.

"Not one sick day," she repeated. "Not the measles. Not the mumps. Not the chicken pox." At least not until the day of Grampy's death when he contracted a case of Hong Kong flu. Within two days the flu was complicated by erratic bouts of fever. At times he found himself floating above the bed gazing down at the sweating, aching ball he had become. He could smell the dry burning beneath his skin, and for a few moments he caught a glimpse of what slow death could bring, the brooding certainty it held — just as Grampy's funeral was about to begin.

"You're not going to the funeral," his mother said after

the doctor examined him. "Doctor Washburn has ordered you to stay in bed for at least a week."

"But Grampy — "

"In bed," she repeated. "You're running a temperature of a hundred and three. And that's final, young man." She fed him two crushed aspirins mixed in a paste of canned apple sauce, kissed him on the forehead and closed his bedroom door behind her.

Lying alone in his bed David felt a wave of chills wash over him. The trees rippled in the wind outside, their silhouettes purled against the patterns of fish and whales swimming in the bedroom curtains. On the wall the clash of shifting shadows absorbed him and dragged him under the rising tide of fever until he was gone, drowned, his body lying lifeless on the damp linen below. Then suddenly he was floating — drifting inches from the ceiling, looking down, seeing everything clearly, perfectly, and he realized that nothing could ever happen to his body that would threaten his soul. No sickness, no mutilation, no pain could possibly destroy him. He smiled and except for the fever that scorched through him he felt like a thin cloud billowing under the roof of their brick house, a house where death had a habit of coming in April.

As he floated there — the thread of fever anchoring the visionary cloud to his body — Grampy's voice began to speak:

"Davy."

David crashed back onto the bed. His body was a vacuum sucking him into a bag of sweating skin.

"Davy?"

He opened his eyes, but they burned in his head. All he could see was the hovering cloud.

"What?" he said but no sound came from his throat.

Healing the Dead

"I've come to say good-bye." David could tell it was Grampy by the burr in his voice, the phlegmatic way he always spoke when he wanted to whisper something important.

Good-bye, he said. But he didn't say it out loud. If this was Grampy then David knew all he had to do was think what he wanted to say; in the cloud, Grampy could hear his thoughts without any words at all.

"There's something I have to tell you."

David waited. It seemed to take some time before his grandfather could move on to a new sentence. Maybe he's coming to take me away, David thought, but he's afraid to say it.

"Something to tell your father."

"Why don't you tell him yourself?" David said aloud at last.

He waited again. "He can't hear me. His ears are stopped with sorrow."

David pressed his lips together and bit them. He couldn't move. Just breathing took all the energy he had.

"Tell him ... tell him that I love him."

He noticed the cloud beginning to shift. It rolled against the line of windows as he watched, then slowly dissipated and slipped behind the curtains into the night. Once it was gone, completely gone, he heard his grandfather calling from the emptiness in a thin, reedy voice blown back into the room by the wind. "And I love you, too," he wailed. "I love you."

At noon they buried him. Rose witnessed the ceremony, and the following day she told David the story exactly, describing everything in careful detail. She closed her eyes as she spoke and began by describing Reverend Brayne. In her opinion, he said nothing that touched the depth of Grampy's suffering — no mention of his arthritis nor the war nor the puréed food he was force fed the last few weeks of his life. All of that was forgotten with his death.

"But his life will be remembered," he'd said, "by the family that survives him. And if there is any meaning we can derive from the death of our loved ones, it is that life continues to flourish in the face of death. That the continuity of life on Earth provides us with the knowledge that in God there is a Life Everlasting."

"But it's not much more than a word game," Rose said after reciting the sermon. She paced in front of David's bedroom windows, twisting thin strands of her red hair in her fingers. "Like Scrabble, except that instead of letters that you put together, there's ready-made phrases like 'eternal comfort,' and 'life everlasting,' and 'the knowledge of God.' And the trick is to fit them all together in a pattern that makes a triple-word score in front of the whole congregation."

"So what did you think of it?" David could barely talk. During the day of the funeral his health improved, but he was still having bouts of fever and chills.

She sat down at his new desk. "I think it's strange they put us in the ground. I mean everybody believes that heaven's in the sky and hell's in the middle of the earth, right?"

"I guess so."

"So then after half an hour of sermons which are supposed to make us believe that we'll all go to heaven, they stick you six feet into hell. Either that or they cremate you, which is just a start on burning in hell."

David rolled his lips and considered Rose's new theory. It made sense, but it was so bleak. "But you don't really believe in hell, do you?" Somehow only heaven had any reality. Either that or Nothing-at-All.

She looked at him very carefully, measuring him again, trying to test his strength and endurance. "Do you want to know something? Something ... personal."

"Sure."

She spoke very softly and pushed her head forward a few inches. "I know there's a devil."

Neither of them said anything for a moment. They both glanced through the bedroom windows at the sky and watched the clouds tumbling toward them.

After a minute she turned to him again. "I've talked to him," she said.

He nodded slightly and looked at her. "And I talked to Grampy," he whispered. "Last night." He hadn't told anyone about it. He'd promised himself to keep the visit secret, but now it seemed important to tell Rose. Maybe she knew something about the cloud, too. "He was in a cloud. Just under the ceiling." He pointed to the exact location where the cloud had floated through the windows.

"Really?" She cocked her head and stared at his eyes.

"He said I'm supposed to give Dad a message."

She raised her eyebrows and David thought she was going to laugh.

"So what's the big message?"

He pressed his lips together. They were very dry, and he took a sip of water from the medicine cup. "It's personal," he said. "It's just for Dad."

She moved her head away. "So what'd he look like?"

"Well, nothing, really. There was just this cloud. And he was in it."

She bent forward again and stared at him. "Prove it."

"Look, he came right through ... " He closed his mouth.

It was impossible to prove a word of what he'd said. Especially to Rose.

"Didn't you take a picture? You're always taking a picture of everything."

"No, I didn't." Jayne had taught him to say "piss off" in situations like this and he felt like yelling it at Rose. But instead, he thrust the burden of proof on her. "Prove that you talked to the devil."

She stood up and walked to the window and then to the door. She thought that he was going to call her a liar. People had been calling her a liar at school lately. She didn't need to hear it from David too, not from her own family. She turned to him, to tell him this — the truth — when she saw two dots of glowing white light, just above his forehead. Suddenly they arced across the room, pinging from wall to wall in tight, sharp angles, threatening to smash into her. "Stop it!" she screamed. "Stop it!" She slapped both hands over her mouth as if to stop her own screaming and force it back down her throat.

"Stop what?" David yanked his sheets away and looked at her contorted face.

But she ran out of the room without saying anything and slammed the door behind her. As the door banged into place, David felt a new wave of fever roll through his body. Then he heard his grandfather's voice booming through the windows and up into the sky: "Don't grow old."

That night, after Catrina gave him another dose of crushed aspirins and apple sauce, David decided to stay awake all night. He snuck out of bed and got the Brownie Bull's-Eye and checked the flash to ensure it was properly fixed to the camera. When he was certain the camera was ready he set it next to the medicine cup and waited. If Grampy visited again, he was determined to take his picture.

He listened to the house, to the silence that covered them all. He listened for Harris's crying, the muffled crying he'd heard for the last two nights. There was not a sound now, and he wondered if his father's sadness had been replaced by emptiness, the same emptiness that had been squeezing them all one by one into tiny black boxes.

He felt himself drifting, floating, and eventually he decided to bite his lip to stay awake. Once he'd watched a John Wayne movie in which John Wayne had taught an unreliable soldier how to guard a wagon train through the night without falling asleep. "If you're gonna survive," John Wayne said, "you gotta suffer, soldier," and he opened his mouth and bit into his tongue until it bulged. But the soldier didn't have the inner strength to bite his tongue — *hard* — and during a momentary lapse a renegade Sioux slit his throat from ear to ear. David thought of the Indians crawling under his bed with long knives clasped in their mouths, and he pulled his lower lip between his teeth. Then he thought of German boys, boys his own age with Nazi daggers like Charlie Watson's — the same one that Brad Watson had used the day Rose shot him.

After a moment he forgot the pain of his teeth biting against his lip and fell asleep. It was like falling from a cliff into a dark pool of warm, warm water. There was no cloud, no white mist rising above the bed. Only blackness and then the voice whispering: "Davy."

He said nothing. Everything came from the emptiness.

"Davy, you must tell him that I loved him."

A breeze slipped over his chest and head, and he began shivering under the bedcovers. No.

"You are the vessel of love and forgiveness."

David's jaw shook and he tightened his mouth. *No.* The fever burned through his eyes and his teeth bit into his lower lip cutting hard into the skin. *No.*

"You are the vessel of — "

"Shut up!" The blood burst from his lips. Suddenly a slash of pain ripped through his mouth and he screamed again. But there were no words — only the pain came out, surging from his throat and eyes and ears.

"David! What is it? What's wrong?" His father bent over the bed, his hands searching through the twisted blankets for his son's face. "What is it?" he cried wrapping him in his arms. "What's wrong?"

"I ... " The blood oozed through his mouth as he sucked on his lip and pressed his tongue into the open cut.

His father could feel the moisture on David's face and hands and he clicked on the night lamp. "Oh God," he whispered when he saw the blood on his palm. He pulled his son to his chest and ran his fingers back and forth over David's hair. You're getting so big, he thought. And he buried his boy there, tucked him into the cave formed by his arms and chest, and listened to him crying. Somehow the crying and whimpering of his child made him feel complete. Harris held him there and thought about his own father. Had he ever comforted him like this? Tighter, tighter.

"It's okay, it's just a dream," he whispered and he started rocking back and forth as though they were two wheels trying to cycle up a long, broken hill. "Daddy's here," he said. "He loves you very, very much."

For a few moments they held onto one another, starring into each other's eyes. Looking into his father's face, David felt all of the past opening before him and the pain in his mouth, his fevers and chills, his aching head and neck — all of it slipped away. Then he felt the urgency of Grampy's message, the one last message linking the three of them together.

"It wasn't just a dream," David said after a little while. "Grampy said he loves you."

"Grampy?"

"Yes. He told me that he loves you."

"What?"

"I'm supposed to tell you. That he loves you."

But his father could not understand what David was saying. The message came too late, from a voice far too distant to mean anything.

Chapter Eight

For his thirteenth birthday David's parents bought him a new camera. It was a Canon 7, a 35-mm range finder that would shoot up to thirty-six pictures on one roll of film. Within three months he'd learned how to use it well enough to enter the Kandid Kamera division of the Ontario Junior Arts Festival. Jayne explained that "candid" meant "truth" and that if he wanted to win the prize David should take honest pictures of people doing things they'd never let you see if they knew you had a camera pointed at them. She also told him to give every picture a name. A name provided meaning, and in art meaning was as important as honesty.

Then Rose taught him to develop a theme. Over the past year she'd been developing themes of her own. She'd started writing a book of poems about love, although most of the poems were really about broken hearts. "Same damn thing," she insisted, "and the faster you fucking learn it, the better." She was swearing almost as much as Jayne now, at least in private, and he realized that rather than imitating their oldest sister, Rose was trying to outdo her.

David couldn't think of a theme at first, so he took pictures of whatever interested him. And what interested him most recently was the sight of his sisters' breasts.

Jayne was nineteen and Rose almost seventeen. Being the oldest, Jayne broke the romantic ground in the Sykes family. She and Grant Preston had been "an item," as Rose put it, for almost two years. And now Rose was very excited about developing a romance of her own. She studied Jayne and Grant carefully, and soon Rose began to share items with a boy named Billy Lugosi. Billy Lugosi had a sensitive, masculine face, but he knew absolutely nothing about love poetry. However, he seemed to know a fair amount about worming his hand under Rose's blouse and decorating the side of her neck with rings of purple hickeys. From David's vantage point (behind the swinging door of the basement bathroom), the amount of necking and petting going on in the house was fantastic.

"David! Knock it off!" Rose pulled herself from Billy's dark, smiling face and braced her elbow against the playroom sofa. "Get out of here or I'll kill you!"

"All right." Once she'd heard the camera cocking, David knew he'd lost the element of surprise. He still hadn't found a way of muffling the film winder, so he usually waited for the scene he wanted and then cranked off as many pictures as possible before the complaints started flying.

"I said hike your ass outta here or you're dead!"

He jumped out from behind the doorway and banged off two more shots.

"That's it!" A pillow flew by his face and brushed the camera from his eye. "You're meat, buster!"

"Okay!" He folded the camera into its case and walked upstairs to the kitchen.

His parents were in New York, and Granny was going to

cook dinner and stay the night. She hadn't arrived yet, and Rose, Billy and David were on their own. Earlier that afternoon Jayne had roared off with Grant on the Harley. "Goin' fishing," she'd said and laughed.

David leaned against the sink and gazed through the window. There's nothing to see here, he thought, and he felt the emptiness sift through the house, across the oak floors and into the kitchen. He heard something strange, a rasping noise, above him. He wandered into the front hallway and stood at the foot of the stairs and listened. Then he heard it clearly. Was it an animal panting?

He advanced the film to the next frame and quietly moved up the steps. The panting had stopped. He turned the landing corner and listened. Nothing. Then he heard it again. A shout and then a soft moan coming from the attic. Since Jayne had moved into her own bedroom in the attic, they'd discovered all kinds of animals up there. First a nest of squirrels, then a bat, and lately Jayne had mentioned the possibility of raccoons. David eased his foot along the floor and looked around the corner. The attic stairs rose at a steep angle straight up to her bedroom door. It was closed. He slipped his shoes off and put a foot on the first step. The stairs were very old and dry and every board creaked unless you knew exactly where to place your feet. But he'd practiced it a hundred times and pawed up the stairs soundlessly. He pressed an ear to her door and listened. Through the wood panel he could hear them: "Sha-sha-sha." *The sound of raccoons shucking nuts.*

It occurred to him that "Nature" might be a good theme for his entry into the Kandid Kamera division of the Ontario Junior Arts Festival. In the last year lots of wild animals had been spotted in Toronto, and now he knew he was going to get some very special shots for the photo competition: raccoons shucking nuts inside Jayne's bedroom! This could be the centerpiece of his whole portfolio. He'd call it something very straightforward: "Shucking Season," or simply, "Shucking." He listened again, trying to pinpoint exactly where they were working. If he could pop the door open and snap off three or four shots right away, he knew he could get something wonderful. But it had to be fast. His dad had warned him never to corner an animal, no matter how small. Even a rat could tear his throat out. So just in case the raccoons got rowdy, he planned to bang off four exposures, slam the door and beat it down to the basement to get Rose and Billy.

He heard them shucking again. "Sha-sh-sh." They were right on Jayne's bed! He pressed his ear to the door once more to make sure. He heard the bed squeak. Yes, definitely on the bed. He moved the camera to the door jamb and eased it open three inches, just enough for the lens, and then — click. Cock, click, cock, click, cock, click. Four shots before he even looked.

"David!"

He fumbled the camera, then caught it again.

"What the hell do you think you're doing?"

He looked. Where were the raccoons?

"Jesus. Get out of here!" Jayne screamed at him, her blonde hair flashing in the shadows of the room. But it was her body that absorbed David. Her breasts jacked back and forth as she yelled, her brown nipples nut-hard and insistent. And beneath them, Grant Preston's ever-cool mouth, wet along the lips.

"Sorry," David groaned in confusion. "I thought you were out."

"Christ! Just go." She wrapped the bedspread over her

chest and legs and brushed some hair from her eyes. "And stay out of here!"

"David, would you come here a minute, please?"

He was walking through the kitchen towards the backyard when his mother spotted him. Even before she said a word, he guessed there was trouble coming. He could tell by her white face. It looked very dry and empty.

"Sure, Mom." He smiled, mounting a hopeless but necessary defense.

"Wipe that grin off your face," she said. She shoved an envelope from Reich's Photography Shoppe towards him. "What are these?"

"Uh, my new set of pictures, I guess." Then he knew what she had. For the last year she'd picked up his prints from Reich's Photography, brought them home and looked through them. But he'd taken in this roll of film and picked up the prints himself. Then he'd hidden them under his bureau, under the little slot of wood where no one could find them.

"Pictures? This isn't photography — it's pornography." Her mouth cut at a severe angle. "Why did you take these pictures of your sisters — these *nudes* — and send them into town to be leered at by everyone?"

He looked at her teeth, the way she was spitting every word into the air. There's going to be hell to pay for this, he thought.

"Why are you destroying my life?"

He couldn't say a thing. He felt a surge of pee building in his bladder, pee that could possibly burst through his pants and onto her white shoes.

She slapped the envelope onto the counter and then

pointed her finger at the ceiling. "Now get up to your room and stay there until you hear from me."

"But ... "

"Go!"

He started to cry, but it didn't stop her. She pushed him into the hall with the palm of her hand; he ran up to his room and slammed the door.

He heard her call the girls down to the kitchen. One at a time they slumped down to her, their bare feet thunking onto each wooden stair. Then there was more screaming, and they came back upstairs and cursed through David's door before shutting themselves into their own bedrooms.

Jayne was angry, but she seemed to pity him more than anything else. But Rose was furious. "You might as well be dead, Daydoe. And six feet into Hell."

When his father returned home, they were given separate punishments. David had his Canon taken away for a month. Jayne lost her car privileges for one month and was not permitted to see Grant for two months. And Rose was forbidden to date again until she turned seventeen — another ten weeks away.

When the high school Valentine's Day dance was announced three weeks later, the girls begged for a reprieve.

"You're not going out with those boys, and that's final." Their father balled his fists in his pockets and stared into their eyes.

"But it's Valentine's Day! " Rose screamed from the top of the stairs.

"You should have thought about that while you were stripped naked on the sofa," their mother bit back and stood beside her husband in the hallway. A boozy vapour enveloped her as she braced herself, one hand reaching to her husband's shoulder for support. She felt everything she loved was melting, draining through the tiny cracks in the floor. They both sensed that now was the critical time to make a stand. But a stand against what? Harris wondered. For a moment he thought that he was battling time itself and that he would certainly lose.

By Valentine's night David had given up any hope of peace. Every evening that week he sat in the living room watching TV until Rose and Harris started screaming. He told her to get back up to her room. She told him to go to hell. He told her to come downstairs and say that to his face. Rose walked towards him, her lips tight like her mother's.

"Go to hell." It was a whisper, a breeze. "I hate you!"

Harris felt an immense rush of blood rise through his chest and arms. Then, suddenly, his open hand slashed across her mouth.

Rose held her fingers to her chin to stop the pain. "I'm going to the dance, and there's nothing you can do to stop me!"

"Sweetheart — " Harris tried to embrace her. He needed to hold her, but she turned away. She bit her lip to stop her tears.

"Darling ... Rose. I'm sorry, but I can't let you go. Can't you see that?" He thrust his arms around her but she broke loose and ran upstairs.

For the next hour a kind of quiet returned. David heard Catrina and Harris in the dining room talking secretly, and at last he could breathe easily again. He inched his way into the front hall and pressed his ear next to the dining room door.

"I'm telling you, Harris. If one more thing happens now —"

Healing the Dead

"Don't even think that way," his father cut in. "Why are you always planning for a disaster? You're building your whole life around it."

"I'm not planning anything!" she whispered emphatically. "I'm just telling you that if anything more goes wrong, I don't know what'll happen to me."

"What do you mean?" his father's voice dropped to a deeper tone.

"I ... I don't know." She paused, and for a moment David thought that he shouldn't be listening to any of this, that what he'd heard was forbidden. "It's just that in the last month ... I've been thinking more about Jean."

"Jean?" Harris coughed lightly. "But you weren't responsible for your sister's death. That was a car accident."

"I know. But it just left everyone so unprepared." Her voice broke slightly, and David quietly tiptoed back across the hallway to the living room and sat next to the TV.

He turned up the volume and watched Rin Tin Tin race through a forest. David felt himself entering the world of the television as he tried to vanish into the woods with the dog. Running, running, running — tirelessly, and always for the good.

Then an explosion burst through the air. David slipped into the hallway and looked upstairs. Harris appeared beside him, leaning against the banister. They glanced at one another and ran up to the landing and stared at the hole that had been punched through the glass door. Glass had shattered across the carpet and down the first few steps of the staircase. A motorcycle wrench lay on the floor just below the door, and when they looked across the balcony above the back porch, they saw two bedsheets knotted to the railing where they fluttered in the breeze. Then they heard screaming coming from Rose's bedroom.

"Oh God." Harris ran along the hallway to her bedroom. He cranked the doorknob back and forth. The door wouldn't open. Suddenly David knew that the huge block of ice that had frozen them all in suspension for so long was fracturing, fracturing hard and loud, grinding across the bedrock. He felt exposed and very cold.

The screaming came in a raw primal fury. Harris broke open the bedroom door and there, shoved against the wall as though someone had thrown her, Rose hammered her fist into the palm of her left hand. Her mouth stretched wide open and her lips narrowed against her teeth. The shrieking had stopped and only one sound filled the room: her hands smacking together with wet slaps as ribbons of blood danced from her palm along her arm onto the floor. David could see the safety pin she'd straightened into a long needle as it caught the light from her study lamp. She jabbed it into her hand again and again before Harris could pull the steel pin away and wrap her carefully in his arms.

Chapter Nine

Catrina wound some gauze around Rose's palm and taped it to prevent any slippage. Although she'd trained as a nurse she'd lost the forced calm that most nurses possess as they stare into the accidental mash of flesh and bone. When she saw that the safety pin had punctured an artery and punched through the back of Rose's hand she started to cry. Then Harris guided them both in his arms. David led the way to the car and opened and closed the doors for everyone. As he walked around the car he thought, this is the way Jesus had it — nails hammered right through His hands.

But Jesus went to heaven and he knew the hospital psychiatrist was telling his father that they were all going straight to hell. It was just a question of how hot things could get before somebody cracked. And somehow he knew that it was going to be his mother. She was the one who was really hurting, and he could see the pain rising in her throat and then into her face as they waited in the hospital lounge while Harris and Rose sat in the psychiatrist's office.

"I don't know why she did it." His mother gazed at the wall studying it for answers.

"Me neither," David said. He could still smell the Dewar's scotch on her breath and he thought it was probably best that she'd had a couple of drinks before everything had blown up.

"It's just despicable!" she whispered, the anger tucked furiously under her breath. "To think that she could cause so much suffering."

"Maybe it's not all her fault." David had read enough about Harry Houdini to know that people could slip into unconscious states and endure immense pain without any awareness of discomfort. "What if she was in a trance or something, and she just didn't know what she was doing?"

"Smash a glass window in a trance?" Her eyes were bloodshot and unforgiving. "And then wrap the bedsheets over the railing and run off into the night like a common tramp? Don't be a fool, David."

Then David realized that she was talking about Jayne while he was talking about Rose. He shook his head and tried to relax on the wooden bench.

Harris rounded the corner with his arm across Rose's shoulder and led her down the hall. "Okay we're ready to go." He half smiled, but Rose's mouth thinned into a narrow line. Her face turned cakey and white.

As he turned the ignition key in the car, Harris glanced at has wife. "So the doctor wants us to come in again next week."

"Oh? Which doctor is that?" Their mother looked out into the night traffic. The red and white lights reflected all over the windshield dancing across her face like sparklers.

"Dr. Ramsey." He pulled out into the stream of flashing lights.

Sitting in the back seat, Rose and David stared out the windows and listened.

"You mean Dr. Ramsey, the psychiatrist." Their mother's voice dropped and then she laughed a little.

"Look, I'm just trying to help you."

"Well, I think I can look after Rose's hand on my own. I was trained as a nurse, you know and — "

"All right!" Harris punched his foot into the brake. The car lurched, but he managed to pull over to the curb. "If you think you can handle it, fine!" His face glowed in the darkness, the amber sheen flickering over his skin. "You do it then. But do it, goddammit."

She tried. Twice a day she bathed Rose's hand in disinfectant solutions and each time she said that the wound was healing. After three days Rose unravelled the gauze and let David examine her palm.

"Wow. It went right through your hand." He'd never guessed the hole had cut so deep. The skin had been stitched together and a burgundy scab had formed in her palm. On the back of her hand tiny pointillist scars dotted her skin. He took a deep breath and examined it carefully. "Holy shit," he said hoping to please her.

She frowned. Her hand seemed detached from her, as though it belonged to some other creature, an alien.

David thought of Harry Houdini again, and he was certain that Rose had fallen into an unconscious trance. He wondered how strange it must have felt. "Can I ask you for a personal favor?"

"What?"

"Can I take a picture of your hand?"

"Are you kidding?" Her eyes widened. "Of course not."

"Just one shot." Her hand looked so unusual with its fresh scab and the pale skin around it. He held a thumb and finger in the air, an inch apart. "Come on, just one little picture."

"You sadist."

"It's part of a new theme I'm going to do: hand holes."

She smiled. Christ, hand holes now. She examined her hand again and said, "All right, but only one picture."

David believed she consented because she knew that the picture would give her a way to remember her insanity. And that perhaps the memory would be enough to make her hesitate before she tried to go crazy again.

In the end she permitted four pictures. It was the first time David was allowed to use the Canon in a month, and he felt very excited looking through the eye piece once more. He found that the camera added a certain richness to seeing the world: the split image in the range finder, the focus, the blown-up enlargements. With a camera he could see things that didn't appear to him in any other way. And, of course, it helped him to remember. The pictures remembered the truth, the exact way life happened without the soft filters of nostalgia and hope blurring the hard edges of reality. The facts: Rose's punctured hand and Brad's dead body stretched on the basement floor.

Two days later Catrina got a call from Granny. Jayne had arrived at her house that morning. She was nauseous, and Granny promised to drive her over. They planned to come with Reverend Brayne and they had something important to say. "So," she asked, "could everyone please be ready in about half an hour?" David heard it all on the upstairs telephone as he eavesdropped with his ear pressed to the receiver and his hand wrapped over the mouthpiece the way he'd seen Jayne do it.

When they arrived, he was surprised to see Reverend Brayne without his robes. He did wear his white collar, but the rest of his outfit was casual — a tan shirt and brown corduroy jacket. Still, he came into the front hallway and smiled with the same comforting smile he used whenever he climbed into the St. Mary's Church pulpit.

"Hello, David." He touched him on the head and then turned to Rose.

"Hello, Rose. How are you?"

"All right." She looked at his shoes.

"You have such a lovely name," he said, touching the top of her head, too. "If I had your name, I'm sure I would think of God's beauty every day."

She didn't say anything more, and in the silence everyone noticed Jayne standing behind Reverend Brayne and Granny. An awkward hesitation filled the hallway for a moment before Catrina invited them into the living room. She'd spent the last twenty minutes running up and down the rugs with her carpet sweeper. The room was immaculate.

"Whiskey?" Harris offered. "Or scotch?"

"No." Reverend Brayne waved a hand and smiled again. "Not right now, thanks."

Something was building, but David had no idea what. Jayne wouldn't look at him. She was very pale, and she bit along the edge of her lower lip. Granny smiled and said nothing. Somehow she'd grown younger now that Grampy was gone. Her face seemed soft and full.

"Harris," she said, turning to her son once everyone was seated, "I was thinking that perhaps there might be something for Rose and David to do upstairs."

"Yes, there is!" Catrina jumped at this. "There's beds to be made and linen to be changed!" She stood up and whisked the children ahead of her. "Come on, David, Rose — upstairs. You know where the fresh sheets are kept." She escorted them to the linen closet and stripped the bed in the guest room. No one had slept there in months. "You two are not to come downstairs until you're called." Her face was stern and her eyes bloodshot. Rose didn't say a word. She started spreading the bedsheets over the bed and smoothing them flat with her good hand.

"What's going on?" David looked at his sister, but Rose just glanced at him and kept working.

"How come Reverend Brayne's here?"

"Why do people usually bring a minister home?"

"I don't know."

"Well, think about it." She fluffed the pillow and pulled the bedspread over the blankets. David calculated that there could be only two reasons she was stalling: she either knew everything — or nothing.

"*Tell* me."

"Because," she said turning to him, "they believe the devil has come into the house."

"There are times," Reverend Brayne said when Catrina returned to the living room and sat down, "when it's difficult to know if what has to be said is worse than the fact that it must be said." He smiled in a way that turned the corners of his mouth down.

Catrina watched him and sank into the sofa. She'd thought of having the living room furniture reupholstered and just now, as she eased into the pillows and watched the reverend's smiling frown, she made a note to herself to phone the upholsterer as soon as he left.

"This is one of those times," he continued, "when I know that everything is very difficult." He took Jayne's hand into his own. "Especially for Jayne and what she must tell you now."

Catrina sank deeper and deeper into the sofa. Only her ears were able to stay afloat, somewhere up near the surface, two tiny listening holes.

"I ca—" Jayne looked at her hand lying in Reverend Brayne's palm. It was a bird, calmly feeding there, a wild bird picking pebbles from the rows of his fingers.

"Darlin' ... " Harris got up from his chair, but the reverend waved him back with his free hand.

"Please, let her speak."

Catrina's ears were hot bowls steaming on the edge of the well. From deep below, completely submerged, she listened.

"I ... " Jayne took a deep breath. She pulled her hand free and laid it in her lap. She glanced at her mother, then the others. Her stomach was sore and her fingers pressed against the edge of the tiny, growing ball. "I'm pregnant," she whispered. Then she said it again looking directly into the room, looking at no one, but saying it aloud to everybody. "I'm pregnant."

Catrina heard her ears pop: a bright, crisp noise that bounced at the back of her skull. And as her ears sank into the well, she was surprised that she'd stopped breathing, surprised that no one pulled her up for air.

Jayne had two suitcases open on her bed. She started loading one with socks and underwear, then jeans and shirts and skirts. The other she filled with books and records, newspaper clippings, and the academic ribbons and badges she'd pinned above her dresser.

"How come you're leaving before you finish college?" David sat next to the window at her desk. She'd told him that he could have her desk once she'd gone, and now he pulled the drawers in and out, testing their action. "You know Dad wants you to finish college. It's just your first year."

"Because I've got to go now." She held her fingers to her mouth, considering what to take and what to leave behind. Does it really matter? she asked herself. No, nothing matters any more. There's just you and the secret. You and the baby and the secret. But of course the baby is the secret, so it's really only you and the secret.

"That's no answer."

She glanced at him but didn't say anything more. She was going to New York and that was the only thing that seemed to make any sense at all. Harris had managed to find a home for unwed mothers in a small house that was run by an Episcopalian minister. And since he worked in New York almost half the time anyway, he'd told her, he could check on her just like at home.

"I'm going to be free," Jayne said after she had her clothing loaded into the first suitcase. "From now on, all my decisions are mine."

"Yeah, well, what about us?" He pretended that his eyes could see right into her soul and find things there that she didn't even dream were a part of her.

"What do you mean?" She stopped and sat next to him. "There'll still be us. We're still together. I'll be back, you know." She tried to smile but felt the deceit in her lips. She'd always hated faking, and now that she had to mislead him, her contempt for this fraud made her shudder.

"Back forever?"

"Well, at least back to visit."

"Oh, that's *just* great." David knew that he didn't want to be left in Toronto with Rose and his mother while his dad and Jayne lived together in New York. He'd never been to New York, but he imagined it was fabulous.

"It will be great. Just think of me in New York like it's a sister city. You'll have one sister in Toronto and one in New York. It'll be okay, you'll see." Another lie, she whispered to herself. Now that she had lied several times in the last three weeks, she didn't want to dwell on it. She'd agreed to tell him nothing about the baby. Her mother had insisted on that.

"If you don't tell him anything, then it is not a lie." Catrina had rubbed at her ears as she spoke, looking up to the ceiling. "Silence is never a lie."

"It is to me!" Jayne had screamed. She knew that this was one of the differences between them: that the truth could never be a conspiracy of silence.

Her mother had taken a deep breath and examined her daughter. "What if our neighbors find out about this? Did you ever stop to think what would happen if the papers published the facts? Your father has a reputation to maintain. Did you think about that? This is his livelihood. This is how he supports our family. Did you think of any of that?" Her anger had ground each word into a metallic spittle that frightened Jayne. She had never really been frightened by her mother before. Then suddenly she had understood that her mother was the one in danger; that the truth could kill her. At that moment Jayne had decided that life was more important than the truth, and she accepted the lie. She had wrapped her baby in a shroud of silence and buried it in dark quietude. No one would be told about her child.

"Come on give me a kiss okay?" Jayne looked at David as he split the veneer edge of the desk with his fingernails. She already felt a hundred miles away.

He kissed her flatly on the cheek without making his lips pucker. He thought he would cry — he could feel it in his chest and eyes. He couldn't figure out what stopped them both from crying right there. But they didn't. Instead, he ground his teeth together. In the silence he hoped that Jayne would refuse to go and when it was time to leave she'd run back into the house and hold him — hold him and never let go.

Later that afternoon when Jayne drove away with her father in the car she and her mother were both sobbing. The March sun rose high above the snowbanks, and the icicles had just begun to melt. Watching the Chevy back out of the driveway, David could feel the thin heat through the window as it warmed his belly, and he wondered how long it would take all the ice to melt into the gutters and wash down the storm drains. It seemed like a question that no one could answer with any precision. When the car finally drove out of sight his mother closed the front door and came into the living room. She dabbed her tears with one knuckle of each hand. "Well, it has to happen eventually," she said.

For a moment David thought she'd read his mind, that she was talking about the melting snow. But he didn't say anything. Instead he watched the way she tied the apron knot behind her back. She always tied it snugly, without looking.

Then she went into the kitchen, and without soap or

water or the wire brush she got down on her knees and started to scrub the tile floor with her bare hands.

Chapter Ten

"We're moving to New York!" Harris strolled into the dining room with a huge grin on his face, turned and looked at David and Rose, then back to Catrina. "I just found out today. The department wants me in New York and Washington on a permanent basis!"

"Really? ... " Catrina was eating a tuna sandwich for lunch and it took her two or three chews to finish her sentence. "That's wonderful!"

"It is?" Rose dropped her sandwich onto the side plate, looked at her father and tightened her mouth into a little blowhole. Sometimes when she felt threatened she pinched her lips together as though she were going to whistle. But instead of whistling she'd simply blow a stream of air from her mouth.

"Of course it is!" Her mother finally managed to swallow her food and got up from her chair to kiss Harris on the cheek. "This is a very big promotion for your father," she said, turning back to Rose, "and you should congratulate him."

Rose glared at him as she stood. "Congratulations," she hissed and then strode upstairs to her bedroom, banging her feet as she went.

Harris sat down and propped his chin on his fists. Dammit, he moaned to himself. But then he smiled again.

"Will we get to see Jayne?" David asked.

"You bet!" He unrolled his fingers and clapped his hands together.

"Of course. We'll all be together again!" Catrina realized that Harris had found a way out of Toronto, a way out of their haunted brick house, and her face began to pink as she dabbed her eyes with the corner of her napkin.

David watched them for a minute, and he sensed their relief. He got up from the table, walked into the living room and looked at the fireplace. It had been a year and a half since Jayne had left. She was living in Queens, and although he'd never been in the United States, David thought that Queens would be a good place for her. The name made it seem very green and well tended, with long driveways curling through riverside parks. Jayne had mailed him a few postcards of Manhattan. She loved New York. It was the "center," she wrote. But the center of what?

"The center of loneliness," Rose said once she was willing to talk about the fact that they were really going to move. "And the center of crime and misery."

"And Ed Sullivan and the New York Rangers."

"And over ten million people. Did you know that?"

"So what's wrong with that? I thought you liked people. There's lots of people to be popular with there." David also thought that moving to New York would give them all a chance to start new lives. And more than anyone else, Rose needed a new life.

"Nothing's wrong with it. It's just that I happen to have friends here." They sat on the porch steps looking down at the FOR SALE sign staked into the lawn. As she spoke Rose tapped a small rock against the flagstone sidewalk. "Just because you don't have any friends doesn't mean I have to suffer."

David could feel the blood rising in his face. Friends? He just never wanted to bring any friends home — specially when she was around. But he didn't say any of this. Most of the people he knew believed Rose was half crazy and some of them — Michael Van Durr and Don Dimeon — said nobody wanted to visit because there was always an outside chance of being shot in the face. Besides, except for Billy Lugosi, it was Rose who didn't have any friends. And Lugosi only came around whenever Catrina and Harris were out because he knew he could take advantage of Rose's ever enlarging breasts.

David tried to shift the subject, tried to invent compelling new reasons why they would all love New York. "What about the New York Yankees? Dad said we could follow their home games right through the fall season."

Rose pinched her lips a little. She was interested in the Yankees. She always liked the overlapping initials on their caps: the Y placed on top of the N. They could stand for Yes and No. She smiled. Yes and no, yes and no, she whispered to herself. She thought about Mickey Mantle. He was very sexy. "Yeah," she agreed, "the Yankees are a gas."

It made David happy to hear her say that. *The Yankees are gas* — a concession from her that things just might be okay. Whenever she started to brood about leaving all her friends behind he reminded her of the New York Yankees and what a miraculous team they had.

Harris eventually sold the house. While the Allied Van Lines men loaded their furniture into the truck, Catrina vacuumed and scrubbed the last vestige of their existence from the floors and walls. Finally they all sat in the Chevy at the foot of the driveway and looked at their old home. This made David very happy, too.

But at the moment they began to drive away Rose started to cry. Catrina wrapped an arm around her and began murmuring, "Don't cry, Rosie. Don't cry. We're going to leave it all behind, sweetheart. It'll be all gone as soon as we drive down the road." And although she settled Rose down, Catrina soon had tears running from her eyes, too.

"Amazing," Harris said turning the car onto the street, "how we're all just so damned pleased to be leaving."

Chapter Eleven

Rose sat on the edge of the Palisade cliffs and stared over the Hudson River towards her new home. Her eyes scanned the horizon where she thought their townhouse should be, but there were clusters of buildings everywhere, with nothing to distinguish their corner townhouse from other identical buildings, each with stone facades around the dining room windows and over the back patio doors. From the west side of the river, she couldn't be sure of anything. She'd only been in New York a few months and this was her first trip across the Hudson to New Jersey, up to the top of the cliffs.

Rose first saw the Palisades from the den window in their new townhouse in Hastings-on-Hudson, a Westchester bedroom community fifteen miles north of the city. From inside, through the west-facing windows, she looked across the Hudson River to the New Jersey side at the Palisades, a continuous wall of sheer cliffs that rose from the Hudson. At their top Rose could see a line of trees that she thought might be a park or an estate.

"This is New York?" she'd asked as her family stood together gazing out the window.

"No, this is Hastings," Catrina said.

"-on-Hudson. Or H-O-H, for short." Harris flattened the palm of his hand on the freshly painted drywall and smiled. He and Catrina had picked out the townhouse during one of their trips to the United Nations.

"I thought we were moving to New York. Where's the Empire State Building, the Statue of Liberty," Rose paused, "the poor, tired, huddled masses?"

In Hastings-on-Hudson nothing resembled the poor, the tired or the huddled. Not remotely. To get near them she had to take a commuter train that shuffled through suburb after suburb until it crossed the Harlem River and then slipped underground. After another fifteen minutes jiggling through the black tunnels of Manhattan, the train arrived in Grand Central Station on 42nd Street. There the masses began.

Later that night, after they set up the beds, Rose told David about the history of the Palisades. Driving down in the car, she'd read the tourist brochures that Harris had given her. "That's where Aaron Burr had a duel with Alexander Hamilton." She pointed out a spot on the far side of the river to authenticate the story. Her bedroom was smaller than David's, but it had a corner window looking across the Hudson.

"Nobody really knows what the duel was about."

"Did they use swords?"

"No. Pistols. Burr shot him right through the belly." Her eyes locked onto the cliffs and her head dipped slightly. "Burr was a soldier during the Revolutionary War. In fact, he even led a Yankee attack on Canada, but we beat the shit out of them. Anyway, he knew what he was doing."

"Then what happened to him?"

"To Burr? Nothing. In fact, they almost elected him president. In the 1800s murder didn't matter so much." She stubbed her cigarette against the aluminum window frame and then flicked the butt onto the back lawn where it could be mistaken for one of her father's.

But now that she'd had long enough to think about it, Hamilton's murder did matter. She wandered around the cliffs for an hour looking for the exact place where he'd been shot, but it was useless. She'd hitched a ride with some of the other kids skipping school and wandered over to the cliffs on foot, half lost except for the fact that she could see the river below her. She'd had to cut school to get here, but lots of people were doing that; with the atomic bomb about to drop, who wanted to stay in school?

Her stomach began to roll. It felt like a small nest of worms the way it churned in a mass and then settled again. Starve, you buggers, she thought. If they got hungry enough they'd have to crawl out for food, wouldn't they? She'd heard the standard therapy for a tape worm. (Starvation diet: when the worm started to climb up the esophagus, you lay flat on a bed with a small dish of sweetened milk just beside your opened mouth. You kept your mouth open, and when the worm smelled the milk, it crawled over your tongue out to the milk, and when two or three feet emerged, the doctor grabbed it and jerked the rest of it up your throat.) Christ, that has to be a lie, she thought. They used drugs now — poison to kill the beast that kills you. But drugs or not, you had to make them starve.

She took a cigarette out of her purse, lit it and tossed the match over the cliff edge. It caught a little eddy of wind, pulled away from the cliff and curled into the water. She looked downstream to where the city would be. None of it was visible in the smoggy October haze, but at the end of the river she knew New York was there, hiding — trying to make itself smaller, now that the Cubans and Russians and Yanks were really going to do it: start dropping their bombs.

She sucked on the cigarette and watched the cloud of smoke billow from her mouth into the air. No, it won't be like that. Not a little puff of smoke in the wind. Nothing so simple. It's a complicated mushroom shape, that grows and grows.

Suddenly a tight gust of wind sucked a sheet of dust from the cliff and she saw herself flying over the river, pulled right out of her shoes. There was the heat and the wind and nothing left behind but her shoes. She was whirling over the river and looking down at New York, at the huge mushroom firestorm devouring the steel and glass. She glanced back at her two black loafers sitting neatly on the edge of the cliff while she soared up and up. A voice came from her mouth, a deep, masculine voice trying to warn her. She knew it was a new poem emerging, with the poetry dictated to her, already formed in lines hanging in the sky beside her, laid out in an exact pattern of the mushroom cloud. She felt herself burning, her hair crackling into brittle stubs, her breasts melting away from her chest in hot gobs and she was falling-falling-falling until all that was left were the words of her poem tattooed into the boiling sky.

The furnace room was the closest thing to a bomb shelter in the Sykeses' new townhouse. It was concrete on three sides. The fourth side was made of paneled wood and had a veneer door which led into the basement den. The ceiling was wood and, due to a flaw in the joists, slightly convex. Whenever anyone walked across the living room floor the ceiling of the furnace room sank and squeaked under the weight. Two walls were lined with storage shelves; Catrina had put most of her preserves along the north wall where they would be coolest. One of the walls had a window built into the middle of the concrete. Harris taped the window in a big X and then covered it with an old sleeping bag that he nailed to the frame.

On Tuesday Harris came home from the United Nations early in the afternoon. He sat in the den with Catrina and David, watching Walter Cronkite report on the Russians approaching the American blockade zone. "This evening," Cronkite said, his voice stony, resolved to this test of masculinity, "the world looks to its leaders for resolution — or total annihilation."

It was the sixteenth of October, and they didn't know anyone on their street except Mr. Hermanns, the neighbor who told them not to walk on the yard because he'd just sprayed it with DDT. Rose had locked herself in her bedroom. No one knew where Jayne was. Catrina phoned her apartment in Queens every half-hour, but there was no answer.

"Maybe she's coming out on the train," David said.

His mother stood in front of the TV after hanging up the telephone. "No, she's not coming out." She rubbed her hands over her face and looked at Harris. Maybe he would find her. "No," she said again. Harris couldn't find her, she told herself. No one could.

Harris's forehead furled into a dozen ridges, and he clicked the TV off. They'd moved all the way to New York to be near Jayne, and now who in hell knew where she was?

Healing the Dead

He felt the emptiness widen in his stomach. His stomach was always sore; the Russian ships were steaming through his guts. "She'll be fine," he said after a moment. "David, why don't you get Rose and Mom'll show everyone how she's set everything up." He loaded the last box of tinned food into his arms and walked downstairs to the furnace room. "Okay? We'll have a little drill." He tried to make it sound like fun, but his voice fell flat. Instead of smiling, he turned his head away and thought about his stomach.

David walked up the stairway to Rose's room. Because the townhouse was a split level, the stairs crisscrossed in three flights from top to bottom. When he reached the top level, he called to her so that she wouldn't have to throw out her cigarette because she suspected he was Harris or Catrina.

"It's me."

"What d'you want?" Her door was locked.

"Dad wants to show off the bomb shelter."

She opened the door. "What a bunch of crap," she said and waved him through and relocked the door behind him. Then she flopped down on her bed and tucked a pack of Marlboro cigarettes under the pillow. She'd had to switch from Players to Marlboros because that was the American brand Harris smoked. She thought Yankee smokes were lousy. "Want to read a new poem?" She passed a sheet of paper to her brother and braced her head against the pillow. "It's a hate poem."

"I thought you were writing love poems." He looked at the title, "War Cry of the Worm."

"I quit that crap." Her voice hardened. "Love is an escapist fantasy in the face of total annihilation."

Total annihilation — exactly what Walter Cronkite had

just said. There was a raspiness to Cronkite's voice that loaded the Cuban missile crisis with the weight of inevitable doom. And it was Cronkite's voice, the sound of it, that made David realize Rose was becoming more masculine. The change was not in her physical appearance. In fact, now that she was eighteen she had developed very full breasts and a narrow waist that she cinched with a wide black belt. Her red hair was long but very fine. Every Sunday night she curled it to perfect its dancing, ribboned fall from her shoulders. Because she looked so much like a model, it took David months to realize that it was Rose's voice, not her body, that made her seem so masculine. Although it didn't resonate in the chest or rise deeply through the throat, her voice was severe and had a shell that coated every word and eliminated any possibility of tenderness.

"Read it. Don't you know how to read?"

David didn't know what to say. It was impossible fighting Rose with words. When she was like this he found it difficult just being in the same room with her. A rush of prickles ran along his spine and over the top of his scalp. He looked at the poem and pretended to read it. But the whole time his eyes blurred and he kept telling himself, just get her down to the basement, just get her down there as fast as you can. Maybe Dad will know what to do, especially if she's going to go crazy.

"You don't have to tell me you like it," she said after a minute. "You're not supposed to. You're just supposed to hate yourself for being part of it all." Her chin stuck into the air and her pupils dilated. Be honest, she thought. Just be honest about how you feel about the end of the fucking world.

"Oh. I guess ... I do."

"Do what? Hate yourself? Ha! That's a laugh." She lifted her head from the pillow and sat on the edge of the bed. She could feel her skin tingling. She was in a vacuum, the same one that was sucking them all into eternal death. The feeling was exactly the same as when she stood on the edge of the Palisades and the vision of the bomb came to her: she felt disembodied but free. Then she looked at David and saw that he was stranded far, far below her. "You love yourself. More than anyone else I know."

"We'd better go downstairs," he said to her. "Dad wanted — "

As he spoke he saw her eyes disconnect. First she was staring at him, then he realized that her eyes had lost focus. He couldn't decide if she were just thinking or if her soul had become unhinged and disappeared. She'd done this before, when Jayne was there with him, but never when he was alone with her.

"Look. Let's just go."

She didn't move.

He went to the bed and touched her sleeve. He rubbed the top of her shoulder. "Come on, Rose. Let's go downstairs."

She felt his hand reaching up to her. Maybe he wasn't so far away after all. Then she felt his fingertips, the lightness of them through her cotton sleeve, and she decided, yes, why not go downstairs and tell them. She was quiet as they walked down the three flights of stairs and into the furnace room; she was quiet as her father closed the veneer door behind her. When she looked around the room, she saw everything laid out in a way that only her mother could arrange: tins of food stacked neatly against the wall; preserves all labelled and shelved; bottled water wrapped in layers of paper; blankets folded together and tied with twine; plates, cups and utensils stacked in a wicker picnic basket; and five cots collapsed and stacked next to the furnace. Everything revealed a perfection of sanitary organization.

Then she heard the silence. She realized they were all waiting to die. They'd sealed themselves in this tiny cubicle, a minute box arcing through space, and if they opened the door and looked out they'd see nothing at all — just the emptiness sucking them into the void. She drew a deep breath into her lungs and looked at her family. She saw each one of them very far below her, mere specks of light, far, far away in the dusk. Then she thought that she would scream it out, but instead her voice broke into a whispering chant, a psalm penetrating the immense silence among them:

This war is a prayer.
This war is a prophecy without soldiers
a machine that has fabricated a nightmare from the sun
and torn the eyes from children who watch their parents'
helpless preparation for life
as though life is death
and death is death
the suicidal gift
of machinery.
This war is a prayer.
It is the scissor dance
of legless invention
the crawling child
of greed
the broken conception
of a wild dream
an infant given up
to strangers

Healing the Dead

who wander
humming this hymn
offering
the child
for sacrifice.
Their hymn is the war cry of the worm.

Chapter Twelve

The year following the Cuban missile crisis, Rose began dating Robert Houliman. Robert was most famous for his prize-winning design of the 1962 Dwight D. Eisenhower School Yearbook cover. Falling in love with "Hooligan," as he was known, tended to color Rose's judgement about a lot of things. After she announced that they'd become an item, she started writing love poetry again, and David thought that Robert Houliman was the only person who could keep her sane.

In memory of his World War II nickname, "Ike," Dwight D. Eisenhower High School was called Ike High by everyone who went there. Everyone except Robert. "Anyone who's working on the Kike High Yearbook has to have a sense of what this place is really all about." This was the first thing he ever said to David. "And as the name implies, it's all about kikes."

David looked down at his camera and pretended to adjust the lens. He could feel his feet sweating in his socks as he stood in the entrance to the yearbook office. He spent one afternoon a week working on the photography section of the yearbook. At the time, he had no idea what a kike was. At first he thought that Rose had fallen for an arts editor with a JFK haircut who couldn't pronounce the name of his own school properly.

"Kikes? ... kikes?" David wondered aloud. "He must mean kites!" And he spent the rest of the afternoon trying to find the school Kite Club so he could photograph the members for the yearbook Clubs Section.

"Not kites, Daydoe, he means Jews." Rose looked at her brother in amazement. How could anyone be so bloody naive?

"Don't call me that."

"Why not?" She turned her head back to the desk where her German language book lay open. "It suits you."

"Because it shows how ignorant you can be." He slammed the bedroom door on her before she could come back with another answer.

Robert Houliman was a very good artist, the best in the school. Nobody questioned the work he did for the yearbook. By the end of his senior academic year, he'd become an art prodigy. After the Fitzhenry Fund for the Arts awarded him a three thousand dollar art scholarship, The Westchester County News quoted him saying, "In the next twenty years the most important art will carry the observer into his own mind. What the artist discovers through this aesthetic introspection will be as important as the work of DaVinci, Raphael and all the so-called Masters."

This was the kind of self-confidence that captured Rose and bound her to him completely. At the time, nobody worried about their relationship. Catrina was all for it. "There's no one else she can talk to," she told Harris one night. "After all, she doesn't ... fit in with the crowd." He nodded thoughtfully, slowly lifting his food to his mouth at the dining room table. They ate late most evenings, after ten, when he got home from the UN.

"I know," he said. But she didn't know if he was agreeing that Rose didn't fit in, or that she had no one to talk to.

David realized that it didn't matter what his parents thought. Rose was just too much for them to handle. Robert appeared as a savior, the only person capable of talking to her, the one person who seemed able to convince her to move ahead with her life. And while he was at it, Robert decided he should help David along, too.

"What you want to do, David," he advised, leaning against his desk in the yearbook office, "is use your camera to penetrate the other side of the window." The "window" was what he called the camera lens and everything worthy of being photographed. "Don't just capture the surface of things. Fuck, anyone can do that. And don't go for the meat and bones either. All the bloody realists have done all that, and it hasn't meant a nerd of shit to anyone. You need the will to go further and deeper than anyone before. What you have to do is permeate your art with intelligence. And look for it first in the heart. That's where you'll find the goddamned truth. Read Nietzsche's *Antichrist*; he explains it perfectly."

David thought that Robert sounded a lot like Rose, especially with all his swearing thrown in for impact. But as he spoke, he had a smile on his lips. It was a smile that curved across one side of his mouth and left the other side flat. David first noticed it when he developed a few pictures of him in the school darkroom. He held a sheet of paper over one half of Robert's face. Then he switched sides. Strange.

Healing the Dead

The two sides of his face didn't match. One part was smiling and the other looked almost angry. And his eyes were different, too. Each had the same deep brown irises, the same long eyelashes, but the eyes and eyebrows were starkly dissimilar. On the right, his eye sparkled above his half-smile and the eyebrow arched as though he'd just told a very good joke, one which required his cleverness to understand. But the other eye was a deep, penetrating hole. This was the eye he used to dig inside people, David thought. Then he hammered them.

To make the division more obvious, he cut Robert's picture along the midline of his face. Then he placed the two halves an inch apart on a black mounting board and photographed the split halves together in one frame. When he developed the new picture, he couldn't believe what he saw. It looked like Robert Houliman was two distinct people.

"Hey, Mom, look at this!" As soon as he got home David ran up the stairs to the kitchen with the pictures tucked under his arm.

"What is it, David?" She sat next to the telephone on a bar stool, staring out the window at the Palisades. The moon was up and a fog bank had settled against the bottom of the ridge.

"Who do you think this is?" He held the picture under her face, but she just gazed at it, unblinking. "I call it 'The Divided Eye.'"

"Why'd you cut your picture in two?"

He looked at her. She didn't notice any difference. Then he smelled the scotch on her breath, and for a moment he thought she was two people, too.

"It's Robert Houliman. Both of them. Can't tell though, can you?" He walked around the room and considered that he was possibly the only person who really saw the truth about Robert.

"Don't be silly. Robert's upstairs with Rose, studying for their history finals."

"Really? I got to show them this."

"Don't you dare. They're studying."

By the time David walked up the stairs and halfway along the hall, he could hear their soft moaning. A muffled laugh sputtered into the corridor and then he heard Rose panting. He pressed an ear to her door and listened. They're doing it, he thought. Screwing right under Mom's nose. At first he felt like barging in on them and screaming at the two-faced bastard. But he'd interrupted his sisters before, and that had resulted in disaster. So instead, he stood there listening to the taut noise vibrating through the panel door. He thought maybe this was what Rose really did need, that Robert would get to the heart of her and make everything right. But at the very least, he thought they should know what he'd discovered about Robert's face.

He slipped the picture under her door and walked back into the kitchen where his mother had begun stacking the freshly ironed laundry into piles. Her hands folded each piece of clothing with a rigid mechanical energy. Her jaw was set as she looked at him. "I want you to help me carry this upstairs." She handed him the hamper of socks and leaned against the door.

"Right now?" He listened for Rose. Couldn't his mother hear them too? How could she miss? They were banging away like slap-happy beavers. Probably old man Hermanns could hear them two doors down. He decided to stall for time. In a few minutes maybe Rose would be quiet and their mother would never hear a thing. "Wait a sec," he begged her. "I need a Coke."

"Get a drink later. This is heavy, David." She could feel the weight of the laundry pulling the tendons in her arms, and she wanted to lie down. She'd spent half the morning in bed, and now she just wanted to get the laundry over with and lie down again.

"But if I wait, I'll die of thirst." He tried humoring her. If he could get her laughing, then she'd wait. "And if I die, I'll be useless as a laundry slave forever."

"March!"

"Oh, all right." He took the wicker basket and led the way up the stairs. Maybe it'll be best for her to hear everything, he thought. Then she can do something about it herself.

But nothing happened. As Catrina climbed the stairs, she heard her daughter panting, and in an instant she realized that Rose and Robert were making love, right beside her, in the bedroom. And at that moment she knew that she'd lost control of them. She couldn't go through the door, she thought. She'd gone through that door once before with Jayne and she'd lost her. Did she want to lose them all? All of them? She could feel the tug of the laundry on her wrists as though the clothes were slipping to the floor, and she locked her arms tightly in place.

Suddenly Rose barked out a long series of gasps. Catrina braced herself with the stack of Harris's ironed shirts and pants and walked straight past Rose's doorway without missing a step. When she reached the master bedroom, she breezed past David and closed the door. Then carefully, without a trace of emotion on her white face, she hung all of Harris's shirts in his closet: solid whites on the left, then off-whites and blues, then stripes and checks and finally the Arnold Palmer golf shirts on the extreme right. After all the pants were hung and his socks dispatched she opened the window and stuck her head into the spring air. "My there's a lot of traffic out on the street today," she said. "So many cars."

When it was quieter she deftly worked her way downstairs and into the kitchen. Leaning against the stove, she started to worry that the blood might stop flowing to her legs, and it occurred to her that one day soon she wouldn't be able to walk at all. With one hand pressed against her forehead she reached into the cabinet above the refrigerator for the Dewar's scotch. She'd managed a new discipline in the last few months, one that ensured a reasonable appearance of sobriety: depending on when Harris was expected home, she'd make long or short drinks — long on his delays, short on his pending arrival. She stared at the golden reflection in the bottle. Was it her face she saw or Rose's? Or was it even Jayne's lost little baby? Her fingers covered the reflection so that she could think straight. Time to make some fine adjustments she thought. Think straight or stop thinking at all.

Chapter Thirteen

The day before David turned seventeen Jayne invited him and Rose downtown to her new apartment in Greenwich Village.

"Look, how 'bout if I treat you on your birthday? In fact, I'll treat all three of us to lunch. Let's just go out on the town and blow it off!"

She sounded very persuasive on the telephone, almost persuasive enough to get them out of the house without a second thought.

"Okay. But I have to check with Robert." Rose hoped that Robert would take her out, but she knew he had to study.

"And Mom," David added from the second telephone.

"Don't ask. Tell her. Shit, it's your birthday." Jayne couldn't believe they wanted to ask for permission. Especially her sister. But she thought about it a moment and decided not to mention Robert Houliman at all.

On the way downtown David sat next to Rose on the commuter train and tucked his new camera between them.

For his birthday his father had given him a Canon FX, a 35 mm SLR which made his old range finder seem like a toy.

"Don't you think Mom's overdoing it with the booze?" he asked, testing his sister's mood. "Last night she almost fell over."

"Define 'overdoing it,' " Rose said. "Everybody knows that the meaning of excess is subjective. Besides, she should do whatever she wants. She's forty-seven, you know."

"Really?" That meant she was thirty when he was born. He looked at Rose and wondered if she'd ever have a baby. "Hey, let's have a cigarette." He glanced at the package of Marlboros tucked in her open purse.

"Why should I give you a smoke?" Rose turned her eyes away from his face and followed the conductor as he swayed down the aisle.

"To celebrate."

"Get off it."

"Simple Christian charity, then."

"Dry up."

"And it's my birthday."

"I already gave you a present," she said, handing him a Marlboro and then lighting one for herself. "Here. And make sure you light the right end."

Her gift to him was a copy of Hemingway's *For Whom the Bell Tolls*. She'd considered giving him a copy of Sylvia Plath's poetry, but decided on the Hemingway. She explained that Hemingway had shot himself and that Plath had stuck her head in an oven and turned on the gas. To Rose, Plath had more guts because it took considerable determination to hold your head in a gas oven and wait. Because a shot in the head was instantaneous, old Hemingway never gave himself the opportunity to savor "the dark color of the gate ahead."

David looked at her. "What's 'the dark color of the gate ahead' supposed to mean?"

"That's how Robert described death's door. Not a bad metaphor for a mere painter, huh?"

Worse than bad — awful, David thought, but he knew there was no point in telling her his opinion of Robert Houliman. His head was starting to spin from the smoke of the Marlboro, and he could never explain the finer points of Robert's madness. Besides, she'd heard it all before. The first time was when he'd slipped the picture of Robert's split image under her door. She'd screamed at him after that: it was malicious, slanderous — cutting somebody's head in two and then flashing it around. So instead of focussing on Robert personally, David commented on the fact that he actually managed to let her loose for a day.

"He didn't let me loose," she said as the train crossed the Harlem River. "Nobody holds a key on me."

David laughed and sucked another cloud of smoke into his mouth as he watched the city spin past the windows.

"He's working on a term assignment this weekend and needs the time to get everything right. Columbia University's no joke, you know. One day he's going to be famous." She gazed out the window and David thought the conversation had stopped. But then she added something as though it was meant to be part of the same sentence: "And, while he's doing that, I'm working on the final draft of my poetry collection."

David hadn't read any of her new work, but she'd told him that she'd switched from hate poetry back to love poems. As the train slipped underground, it picked up speed and rattled the dizzy, smoky feeling in his head. Watching his reflection in the window, he tucked the cigarette into the corner of his mouth and let the smoke sting his eyes as it rolled up his cheek. Love was supposed to make you feel just like this — dizzy. Maybe that's what love was all about: a deck of Marlboros and a long ride through a dark tunnel as you stare at your own reflection in the glass. That, and the faith that love will change the way you feel. In Rose's case, he hoped it would work.

After the train arrived at Grand Central Station, they took a bus to Greenwich Village and walked over to Houston Street, to Jayne's new apartment in a five-story walkup. It was just two rooms and a bathroom, with a little kitchen area hidden behind folding doors. The windows overlooked a courtyard where a huge maple tree grew through the cracked asphalt and reached up to her fire escape.

"Don't you love that tree?" Jayne chewed on a piece of dry toast and combed the hair from her eyes with one hand.

"Yeah, it's outstanding." A gust of wind pulled the branches into the air. David held his camera next to the window and twisted the focus ring until he could see the leaves floating in the lens. Then he turned it just a little off-focus so the leaves looked like butterflies.

"Isn't it?" she asked again. "Look, you know what I'd like to do? Let's take a thermos of coffee and sit out in Washington Square and soak up the ambience. You want to do that? There's musicians — and lots of photo opportunities."

"Ambience? As long as it's open-air ambience." Rose hadn't even taken off her jacket. The smallness of the apartment made her want to leave as soon as she arrived. She started coughing and walked to the window and pressed her face to the glass. Outside she saw two bullets flash in front of the tree then straight into the sky. She stepped back and felt her ribs gnawing at her heart.

It took them ten minutes to find an empty bench in Washington Square. Hundreds of people had come down to the park, and while most walked idly by, many had claimed the benches as their own. Rows of older men sat around a series of chess games set up on small collapsible tables. On some of the benches, couples were hugging and kissing while pigeons fluttered about their feet. In the middle of the square a dozen boys bounced a basketball up and down the pavement. Beyond them, next to the Washington Square Arch, five musicians played guitars and sang in the middle of the rings of people that spilled across the sidewalk.

"The music here at night is fantastic," Jayne said, pointing across the street to Small Libertys, a coffee-house restaurant decorated with a dozen plaster imitations of the Statue of Liberty. She worked there as a waitress and, more than anything else about her job, she loved the restaurant's vibrant atmosphere. "Every night a couple of folkies prop themselves on stools next to the front door and play right into the morning. It's so wild. You should stay down just to hear them."

"I don't know." Rose rolled her shoulders up towards her ears. She felt vulnerable, waiting for something to hit her. She shivered. A few yards away two boys threw a baseball back and forth. They hammered the ball at one another and caught it barehanded. She wondered how much pain they could take as the ball slapped back and forth into their hands.

David didn't say anything. They sat there drinking coffee and smoking Marlboros as they watched the spontaneous circus whirling around them. The sun was warm and David took off his jacket. The leaves were yellow and brown, and whenever the wind caught them, a few would break free from the trees and spiral through the air. The breeze was damp but not cold, and the wind flashing on his skin felt perfect. He thought that they were in the pitch of fall, sitting on the wooden bench on the one day that was both the end of summer and the beginning of winter. He tried to remember the last time the three of them had done anything together without their parents. He smoked another Marlboro and thought of his father. Marlboro was his brand, too.

"Happy birthday, David." Jayne broke his trance and passed a small package to him.

"Thanks." He smiled and opened it slowly and very carefully; the longer he took, the greater was his sense of her giving. Inside was a Hoya yellow filter for his camera. He screwed it onto the Canon lens and took a picture of the two boys throwing the baseball.

"Ahh, Jayne." A voice called from the center of the square. "Jayne!"

Jayne turned her head and looked along the walkway.

A lady with a red-and-white bandanna wrapped around her hair approached them from behind the bench. Her cheeks were pink and lined with creases that tucked behind her ears. David couldn't decide if her cheeks were naturally colored or cleverly rouged. But the lines in her face were real: the scars of happiness. "So. This must be the birthday boy!"

"Hi, Sam." Jayne smiled. "Yeah. This is my brother David. And Rose, my sister."

Sam shook everyone's hand and explained that her working name was really Samantha, but that friends just called her Sam. Samantha was a clairvoyant, a tarot card and palm reader who worked from a corner table in Small Libertys every Tuesday afternoon.

"I love birthday readings," she said, looking at David. "Things can become very clear on anniversaries." A trace of accent rippled through her voice, a throatiness that rolled over her words before they emerged. "Please. Let me see your hands."

David rubbed his hands over his legs and looked at Jayne. She arched her eyebrows and shrugged.

"Come, come. This is my birthday present to you." She reached for both hands and unwrapped his fingers in her palms. Then she ran her thumbs over his skin, spreading the palms open, and gazed into the pattern of crossing lines. She held them there a moment and wiped one end of her bandanna across her mouth. "Hmmm — " She looked at his face, then pulled a deck of cards from a satchel that was looped over her shoulder. "Let's try the tarot. How old are you?"

"Seventeen."

"Good. A prime number." Her head nodded as if this were an important technical point. Then she passed the deck of tarot cards to him and asked him to shuffle them and think of a specific question to ask. David mixed the cards together, but no questions crossed his mind. Then he wondered, what'll happen to the three of us: Jayne, Rose and me?

While he did this, Samantha unravelled her scarf and spread it on the bench. Her short hair was streaked with brown, grey and red. "Now put the cards out like this." She showed him how to lay the cards face up, then she took a deep breath. Two couples stopped at the bench and stared at the cards.

"So." She looked into his face with surprising tenderness. "You see ... " she paused, "somebody is not being honest with you." Her voice emphasized her seriousness. "It is not a question of lies, but more like a truth that is hidden. Do you know who this person could be?"

"No." David looked at Jayne. Was this a joke? But there was a gravity to Samantha's voice that was completely convincing.

"Well ... eventually this truth will be revealed." She frowned a moment. "And the fact that you do not know the truth will not harm you. You see, the truth is held back for now. It's like a fog has blurred reality. The truth is the sun; eventually it burns away the mist and there is clarity. Be patient. Until the fog lifts you may feel betrayed and depressed, but it will pass. Do you understand?"

"Yes, I guess so."

"Mostly you will be protected by the love that surrounds your life. You have it here with these cups." She pointed to the cup cards — two of them. "And you will have money, too. That is certain."

She took David's hand again and opened his palm. "Yes. You can see love is everywhere. But you must treasure it. Do not forsake it or take it for granted. If you spite love, it will become a poison." She twisted his palm and held her head back to look along one line. "And there is a cross. I see an injury. A hospital. But that comes when you are much older. It's hard to tell if you will die there or not. Still, don't concern yourself: death is a mere toy of immortality." She smiled. Her gift was complete. She dropped his hand suddenly, disinterested now.

"But what was your question?" Rose looked at David and then Samantha.

"Oh, yes." Her curiosity sparked again. "What was it?"

"I wanted to know what would happen to all of us." David looked at Rose and Jayne.

"Your sisters?"

"Yes."

She frowned. "You ask the one question that forces me to do more work!" She said this in a very loud voice. But then she smiled and all the creases around her eyes flared open like a fan. "Rose, shuffle the cards." She passed the tarot deck to Rose who obediently shuffled them together. "And think of a question," she added. She lit a cigarette and glanced at the circle of people that now surrounded them.

Rose laid out the cards. Samantha hunched forward, looking at them carefully. For a while she said nothing and snorted two or three times while she finished her cigarette. Then she sat back and tilted her head to one side, as if this was the only true way to examine Rose.

She said, "You are very complicated."

Rose pinched her lips a little and waited.

"But it is a cover-up, hmm? Inside you there is simplicity, a simplicity of feeling and need. And this is something that you must recognize and accept." She took another long drag on her cigarette and blew the smoke out narrowly. "But more than that, you must nourish your needs. Otherwise, you'll be like a flower in the desert. And a desert rose is rare!" Sam laughed. She thought this was a very good joke, and Jayne laughed, too. But Rose remained solemn, almost offended.

"All right. And what about my question?" Rose pushed the tarot cards together and turned them face down on the scarf. "I want to know about my writing."

"What about it?" She opened Rose's hands with the same care she'd used on David: her flat thumbs pressing the skin, smoothing it into her own hand. "What do you need to know?"

"If my poetry is any good." She looked at Jayne and laughed a little. "If I'm going to make it."

Samantha looked into her hands and then dropped them. "You can make it good if you do as I told you, nourish the roots of your soul." She picked up Rose's right hand again and glanced at it. "There is ... " But she didn't finish. She shrugged again, a habit of hers, and spit onto the sidewalk.

Jayne laughed. "Sam! You're not supposed to gob on Washington Square!"

"Why not, darling?" Now she took Jayne's hand in her palm and began to spread the skin with her thumbs. "Are you so fond of the nation's father?"

"Because nobody believes an expectorating clairvoyant." Jayne pulled her hand away and whispered, "Not now."

"Oh?" Samantha was surprised that Jayne had pulled her hand back so suddenly. "Who believes what, these days? And who is hiding the truth?" She looked from Jayne to David and then back to Jayne.

A girl walked behind Samantha and dropped a hand over her shoulder. "Baba, it's time," she said, then looked at David and nodded at Jayne.

"Ahh, it's always time." Samantha wrapped her cards in the bandanna and tucked them both into her satchel. "This is my grandniece, Sandra, and this is David and Rose." She stood up and pointed. "Jayne's brother and sister. It's David's birthday today. Jayne told me she was going to give him something for his camera."

Sandra looked at David again and nodded. Her hair was very dark, and her eyes were wide and brown. "Oh?" She tilted her head in the same way that Samantha had when she saw the hospital cross in the palm of David's hand.

"A light filter," Jayne said. "Show her, David."

David froze. He couldn't open the camera case or talk

or even breathe. The dizziness from all the Marlboros whirled in the back of his head, a small tornado spinning down his spine and into his stomach.

"Yes, let's see it," Samantha said. "I don't know anything about cameras."

Finally he managed to breathe. He felt like a stone dropping through space. Maybe Sandra would catch him.

"Why don't you take our picture?" Sandra said to him. When she spoke, he saw that her teeth were uneven. He stared at her, at her teeth.

Thank God, he thought. This slight imperfection made it possible for him to move.

"All right." He stood up and walked a few feet away so that the sun was behind him. Jayne and Rose stood between Samantha and Sandra and the four of them looked into the camera lens without smiling or posing. In the background were trees and buildings, clouds bunched together above the Washington Square Arch, and the crisp rarity of the fall air. The composition was perfect; he didn't have to do anything but depress the shutter. He took three shots: "Angels of Washington Square."

All of them close ups of Sandra.

Chapter Fourteen

David thought the three pictures of Sandra were fantastic. Perhaps because of the light that day, a kind of luminous vitality had emerged from the people and trees, even from the cars and the concrete sidewalks. The brilliance was most radiant right after he met her, when she said that she'd like a copy of the pictures if he ever had a chance to duplicate them.

Yes, certainly. If he had a chance. But first, he had to be careful to extract all the best qualities from the negatives. It took him weeks in the school darkroom playing with the timing of the exposure in the enlarger, cropping the prints, matching the sizing of her face in each frame so that when he mounted them side by side, "The Three Sandras" were perfect.

But he didn't show them to anyone. He mounted the three pictures on hardboard and kept them on his closet shelf. Every night he took the photographs into bed and stared at her. Her hair rolled over her shoulders, spiraling past the clean, dark walls of her neck. The curves of her

I supposed to do with the damn thing? he wondered. The evidence of his lust was smeared into Rose's Maidenform. He stood beside the bed and considered the possibilities: flush it down the toilet? Burn it in the fireplace? No, no, bury it behind the preserves in the bomb shelter!

The next morning, Saturday, he stuffed the bra into his jeans and quietly worked his way downstairs to the kitchen. He'd decided the best strategy would be to shove it into the garbage. Nobody would look there, especially if it were covered with yesterday's rot. But as he opened the trash can lid, he could hear his mother coming up the stairs. He jammed the bra into the garbage and buried it as far down as possible, past the remnants of soggy cereal, coffee grounds and wet grapefruit rinds. As he yanked his hand free, a banana skin caught his watch band and stuck to his hand. He whirled around to face her.

Catrina eyed him suspiciously. Something was wrong, but what? She frowned and held up a pair of corduroys worn through at the crotch. "Look at these. This morning, we're going to Sears to get you some new pants."

"Sure, Mom." He smiled.

She looked at him, her head jerking unsteadily. "What's that?"

"What?"

"That." She pointed at his hand, to the banana skin dangling from his wrist.

"Oh!" He pulled the wet peel from his hand and dropped it into the trash can. "I just thought I'd have a little fruit for breakfast."

She didn't say anything. She walked over to the garbage pail and pulled the plastic bag from the container. He was certain she was going to dig into the litter, pull out the inseminated bra and press it under his nose. But instead, she face curled into ovals: her eyes, her hollow nostrils, the swirling ridges of her ears. The flatter planes of her cheeks cut across the firm line of her mouth and her lips squeezed together to hide her crooked teeth. She probably worries about her teeth, he thought. That's why all the affection comes through her eyes. "I love you," her eyes whispered, "I love you, David."

These three pictures, which emphasized the quality of her skin — its dark, oiled texture — inspired a remarkable wet dream. Rose had warned him about wet dreams. "Semen is the last, but most important, bodily fluid to come out of your body," she'd said. "You might as well tell me when it happens. That way you'll have an objective view on how you're developing, and you won't think you're leaking into some ejaculatory degenerate."

The first time it had happened (three years before, when he was fourteen), David thought his penis was bleeding. But now his vision of Sandra managed to sustain his erection longer than he'd ever experienced. When the semen finally burst into his hands, he was certain he'd lanced an artery and blood was pouring onto the mattress. He jumped out of bed, desperate to find something to wipe off the bedsheets. In the darkness he stumbled into the bathroom and reached into the laundry basket. He could hear his father snoring, Rose grinding her teeth. Grabbing the first thing that came to hand, he crept back to his room and began wiping up. It was awful stuff: a slick, gluey ooze. With the mess mopped up, he turned on the light and examined the sheets closely. Then he noticed what he was holding. The rag was Rose's bra, with fresh semen smeared along the left cup. A little caught under his fingernail: Maidenform, 38-D. Were breasts really this big? He shoved both fists into the dr' and pressed his nose to the lace and sniffed: salty. Wh twisted the bag around and tied a knot at the top. "This is your job, you know." She held it up to his chest. He could see Rose's D cup bulging against the plastic.

"Sorry, Mom." He grabbed the bag and carted it downstairs to the dumpster. Then he pulled open the knot and stared into the debris. There it was, the damp lacy bra staring back at him. Damn. He jiggled the plastic bag once, twice, and made a final adjustment to ensure Rose's brassiere was completely buried. Then he looked at it one last time and thought, what the hell am I doing?

Sears was at the far end of the local shopping mall. Catrina drove there once or twice a week in the Buick Electra that Harris had bought for her. The Electra represented a new kind of freedom to her, and even though she didn't take advantage of it, she cherished its potential. She often stood at the living room window and gazed at the car parked in the driveway. Just to look at it reassured her. She only used it for shopping and she never drove into Manhattan. The drive over to Sears was as far from home as she ever went, but distant enough to provide an opportunity to talk to David about Rose.

"I don't think she should be spending weekends with Robert," she said, pulling the Buick into the fast lane. She lifted David's window a quarter inch to cut the draft from her increased speed. The feature she liked most about the Buick was the electric windows; she slipped them up and down to create a balanced air flow through the interior of the car. "Just because they're in college and that boy has an apartment now, she thinks she has to be downtown with him all the time." She looked at her son for confirmation.

"At least they're loyal to one another." David wasn't sure

if defending Rose was a good idea — especially if his mother had started drinking already. He didn't want to think about Rose or his mother. He looked at the traffic and imagined Sandra sitting in her home: the small apartment she shared with Samantha, all the heavy furniture and area rugs just as Jayne had described them to him.

"You know, ever since that incident with Brad, it's been very hard on me." She stopped at a red light and glanced out her window away from David. "You really can't imagine what your father and I have been through because of it."

Why was she saying this? he wondered. Brad died years ago.

"It's important for you children to go on with your lives." Her head flicked slightly, like a small tic had invented some clockwork in her neck. "Especially Rose, but — "

"What about Jayne?" he asked suddenly. "She's hiding something, isn't she?"

"Jayne? I'm not talking about Jayne!" When she realized she was screaming, she clamped her mouth shut and gunned the Buick through the light. "I'm talking about Rose. About what you can do to help."

"Mom, that was a red light."

Catrina's face tightened and she checked the light in the rearview mirror. "Please — just listen to me. You're the closest person to her. I think you should say something to her."

"About what?"

"About" — her head ticked twice — "about living an acceptable life."

David didn't know what to say. Rose never listened to anything he told her. Besides, what did "acceptable" mean? Just one blast of scotch first thing every morning — instead of the standard double?

"I'm sorry." Heaving on the wheel, she pulled into a parking slot in front of the mall. "I don't want to say anything more about it right now. Just have a word with her when you get a chance." She cut the engine and turned to him. Do it as a Christian, she thought. But instead she said, "Do it as her brother, David."

She picked up her purse and opened the door. Somehow it seemed a very long way from the car door to the ground. Her foot reached out and dropped down, down until it hit the asphalt. Why is it getting so hard just to walk any more? Trailing him by ten feet, she followed David through the mall to Sears. He's embarrassed, she told herself. It's what Rose is doing that embarrasses him, though. It's just humiliating everyone involved. She felt her cheeks flushing and she opened the collar of her blouse.

They turned a corner and passed a shop called The Maternity Nest. In the store window a mannequin held a baby to her chest. Behind the mother and child, behind the flowers and linen, a single point of light caught Catrina's eye. The grandmother: lingering, smiling, knowing. Catrina stopped and looked at the grandmother's face. A feeling of emptiness washed through her body, through her legs and feet and onto the floor. It's gone, she thought. It's all gone. She could feel the great cycle of life bleeding from her body.

"David." She opened her purse and dug into her wallet. "Buy some corduroys on your own." She pressed twenty dollars into his hand, then snapped her purse shut. "I've forgotten something very important. I'll meet you in the car after you get the pants, all right?"

He looked at her face. So white, so empty.

"All right?" Her lips pinched together.

"Sure." He folded the money into his pocket and frowned. There was something that he hated in her.

Catrina wheeled around toward the exit. As she strode down the mall, her heels clicking against the marble floor, she heard everybody whispering: *She lost the baby. First they shot the boy, then they lost the baby. And she gave them both away.*

David heard nothing. Blood flowed in his ears, rushing minute doses of testosterone through his body, flooding every cell with wave after wave of hormones. He stood there completely helpless. Instead of walking into menswear he breezed through the lingerie department. Posters of women dressed in lace bras and panties hung from the ceiling. Two ladies slipped past him into the change booths. He walked towards the yellow doors and waited. They were in there changing right now. Two naked women slipping bras over the tender globes of their breasts, both of them just inches from his hands. His palms perspired; he curled his fingers into tight fists. He imagined his hands touching them, treasuring them all day long, nursing their aching beauty day after day.

He rubbed his hands against his jeans and noticed himself in the display mirror. God, he thought, Rose was right, he was going insane. Then suddenly the tide of testosterone ebbed, and he pulled himself away from the aisles of lingerie and moved down the walkway to men's pants.

Think of something serious, he told himself. He thought about Brad lying dead on the floor, and then he remembered Grampy, that Grampy wanted him to talk to his father. "You are the vessel of love and forgiveness," he'd whispered — straight into his heart. Now his mother wanted him to talk with Rose. Both of them were pushing, squeezing him into a tiny, dark cubicle. As he tried on a pair of corduroy pants, he felt his chest tightening, pressing into his lungs. For a few seconds he could hardly breathe. He knew it was all because of his mother. It was coming from her. She was the one pressing everyone, forcing them into small, meticulously clean boxes.

After he paid for the pants, he wandered into the mall and sat down on a small wrought-iron bench next to a water fountain. He watched the water squirt straight into the air, then collapse onto itself. He counted the time between blasts — exactly fifty-eight seconds — and he thought somebody had blown it. Surely the fountain management had meant to time the gushers for one minute intervals. Any idiot could see the mistake. He shook his head and another rush of testosterone pulsed through his arteries. All he could think about was mistakes — all the bloody errors in life, all the pain accorded to countless fallacies and lies. Then he felt a rush of energy surge through his stomach and chest and when the fountain sprayed into the air again he realized how much he hated his mother. She was killing herself — doing it on the installment plan — making herself pay a little bit more every day. His eyes narrowed as the cascading water slapped down into the pool. But she's not going to get me, he swore to himself. I'm not going to be part of the dying.

As she sat in the Buick all Catrina could feel was the steering wheel pressing against her forehead. The hard plastic moulded her flesh, forcing it against her skull harder and harder until the pain was strong enough to stop the picture of Brad lying there on the floor. His white face stared at her, trying to tell her something, but what was it? What could it be? And then came the sound of the baby. The newborn girl, with her delicate blue head and the blood still clotted around her face, was crying as the nurse wiped the waxy skin clean and the doctor applied the suction to her mouth. Then the baby wailed. Oh God, she could wail. And Catrina reached over and lifted her carefully from Jayne's arms the way Mrs. Takker the social worker from St Paul's Episcopalian Church had told her to do it. She's so beautiful, so helpless, she thought as she placed the baby in the bassinet. She took the surgical scissors and, leaning over the tiny forehead, cut a small lock of hair. It was such a light, glossy blonde. She took the little swatch of hair and pressed it in her fist as though it were the very life of the baby itself. She handed the infant to Mrs. Takker and watched as the baby was carried from the room and the yellow door closed behind her. Then she was gone, too. First Brad and then this baby. Both of them gone in just one breath. And at that moment she realized what Brad was trying to tell her: she had to keep the baby. Didn't she know? It was one life for another. But instead of keeping the bargain, she gave them both away. The picture of the yellow door swinging shut froze in her mind. The yellow door and nothing else. That and the warm, good pain of the steering wheel pressing unto her skull.

By the time David got back to the car, he felt strong and certain. He was ready to tell his mother to go to hell. The words were right on his lips. If she mentioned Rose or Jayne he was going to scream them at her: *Go freeze in hell.*

He opened the door to the Buick. She was leaning on the steering wheel, her head bowed down as though she were praying. He thought that she must have noticed him then, because she looked up and he could see her face soaked with tears. Her head lifted a little, then collapsed. Her forehead bumped against the horn which let out one long blast.

Chapter Fifteen

After she'd spent a month in the hospital, Harris brought Catrina home. Dr. Goddard wanted her to continue therapy in out-patient treatments twice a week. But he wasn't confident. "Depressives don't do that well in talking therapy," he said, passing Harris a prescription. "However, you might want to consider a change of setting, a resort town or some place she enjoys. Failing that we could try ECT."

"What's that?"

"Electro-Convulsive Therapy. Most people call it 'shock treatment.'"

"Oh," Harris said in a whisper, surprised somehow that it had gone this far without any major signs.

But Harris couldn't think of taking her any place other than the townhouse in Hastings-on-Hudson. He just didn't have time for any of this. He could feel his cheeks redden as he helped her out of the car and into the house. Christ, he thought, why didn't anyone see this coming?

By the new year Catrina had improved. She talked, she walked, she didn't sit alone and cry, and she seldom drank before dinner even when Harris flew off to Geneva or Washington or back to Canada. But David had a sense that some vital core in her had vanished. An interior portion of her existence had disappeared in the hospital and never returned. She didn't get angry with him even when she caught him smoking, and she didn't care about Rose and Robert Houliman and the fact that they virtually lived together in his apartment near Columbia University. None of it mattered to her any more. And while it made him believe that he was free, it terrified him because he suspected she was dying piece by piece, as bits of her inner being fell away and exposed a growing hole at the center of her life.

"You're right." Rose nodded when he explained his suspicions. "That's what depression is. Slow cancer of the soul."

"And you, in particular, ought to be careful, Daydoe," Robert said, pulling the lid from a metal flask with his teeth. "The statistical evidence indicates that mental breakdown runs in families." He kept one hand on the steering wheel of his Dodge and with the other he lifted the flask above his face and poured a stream of bourbon into his mouth. In the past month he'd grown a pencil mustache and developed the habit of sipping from a whiskey flask he carried in his pocket. He wiped the back of his hand across his new mustache and smiled.

"That's bull." David cranked his head away and fixed his eyes on the Henry Hudson Bridge.

"David's right, you know," Rose said, leaning her head toward Robert and taking the flask from his hand. She sucked an ounce of bourbon into her mouth. "Just because one in three American families has somebody going crazy doesn't mean it's contagious."

Healing the Dead

"Read the research, Sweetie. I was perusing it the other day in the APA office." The fact that Robert had secured a contract as an illustrator for the American Psychiatric Association was often at the front of his mind. They paid him one hundred dollars a day, plus five hundred as a retainer. As the Dodge rolled over the bridge into Manhattan, his stomach felt very warm and his sense of certainty hardened.

"Balls on the research." Rose pushed her head even closer to Robert. "With that many crazy people everywhere you have to question a little more than their fucking genes, don't you think?"

Robert started laughing. "Fucking jeans!" he yelled and his hand snaked up her Levis into her crotch.

"I mean when this kind of madness" — her arm knocked his hand from her leg and swept towards the abandoned cars, the cluttered sidewalks, the brown brick tenements of Harlem — "when this insanity reaches epidemic proportions, you'd think someone in the APA might consider environmental causes."

David gazed at them over the seat back. He knew they loved arguing. But when he listened to them squabble like this, he hated Robert, hated the way he'd changed her. God, what a bastard.

His hands dropped to his lap. He fingered the portraits of Sandra and decided that if he hand a chance, he would try to feel her breasts today. The third time he saw her he managed to kiss her twice, but feeling her up would be very good. He'd practiced it at night for months. Concentrating on the texture of her skin and the way her nipples would feel, he imagined all the ways he could undo her bra so that he would seem natural and artless, as though he'd done it with a dozen older women.

By the time the Dodge reached Greenwich Village,

David had almost forgotten Rose and Robert. As he jumped out of the car, all he could think about was Sandra. He'd talked to her on the phone and made a date to give her the pictures he'd taken last year. "Let's meet at Small Libertys," she'd said. "I've got something for you too."

"What?"

"You'll see!" she'd laughed.

When he entered Small Libertys, he saw Jayne right away. She was loading a sandwich platter onto a table and nodding to someone across the room. He called to her, but his voice drowned in the swell of noise that rolled through the restaurant.

David sat at a table next to the wall and propped his photo portfolio against the table leg. Jayne sat down and placed a cup of coffee beside him. "Time for my break. Mind if I join you?" She waved a hand inches from his eyes. "You look very preoccupied, little brother."

"Really?" This was not good news. David did not want to look preoccupied. He wanted to look sexy. Sexy and in command of things. "Have you seen Sandra?"

"Not yet." Jayne had heard what this was all about from Samantha: "They have a date," she'd whispered over the tarot deck. "This is their third time. They're getting permanent."

Suddenly David noticed his sister's hair. "You cut it." He swept a hand over his own head and tried to hide any surprise. But it was difficult; her curling blond hair had been cropped in bunches that poked into the air.

"You like it?" Jayne raised her eyebrows.

"No," he said, examining her. She'd grown heavier in the last year. Her face was wider and her arms filled the sleeves of her blouse. The exact opposite of Rose.

"I don't, either."

Healing the Dead

"So why'd you do it?" He sipped his coffee. He didn't like coffee much, but he believed it was essential to cultivate some kind of caffeine habit, and tea was out of the question.

She looked around the room to see if anyone could overhear them. "Oh Christ, I don't know." She watched him and felt an inner warmth. There he was, right in front of her: her little brother, smoking a cigarette, drinking coffee while he waited for his girl. Suddenly she felt old. Tell him the truth, she thought. Tell him. "Look, I flunked out of college."

David knocked the cigarette ash into the ashtray and narrowed his eyes. "How could you flunk out? You're supposed to be smarter than everybody else." He shook his head and then sipped his coffee, letting the flavor sit on the thickest part of his tongue.

"I don't know." She pushed a hand through the few remaining inches of her hair and glanced at the floor. Then she looked straight into his eyes again. "Because I can't remember anything, that's why. I can't concentrate any more." She flicked her wrist and her waitress tray slid against the wall.

David didn't know what to say. He could see her eyes brimming. "Look, what's wrong?" He leaned forward and almost touched her hand. "You're keeping something from me, aren't you?"

She wiped one eye and thought, tell him. Just tell him.

"That time in the park, Samantha knew you were hiding something from me, didn't she?" He wanted to touch her face, but she seemed so frozen and immobile.

She nodded slightly and gazed at the ceiling. "I never told you, did I?" She slipped both his hands into her own and held them on the table top. "About what happened in Toronto?"

She looked at his face and when his eyes flicked away she knew she could begin. All he had to do was let her tell it. Just look away and listen, she thought, pulling her hands free and wiping them on her jeans. "See ... I was pregnant, Davy." She took a deep breath and glanced at the floor a moment. "I was pregnant and that's why I left. You know, without ever telling you what happened."

Jayne closed her eyes and told the story with her face turned towards the wall. She discovered that this way she could talk without interruption because everything ran like a film in the light emptiness of her eyelids. First came Grant Preston and the discovery of her pregnancy, the confession to her parents and the move to Queens, and then everything gradually slipping out of control until she was in the hospital delivering the baby and someone — but *who?* — physically lifted the baby out of her arms and gave her little girl away. Gave her own daughter away to a stranger. And as she told it, explaining only the details that she could fit into words and sentences, a young voice echoed through her mind and she stopped to listen to it singing, then she heard three or four children singing the melody to "Away in a Manger":

Away to a stranger,
A way far away,
The sleeping new baby
Is given away.

Once his sister paused, David wondered how he could have missed this. How could all the confusion about Jayne leaving home, his mother's fits of crying, his own loneliness and despair — how could he not have guessed this one simple truth?

Jayne brushed a hand over her eye and looked at David through the shadow of her palm. "So once the baby was gone," she continued, "then I really didn't know what to do. I started working here and I went to school. For a while I thought I'd just go back to normal and do what everyone else was doing." She wiped her fingers against her jeans and up against her cheeks.

"But now I can't *concentrate* anymore. Everything I tried worked itself back to the baby. I even gave her my name, Jayne, just so I'd never lose the fact that she was mine. At first it seemed to help knowing that at least I'd given her a name. And then I started doing the craziest stuff. I'd go into department stores, and right there in the baby-wear section I'd start to pick out clothes. And it wasn't just in my head, either. One time I actually went up to the cashier. I had all these little pink sleepers. It was Jayne's second birthday, and I'd been thinking about it all day, you see ... I ended up buying these sleepers and telling the cashier about this party we were all going to have. I didn't even realize what I'd done. Not until I was out on the street and I had this package of gifts in my arms. Then I just broke down right there and started crying." Thinking about it now, she could feel new tears oozing from her eyes. But she brushed them away and kept going. She knew she had to keep going and get through it all. She explained how she kept everything a secret and never told a soul. Not once, not a word to anyone. That was the art of living in New York: the perfection of her anonymity.

For a moment David thought he could speak to her, but he could find nothing adequate to say.

"And that's why I'm going to be moving soon, too." The tears sat in her eyes like tiny, wavering lenses.

"What do you mean?"

"I'm moving to the Philippines. To a Catholic missionary hospital. They need people to help out down there, and I was asked."

"A Catholic mission?"

"Look, I have to change things. I've got to do something to make the past come to a stop." She rubbed a finger under her eyes.

"Are you sure about this?" he asked. "It just seems so ... drastic."

"Yes! It's the first positive step I've made in years. And the people are so desperate down there," she added. "But don't tell Mom and Dad yet, okay?"

"All right." He lit another cigarette and shrugged. "If that's the way you want it."

"It is," she said, standing up with the waitress tray tucked under an arm. See, she told herself, you didn't break down and cry after all.

Sandra walked through the restaurant door with a red hat in her hand and a brown jacket folded across her arm. When she saw David, she smiled. Her lips closed and her eyelids rose like two half-moons. With her eyes, she held David in place at the table against the wall. Her skin was still very dark and rich, David thought, exactly the way he'd imagined it night after night against his pillow.

They decided to take a taxi up to the Museum of Modern Art. David didn't have enough money for a taxi and dinner and the train home, but he wanted to impress her. He waved down a Checker Cab and opened the back door, and she slipped past him onto the cracked leather seat.

"This is the surprise I was telling you about." Sandra dug two museum tickets from her purse. "It's just a fluke that I got them. I couldn't think of anyone else who'd like the exhibition. Besides, André Kertesz has just been discovered. He's in all the arts papers." She looked at him. Why wasn't David saying anything? He'd always spoken so clearly before, and now he was just staring at her.

As the taxi rolled around a corner, their shoulders bumped together. David looked at her and smiled. He couldn't get over her skin. Now would be the best time to show her the three pictures. If she liked them, he would kiss her; if not, he would kiss her anyway — and then try her breasts. He reached into the portfolio and drew out the hardboard. He examined the photographs and compared them to the way she looked now. They were good. They were good because he'd managed to get the special light that was in the air on his birthday. He'd captured the light and made it emanate from her face.

"These are the pictures I was telling you about." He turned the board so she could see the three photographs mounted side by side. "From that time in the park."

She lowered her head and looked at them. God, she thought, three close-ups of her face. Her face and nothing else. She looked at her eyes and forehead, her lips and the small crescent of light on her nose. Each picture was a different moment within the same breath, and as her eyes scanned back and forth from one photograph to the next, she tried to hold the air still in her lungs, squeeze it into her chest and trap it there.

"Well?" Why didn't she say something? He was ready to

kiss her as the Checker Cab turned onto Fifty-third. All she had to do was say she liked them.

She let the air slip from her mouth. Then she looked through the window and back to the pictures, then out the window again.

"Well? What do you think?"

The taxi pulled up to the museum entrance and the driver turned his head so his mouth was an inch from the steel mesh of the passenger cage. "That's five-ninety."

"Five? ... "

"Ninety." The driver rolled his eyes toward David. They were bloodshot with dots of pus oozing from each corner.

David opened his wallet. Damn, that meant seven dollars, if he included a tip, and he knew that tipping was a key to sex and mastery. He slipped the bills through the money port, opened the door and guided her onto the sidewalk. At this rate he would soon be out of money.

"So what do you think?" He felt desperate. The taxi wheels spun through a puddle as he slipped the photographs back into the portfolio.

"Do you mean I can keep them?" Her head tilted and she stepped toward the museum.

"Sure. But do you *like* them?"

She stood so close to him that he could smell her. "Of course," she said and leaned forward just enough for her lips to touch his ear. "I love them," she whispered, her breasts nuzzling gently against his arm.

Not exactly a feel, he decided, but those were definitely her breasts nudging into his biceps. There was no mistake about it, she loved the photographs.

Healing the Dead

The André Kertesz exhibit was installed in the west wing of the Museum of Modern Art. As soon as David saw the first set of portraits, he realized that he'd discovered something new. Then he saw the landscapes, the peasants, the shots from World War I and the cityscapes of Paris. As he walked along the wall, he found himself moving through an exhibit of perfected observation. Kertesz captured everything with an eye that saw the world completely. The only thing the pictures betrayed was Kertesz's own sympathies — sympathy for the misery of the war, for the lives behind every face, for the exhaustion of labour, and for the isolated beauty of the land and sky and trees. He had taken pictures that showed everything that existed below and under the surface of things. He'd penetrated the skin of little boys and whirling dancers to expose the guts and bones of life. And he did it delicately, with respect and fondness.

Sandra held David's photo portfolio under one arm and looked at a picture of dozens of chairs and the shadows they cast in the afternoon sun. Funny, but all these wooden chairs arranged in order for an outdoor concert or something — they looked like spires, like a testament. "Do you think he's religious?"

"He has to be. He put God into everything, even those chairs."

They moved along the wall to a set of nudes, women whose skin stretched in long curving ellipses. "And look at these," he whispered. "Look what he's done."

The pictures were called "The Distortions," a series of photographs taken of reflections cast in convex and concave mirrors. Sandra looked at the women's nipples and breasts arching, twisting in long, narrow contortions of rippling light. In one photograph a pair of hands cupped the opening of a vagina. Sandra held a fingernail to her mouth and pressed it against her lips. She could feel her own hands down there, ten fingers waiting to slip open. God, such hunger made so beautiful.

"I'd love to be able to do that." David nodded his head and looked at Sandra. "Even to think of doing it."

"Yes." She let her free hand brush against his. "I'd love to do it, too."

He pushed himself beside her, let his leg press her thigh, his hip wedge against hers. Touch her, he told himself. Do it now, right here. Touch her. But at the same time his body locked together so rigidly that all his joints and muscles froze, and only his hands had any mobility at all. Feel her, he screamed to himself. And a second voice came back, in quiet authority: No. You know better than that. It's impossible. Then his fingers began ticking out a broken rhythm against her wrist until he snapped his hand away from her and shoved it into his pants pocket. He swallowed hard without looking at her and fixed his molars together.

She stepped back slightly and took his arm. She could feel the stone in him, the grey wall that he'd become. "Hey," she said, rubbing his forearm. She felt it loosen and she smiled with her lips held together. "It's so beautiful."

They stood there like that, in the dry filtered air of the museum, for the rest of the afternoon until closing time — looking at Kertesz's photographs, at the broad ribbons of gorgeous skin twisting in the light.

Chapter Sixteen

Harris sat in the living room with a copy of *The Economist* spread over his lap and pressed his tongue against a canker festering on his gums. When he was younger, just after he'd married Catrina and they were living in Ottawa, he used to read *The Economist* from cover to cover every week. He went one hundred and twenty-three weeks without missing a word. He'd stacked them in a row on the den bookshelf and made a little index of critical themes: Keynesian theory, Macro-economics, International trade. But now the magazine collection was gone. Even the index had disappeared over the years. A little plastic box full of three-by-five inch recipe cards with all the pertinent headings printed across the top of each card — that had vanished, too.

He stood up and walked down the steps to the den to look for the index. The bookshelf was lined with hardbound editions of *Readers Digest* and the *Encyclopedia Britannica*. A set of Winston Churchill biographies lay stacked beside them, and at the far end of the first shelf was *Hauser's Pictorial Guide to Family Medicine*. He flipped through

Hauser's Guide until he arrived at "cankers" and saw six black-and-white illustrations of mouth sores crowning the lips and gums and tongues of variously afflicted victims. He held the pictures next to his face and peered into the vanity mirror to examine has own white blister. His was definitely on the smallish side, at least compared to these. But regardless of the size, it stung. Every two or three weeks after one canker had subsided another would crop up. But never on exactly the same site. It was this mobility factor that convinced Dr. Bantum that Harris's cankers could not possibly be cancerous. At his lowest moments, in spite of Dr. Bantum's assurances, Harris still suspected cancer. He believed in cancer. Now that his twenty-five-year-old index to *The Economist* was gone forever, he considered the possibility of his fifty-year-old face rotting from the inside out. Cancer could do that.

He filled his lungs with air and pressed his lips together. Then he walked back upstairs to the living room and looked out the window onto the street. Nothing moved. Parked cars waited along the curbsides, and the doors to all the townhouses were shut and locked. Half the curtains were pulled tight against the windows. He didn't know any of the neighbors. Not like he'd known Charlie Watson, back in Toronto. Most of these people in Hastings didn't even tell you their names.

He heard a door closing and the hallway floor creaking. David appeared at the top of the stairs. He folded his bathrobe over his pajamas and stood there, rubbing the heel of one hand into his eye.

"Hi."

"Hey, glad to see you're up." Harris glanced at his watch. "Only eleven in the morning. What dragged you out of bed so early?"

David picked a bit of sleep from the corner of his eye, tied the belt of his robe and walked into the kitchen.

"Sure hope it wasn't me that got you up," Harris added.

Listening to his son rummaging through the kitchen, Harris realized he shouldn't press so hard. Not first thing on a Sunday morning. He waited a few minutes, waited until he heard the toaster pop and the sound of jam spreading over the toast before he went into the kitchen to pour a second cup of coffee. He sat at the far end of the table so they wouldn't have to look at one another directly.

"What would you say if I suggested we move?" He stared at his coffee mug, then glanced into David's eyes. A bombshell like this ought to wake him up pretty quick.

"Move? You mean downtown finally?"

"Mmmm, no. I was thinking ... out of town. Down the Jersey shore, maybe. To Wildwood or Cape May, one of those resort areas."

David looked up from his toast and frowned.

"So what do you think?" Harris sipped his coffee. This was going to be a major sell job, he realized.

David bit into his toast. "Dad, why would we want to move to New Jersey? Nobody wants to move to New Jersey from New York. It's the other way around. Haven't you ever noticed how the traffic jams in the Lincoln tunnel are always eastbound? You never, ever hear about the rush to get over to Jersey, do you?"

Harris smiled. He lit a cigarette and sipped his coffee. "You want a coffee?"

David looked at him. Strange; his father seldom acted so generously.

"Okay. With cream and sugar, please."

Harris fixed the coffee, and from the vantage of the counter he thought he could approach the subject more delicately. He stirred sugar into the cup. "See, I think your mother really needs to get into a place that's a little ... " He lowered his voice in case she could hear any of this from their bedroom upstairs. "Something a bit more congenial."

"Congenial?"

"Uh-huh. Like a smaller community." He passed the coffee cup to his son and sat down. "Next to the shore. She loves the ocean, you know."

"Yeah, I know." David sipped the coffee and chewed the crust of his toast.

"On Prince Edward Island, back in Souris, the house where she grew up was right next to the ocean." He paused to think a moment. They'd both grown up on the Island, met and married there. "Did we ever take you down to P.E.I?"

"Once. But I was too young to remember it."

"Well she loved it. She was *happy* next to the ocean."

David glanced at his father. How odd to hear him talk about his mother being happy. Then he heard his stomach rumbling. "I think I'm going to make pancakes. You want some?"

"Pancakes? Yeah, but hey, let me make them!" Harris felt a burst of inspiration. The idea of buying a cottage next to the shore, right at the tip of Cape May, had a real focus now that he was actually talking about it. Even the sting of his canker subsided.

"Dad, do you know how to make pancakes?"

"Of course." Ridiculous question. But in fact, he hadn't made pancakes since he was his son's age. "Tell you what. Why don't we make a whole batch, and we'll take some up to Mom. You know, breakfast in bed: juice, pancakes, coffee. Even some cut flowers to go with it. She really needs something like that."

"All right." David felt infected by the enthusiasm. He'd never seen his father like this: actually doing the cooking. "I'll get the juice."

"Okay!"

The two of them worked together. David set up the placemats and utensils, poured the juice and coffee, and cut the flower stems while Harris oiled the griddle and found the jars of flour, baking powder, sugar — everything specified on the recipe card. Once they got going, they started laughing. There was nothing terribly funny to tease them along, but they began a kind of giggling that carried through the room and up the stairs to Catrina's bedroom door. Then the hum of their laughter, the throaty masculine crowing, vibrated through the veneer door and resonated there. Catrina sat up in her bed to listen. What were they doing? She stood next to the door and listened. Then she felt a wave of exhaustion ripple through her legs, a tide of energy ebb from her body and sink into the floor. She slipped back into bed and listened. If you hear it again, she whispered to herself, then get up.

"But can't you picture one of those older places they have in Cape May?" Harris slipped the spatula under the first pancake to check its color. "Remember how nice they look in the summer? One of those old, white clapboard places just a block up from the beach."

"Yeah, they're pretty sweet, all right." David forced the stems of the flowers into the long narrow neck of the vase. "So you mean we'd just go there for summer holidays?"

"Sure. Any time we like. We'd hang onto this place and go down to the shore any time it took our fancy." Harris had convinced himself. He had the money; why not? Besides, seaside real estate made a solid investment. "Hey, how 'bout banana pancakes?"

"Banana?"

"Sure. It's all on the recipe I saw here. You just have to add thin slices of banana before you flip them over." Harris dug through the box for the recipe. When he found the card for banana pancakes, he pulled it out and examined the details. Then he noticed the imprint on the surface of the card, the blue ink stains seeping through the paper. He flipped it over and looked at the writing. He couldn't believe what he read: "Indices of Labour Productivity."

"Hey ... guess what." His fingers began digging through the recipe box, turning over card after card. His entire *Economist* index had been filed right here, written on the back of sixty, seventy, maybe a hundred recipes.

"What?"

"Look at this." He walked next to his son and wrapped an arm across his shoulders.

"What is it, Dad?"

Harris lifted a card into the air. On one side it read "International Current Account Indices," on the other "Raspberry Fluff." He flicked the card with a fingernail and laughed. "All these years your mother's been saving her recipes on the back of my damn index!"

After eight months Harris found the perfect house on the southern tip of the New Jersey shore in the village of Cape May, two blocks in from the beach. It was a two-story clapboard home with a wraparound veranda that had built-in mosquito screens all along the porch. The previous owners, the Chomskis, had kept it in fair condition for thirty-two years, and except for their color schemes (mostly rose and blue), Harris liked everything about it. So did Catrina. She loved the house the moment she saw it. This was a relief to Harris because he bought it as a surprise, without mentioning a word to her. It was dilapidated, Victorian, gracious, close to the shore, and it did remind Catrina of her childhood home in Souris. The day they all arrived to spend their first weekend in the house, she discovered that she was talking — talking to everyone.

"Boy!" Jayne carted her suitcase into the living room and dumped it onto the sofa. "I think you should live here full-time, Mom."

"Oh, come on." Catrina carried a box of food into the kitchen. "We can't live here. This is just for visits."

"And summer." David liked it too. In the summer the town filled with tourists and beach bums and thousands of Philadelphians — an American summer carnival.

"I would," Jayne said, examining the glass chandelier hanging from the ceiling. "You could spend an age patching this place together."

"Well, maybe you could." Catrina came back into the living room and looked at everyone. They were all there, and she stood and examined them, her children, moving through this new home together and each of them happy with it.

"Come on, let's go to the beach." Rose wore cutoff shorts and had her shirt unbuttoned and tied in a knot above her stomach. She knew this beach from a visit two years before, the fine sand and warm rolling waves.

Harris packed three suitcases under his arms and dropped them in a heap on the floor. "Yeah! I second the motion. Let's hit the beach and deal with this mess later."

They dug through the suitcases for their bathing suits. Catrina smiled. Harris looked at her and decided that buying this place might help win her war after all.

For dinner they had Sloppy Joes. It was a recipe Harris found on the back of the "Commonwealth GNP Index" card. The list of ingredients made him think that the meal was fast and easy, and that no one could fault him for screwing up a dinner with a name like Sloppy Joe.

"Pretty spicy, Dad." David sat next to the door of the front porch with his plate balanced on his lap. Everyone sat on whatever was handy: a step, a corner of the coffee table, the wicker footstool. The evening was hot and the smell of salt water clung to his skin. He could feel his facial pores opening to vaporize the spice of Sloppy Joes as his skin flushed with a damp heat.

"Well, the recipe calls for a touch of cayenne." Harris forked a portion of meat and bun into his mouth before it drooled over his chin. "The idea's to get your head rolling." His jaw ground over and over. "A bit like poetry, right?"

"Speaking of which," Rose said, looking up from her corner of the veranda, "I just received a letter from a company called Deep Side Press. And ... you'll never guess what. They want to publish a collection of my poetry."

"You're kidding! A book?"

"Yes."

"Seriously?" Harris dropped his fork to his plate, took a deep breath and sucked the air over his burning tongue.

"I am serious. They want to entitle it *The Cry*. What do you think?"

"*The Cry?*" Catrina asked. She looked at her daughter, at her brilliant, fiery hair.

"Yeah. Do you like it?"

"That's wonderful, Rose." But is it the cry of joy, she wondered, or a cry of pain? "It really is," she added. "Just wonderful."

"Do you think so? Really?" Rose looked at her mother's

face to see if she could believe her. She suspected that it might be a mistake; a book of poems telling the truth about everyone.

"It's tremendous, as long as you're happy with it." Harris prepared another forkful. "That's the main thing." And he chewed quietly in the growing darkness, wondering how much cayenne he'd thrown into the mixing bowl by accident.

Harris pulled off his underpants and slipped into bed beside his wife. "Happy?" he asked, easing his hand under her arm to cup her breast.

She gazed out the window into the summer night. The house would need curtains, eight sets of them, but she had decided on the color for these windows only: blue, either china or royal blue.

"You happy, Cat?"

She rolled slightly, in a way that dropped his hand from her breast onto her stomach. Her body chafed with a dry staleness and she felt light and flaky. "I guess so," she said.

"That's good." He shifted his belly into the curve of her spine and lifted his hand back up to her breast. It would help them so much to make love tonight, he thought. Just to pickle the old honey pie. That's what Charlie Watson used to say about screwing his wife, Diane. "Been up all night pickling honey pie."

"Isn't it nice with the kids home all at once?" His hand slipped onto her stomach, then back up to her breasts. At one time he'd been expert at this.

"Yes." She let his hand work along her skin and felt for any signs that he could open her up. In spite of the handkerchief she'd discovered in his suit pocket, it might still be possible to find something between them, she murmured to herself. She wanted him to find something in her somewhere. Something of pleasure. For a moment she could feel her skin humming with the tension of Harris's hand smoothing the surface of her body into a long, tender flow. Beneath his fingers she felt a current of power easing her down and down and down, draining her energy, unravelling all the tired muscles and tendons beneath her skin and dropping her into the deep dark stream.

"Don't you feel wonderful here?" Harris whispered over Catrina's face. Normally he didn't like to talk if they were going to make love, but it looked like she was fading and he needed to revive her.

She blinked. The handkerchief was perfumed. And smeared with lipstick and chocolate.

"Just the sound of the ocean at night." He listened. Actually he could not hear the waves. He thought he should be able to hear the ocean, but he could not.

"Hmm?"

"You know, sometimes I think of how things were when it was just the two of us." He stopped caressing her stomach and let his hand roll over her pelvis and then lie against her hip. He looked at her; her eyes were half-closed.

Catrina rolled slightly so that his hand fell to one side. On one corner of the handkerchief someone had embroidered the initials G.L. Did he really think that she wouldn't notice? Or worse, that it didn't matter? The veil of sleep was drifting so close to her now, and yet he had to bring up their past. How could he even think about it when he'd found another woman?

"Don't you ever think back to Ottawa sometimes, Catty?"

Catrina could feel her heart moving. What if it stopped?

Just like that? Then she noticed a tiny web of sleep fluttering just ahead of her, through the thin curtain and then into the river of peace. She could see it, right there, with her eyes closed. Gorgeous, beautiful, right through the doorway. *Dream of heav-en-ly peace.*

Harris looked at her without speaking. The light from the window cut across her mouth and he could see the dryness of her skin. He thought about when they were younger when they first lived in Ottawa and used to skate for miles along the frozen Rideau Canal during the winter months.

Pickle yer honey pie.

Harris couldn't get it out of his head. Charlie Watson's goddamn story about screwing his wife Diane echoed over and over through his mind. God, he and Charlie had been close. Men didn't get that close to one another, not the way he and Charlie had back in Toronto. He turned in the bed and pulled the sheet across his shoulder and listened to Catrina's purring. When she slept he could hear the small motors whirring inside her, her engines slowly unwinding while he lay there night after night.

He turned again and thought about the times he'd visited Switzerland, where he'd met Giselle Lamonde. God, she was wonderful. Sucked his cock into her mouth, took it right into her, and then drank from him like he was a river, draining the flood into her tiny mouth, so red and wet and glad when he finally burst through her. She seemed so happy — because he was happy. Later she said that she wanted to love more than be loved. Said it in French and he understood it all especially the importance she attached to loving, as opposed to being loved. Funny, but she had no breasts to speak of. He didn't mind. She was generous, that was the main thing. That and the fact she didn't expect anything in return.

He got out of bed and walked to the window and looked out into the night. The sound of Cat's wheezing buzzed through the room as he stood there, his hands cupped over his ears calculating how long it had been since they'd had any love at all. Two years. Something over two years, and even then only when she'd drunk enough to render herself mostly unconscious. He tiptoed next to the bed and looked down at her purring face. Apart from the fact that her lips vibrated with every breath, he thought that she could be dead. He dropped his hands from his ears to test her skin against his fingers: cold. Cold.

Yes, he thought, she really could be dead.

Chapter Seventeen

Robert Houliman perched the metal flask at his lips, tipped it into the air and drank off two quick snorts of bourbon. "Gawd that's a rush!" His lips puckered as he twisted the cap into place and tucked the flask into his tweed jacket.

"Yeah?"

"You bet, Daydoe. It tunes the sensitivities. Know what I mean?"

Whatever Robert meant, David did not want to pursue it. More talk would just interrupt the speech that Joe Engelmeyer, the president of Deep Side Press had just begun.

"Ladies and gentlemen, I am enormously pleased to see everyone gathered here today." Engelmeyer himself — his belly, his shoulders — was enormous. Everything he did had something gargantuan about it. As he looked around the room he extended his arms in a broad arc that swept everyone towards him. Small Libertys could hold about two hundred but only fifty-odd people had been invited to launch Rose's book, and most of them were milling around the bar where Jayne was busy pouring glass after glass of wine.

"I think that it's fitting indeed that *The Cry* is launched on Rose's twenty-second birthday, a birthday that marks a new maturity, and with it a new voice in contemporary literary art." Engelmeyer glanced around again and when he saw that most of the party had gathered near him, he continued. "If our era is about anything, it is about the world twisting out of shape, about the dislocation of humanity from the great cycle of life. And *The Cry* captures that shift, the fundamental break from the whole history of humanity." He sucked a draft of air into his lungs and held a copy of the book above his shoulder. "*The Cry* is, without a doubt, the best collection of poetry to emerge from a new writer in America this decade. Please join with me to toast a marvelous new poet, and the insights she brings to our attention." Engelmeyer lifted his wineglass with his free hand and smiled. "To Rose Sykes."

"Here! Here!" Robert Houliman clapped his hands together and Harris joined him, grinning effusively, lifting his glass of Beaujolais and clinking it against Catrina's.

"Bravo!" Jayne called out from the bar and clapped her hands. "Whooee!" she shouted in her best Wyoming cowgirl yell.

"The cover's fabulous," Sandra said to David. "Especially since you took her portrait for the back cover."

"I guess so." David didn't really care for the picture he'd taken of Rose: a reverse cameo of her head set over the backlight so that her profile made a foreground silhouette. Too much of the pose emerged, the obvious design of the shot. Besides, all he could think about was Sandra and the fact that he wanted to shoot her. Naked, preferably. She'd already let him take a whole series of facial portraits, everything in black and white to highlight the textures of her skin. But he hadn't mentioned anything about nudes. Not yet.

"Yeah, but it's the front cover that's going to sell this book." Robert pressed between David and Sandra and turned his head from one to the other. "It took me two days to get the abstraction of the bloody thing done just right."

"The abstraction?" Sandra tilted her head as though she hadn't heard him clearly. "What do you mean?"

"That's what we do." Robert crooked his thumb at Rose who stood at the bar signing copies of her book. "That's where you take the subject of a poem, or a painting, or even a photograph," he mused, smiling at David, "and pull the real subject to the surface." He sipped at his wine and wobbled slightly, swaying back and forth. "See, that way you don't just get a picture of some goddamn flower in a vase. Instead, you get a picture that shows you what it means to be a flower." He coughed roughly and wiped his mouth. "What it means," he continued, "to have the inner fucking experience of a flower."

"Interesting." Sandra sniffed the bourbon oozing from his pores. She winced; he smelled pungent, dangerous.

"Yes," he said, and leered at her breasts, "it is."

Sandra looked at Robert's eyes weaving across her chest. "Hold this," she said and passed David her wineglass. "Excuse me, would you?" She walked toward the washrooms.

Robert turned his head to watch her ass as she moved across the floor. "I'll poke her, if ya want," he said, his teeth white and sharp under his lips.

David's hands tightened.

"Just to get her warmed up for ya." He reached into his jacket and pulled out the flask.

David studied his eyes. He felt like smashing him in the face with his wineglass. But nothing happened. His arms froze and his eyes filled with the vision of blood pouring from Robert's head. Instead of killing him he felt a thin wisp of dry air stammering from his lips: "I-i-it's okay," he said.

"Okay? You're kidding me?!" Robert tipped the flask above his mouth and his tongue slicked the bourbon from his lips. "I'll poke her if ya want, Daydoe. But I warn you: once she's toyed with the Houliman snake, she may never be satisfied with anything else!" He laughed and slipped the flask into the inside pocket of his jacket. Then he slowly pulled his jacket lapel open and smiled. Look at this, the smile boasted, it's a banger — a big one.

David stared at the gun, a flat black revolver with a wooden stock strapped into a leather holster against his ribs. All suited up just the way he'd seen them in a dozen police shows. He looked at Robert's face, his rubbery, boozy skin. Death and lies with a grin, David thought. What a bastard.

Rose had signed a dozen books before she saw the silver flashing. They came in two horizontal streaks with white hot trailers skimming through the air. *Whhhiitt, whiittt* — two of them, blazing under her eyes and across the room.

"Did you see that?" She glanced at her mother.

"What do you mean?" Catrina stood in the line next to Rose, and Harris waited behind her with two copies of *The Cry* in his hand.

"Those streaks just now." Rose dropped her pen and scanned the room for the tiny white bullets.

"No." Catrina stepped backward until she felt herself pressing against Harris.

Rose balanced delicately against the bar railing. For a moment she thought she could hear them — tiny pings ricochetting around the room — but they'd disappeared and finally the sound of them faded too. She was left with nothing but the immense horror that they were going to descend from the ceiling and pierce her, drill two perfect holes through her skin and drain her blood onto the floor.

"Sit down, Rose." Robert walked towards her from the far side of the restaurant. In spite of all the laughing and clatter of the music and drinking, the low frequency of his voice undercut the noise and instantly turned her head. She saw him immediately, and one arm lifted slightly toward him and then fell again.

"Just sit over here a minute and forget all this shit." He led her over to a table and glanced at Catrina and then Engelmeyer with contempt.

"What's the matter?" Harris followed them and leaned over the table to examine Rose's face. She looked past him vacuously.

"What's the matter?" Robert reached for his flask again, but this time he forced Rose to take a sip. "I'm surprised to hear you ask that, Dad."

"Dad?" Harris looked from Robert back to Rose. Then he pulled a chair up to the table and sat down.

"It's okay, Daddy." Rose blinked a moment and then leaned back so that her head rested against Robert's shoulder. He took another gulp of bourbon and nodded wearily.

"What's okay?" Harris could feel his blood rising. "Tell me what's okay. Then I'll know what's wrong."

"Life's okay." Robert propped his head onto one fist and smiled so that half his face laughed while the other dropped into a dark funk. "You know, it's like this ... what's past is present. And what's present is future. When you're stuck in one, you're stuck in them all. Ain't that the way the mousketeers put it? All for one and one for all." He dipped his flask into the air again, drained it, then perched it bottom-up on the table edge.

Harris cocked his head. "You're full of crap, Houliman," he whispered. Then he lifted Rose by the waist and braced her against his side. As she stepped away, Robert fell from the chair and his head slapped against the green tile floor.

It took about fifteen minutes to carry Robert out to the street and load him into a taxi. After David managed to flag down a second cab for Sandra, Harris felt relieved. At last he had his family alone and unencumbered. Then he insisted on driving everyone home. Quietly but forcefully, he walked them up the street towards Catrina's car.

"But I am home," Jayne said. "At least just a few blocks from home."

"No, I mean it." Harris held open the back door to the Electra. Rose sat beside David, and Catrina eased into the front seat on her own. "Do it for me, please."

Jayne tilted her head slightly and ducked into the car. She couldn't remember his asking anything so pleadingly. "Well, you're very nice about it," she said once he had the engine running.

"I know. Let's all be nice." Harris pulled out from the curb. He could feel his skin sweating under his suit jacket and his nose full of Robert's boozy vapors. He either had to drive everyone home immediately, or drive his foot into Robert Houliman's unconscious crotch. The choice had been that simple. "I'm gonna try, *try* to be very nice about this, but I need to know *what* is going on."

"Going on with what?" Jayne rested her hand on the armrest. "With who?"

"Not you," he said evenly. The car pulled up to a red

light and he glanced over his shoulder. "But I'd like to know what's going on with Rose and Robert."

A moment of silence dampened the air. Rose could feel her throat tightening, almost choking her, then relaxing into what was to come. The twin flashes of light had disappeared — at least for now — and she felt ready. "What about him?" she sighed.

"I'd like to know ... " Harris had to pull around a double-parked taxi and then back into the right lane to ease around two drunks who had fallen off the curb onto Broadway. "Just tell me what's going on," he said. "I mean, couldn't you just inform us, your family, of how things are developing? You know, what your intentions are? Like most normal families do."

"Who says we're normal?" Jayne asked.

"Of course we're normal." Harris scanned the rearview mirror. "At least as normal as anyone else."

"You mean as crazy." Rose glanced at city hall and then along the walls of St. Paul's Chapel. They were driving into the financial district, far past the turnoff that took them over to Jayne's apartment.

"Look. What I'm asking you — " His voice rose and hit a peak. He could feel himself losing it. He wanted her to tell him voluntarily, not to confess under duress.

Catrina looked out to the sidewalk, then back into the car.

"Harris," she whispered, "please."

"All right," Rose interrupted. "What do you want to know? All the traditional questions, right? Does the young lad maintain honorable intentions? Is there any prospect that he'll propose? Is that right? Is that what you're after?"

"That'd be a good place to start." Harris turned left at Trinity Church onto Wall Street. Rows of brokerage towers lit up the night. He was surprised the street was so empty. Sunday and not a soul in sight. He let the car glide along at an idle.

"Jesus." Rose frowned and shook her head. Then she sat up and waved her hands at the concrete and steel and glass all around them. "Can't you see that we live in a different universe than all that?"

"Not so different. What's so different about love and marriage and children?"

"Oh fuck it! Look, we've been married over two months already." Tiny metal husks fit around every word. "In fact, our three-month anniversary comes up next week. On the twentieth, in case you'd like to send flowers."

The engine purred under the hood, the noise humming into the car along with the sound of Rose's heightened breathing.

"And I guess you should know," she said crossing both arms over her breasts, "I'm moving in with him."

Jayne looked across the seat at Rose. She considered a question of balance: to say her piece now or wait? It's very delicate, she thought. If she waited then it would just mean hitting them with another shock next week. So do it now. Now. Say it.

"I'm going to be leaving, too." Jayne tried to speak without moving her lips, but the words came out so that no one understood her.

"What?" Harris brought the car to a stop right in the middle of Wall Street. There wasn't a moving vehicle in sight. Sunday night in the financial center of the world: a vacuum.

"You're moving?" Rose twisted around in her seat. Finally the focus had shifted away from her. She felt free.

"Yes."

"Where to?"

"The Philippines."

"And just what do you think you're going to do there?" Harris turned around so he could see her. See all of them.

"Work in a mission." Jayne pressed her back into the seat. Could they understand this? "At a hospital where they have a field outpost to help the peasants. We give them clean water and medicine and inoculations for the kids ... and there's a school there, too."

"What are you talking about? It's ten thousand miles —"

"Look! You don't know what I'm going through!" Jayne twisted her face away from him and stared onto the street. "I can't even concentrate any more." She looked back at her father. "I've got to find a new way forward. Doesn't that mean anything to you?"

No one spoke. David could feel his skin bristling. He felt as if he were going to vanish, to disappear before anyone could leave him behind.

"I'm going next month." Jayne looked at Rose and then over to her father. "I'm really going to go," she added. The three of them glanced at one another and then their eyes flicked away.

The light from the street slanted through the windows and David watched a newspaper flap through the air until it caught a lamppost, rattled in the wind a moment, then slipped away. He'd listened to them, their voices coming through the top of his head, and now that they'd stopped talking, the night poured into him. There was just the sound of the car idling, filling the strange silence of lower Manhattan, and the noise of electricity pouring through the vacant buildings and street lights, humming through the uninhabited light.

Chapter Eighteen

Samantha Keppke leaned forward from the kitchen chair and pulled open the drawstrings of her shoulder bag. She hadn't gone out in the snow yet. In fact, she'd waited a day and two nights inside the apartment, hoping the thick slush would melt and that she would not have to contend with it at all. But the snow stayed. It reminded her of her childhood in the Ukraine. It pressed forward in her mind until she felt the presence of her father and mother and sister and then their sudden, empty disappearance. Now she would have to go out into the streets no matter what. She could put off the tarot and palm readings a few days but earning her living could not be postponed. Even with Sandra earning a salary at the studio they had to be diligent with money. She looked inside the bag to ensure the tarot cards were there and then rummaged for her mittens.

"Sandra? Have you seen those mittens?"

"No, Baba." The voice was certain as it echoed down the hallway. "But you can take mine. We're not going out."

We're not going. It was always the two of them doing

everything together now. Her hand reached the bottom of the bag and swept around the sides and back to the top. No mittens. And no scarf either. All right, she would settle for the borrowings. Who cared? And this David is a good boy, too, though younger than Sandra. But at least he is intelligent and sensitive.

"All right, I'll borrow," she said when she reached the living room. "Even though yours is not my color." She smiled to indicate this was a joke, that color meant nothing to her. "And the scarf, too," she added.

Sandra went out of the room for her mittens and scarf as David sat watching, wondering what to do.

"Would you like to have some tea?" He turned the handle of the teapot towards her. He didn't really want her to stay, but if she did, then he'd hear more about the tarot and that was almost worth the time he lost alone with Sandra.

Samantha looked at him and then through the window onto the white sidewalks of Seventh Avenue. "All right." She settled into the chair opposite him. "But only one cup. I have to drink it all day." She turned up her lip to demonstrate her contempt for the circuit of tearooms and restaurants that employed her. Then she laughed at her own scorn and waited for him to pour the milk into her cup. Everything in the world was both dark and light. Allowing her contempt to displace her humor would be a perversion of nature.

The tea was poured and the mittens and scarf arrived. "Ah there." She felt well served. "And what are you two going to do once I leave, hmm?" She looked first at Sandra, then David.

Sandra shifted her eyes away. After two years of David's visits, her great aunt had never asked this. And now she had to ask with both of them together. "Just take some pictures," Sandra said. "You know, like the ones you've seen."

"Ahh! More pictures!" Samantha nodded as though this were a great surprise. "And how many pictures have you got already, young man?"

David's eyes focussed on the carpeting. Hundreds. He'd shot at least ten rolls of Sandra's face over the last six months alone. The photographs were his only legitimate excuse to come into town to see her. "Well ... I've had three accepted by a magazine."

"By *Modern Photography*," Sandra added. "It's a magazine sold right across the country. And David's been accepted in it."

"Yes. You told me about this." Samantha felt a plug of phlegm rising in her throat. She sipped her tea and washed it back down. Normally she'd spit it out, but she knew this would disturb her grandniece in front of the boy.

"Do you like photography, Sam?" David leaned forward in his chair and looked at her. Tiny creases cut across her round, wide face, especially near her eyes. Her hair was a mass of shifting colors, waves of grey, red and brown, all of it bound together by a candy-cane bandanna wrapped tightly around her head. Her eyes were a deep grey and theatrically penetrating. She'd developed this quality to assure the tarot clientele of the accuracy of her insights.

"They're all right." She shrugged. "A good photograph is like anything else in the world. All a piece of the world. If you were an alien from the moon, say — this is something very popular today, isn't it? — and the only clue that you had to the existence of life on Earth was the photograph of a young, beautiful woman, then you would have the key to complete knowledge of the world. Why? Because from this one picture, you resolve everything. From her eyes and mouth and nose, you understand the face of humanity. And from the fact of the woman, you deduce the existence of the man because of the division of the universe into opposites. And from the opposites, you would know about struggle and from the struggle, the resolution of life into death." She sipped her tea and examined David as she placed the cup onto the table. "Do you think so?"

"I don't know. I haven't thought about it that way."

"You don't know? Why don't you know?" she asked, slipping the mittens over her thick hands and nodding her head in disgust.

"Because we're not fortune-tellers, Baba." Sandra laughed, relieved to see her preparing to go.

Sam curled her lips again and walked to the door. "There is a difference between fortune-telling and prophecy, child." Then her mouth flattened into a smile. Best not to chide them as she left, she thought. They were her children, all of them. "And bear this prophecy closely: I will be back by five-thirty, and at six you will have the stew on the table. Hmm?"

"Yes, Baba."

"Good-bye." She closed the door and went out into the snow.

"It's very hard living with her, you know."

"Really?" David bolted the Canon onto the tripod, slipped the metal legs free and tightened the lock collars. "She seems so genuine."

"She is. Maybe that's what makes it so hard. I mean, how can I leave anyone who tells me exactly and clearly and honestly what it is they want out of me?" Sandra combed her hair with both hands and let it fall in a dark cloud over her face. She had to get herself in a mood to be photographed. It wouldn't take long; she loved the camera because it gave her herself, and she liked to talk as David shot her. She talked more in front of the camera, with his face hidden behind the lens, than at any other time.

"I didn't know you wanted to leave." He walked over to the window and pulled the curtains wide open. With the snow outside, the winter light cast a cool brightness into the room. He could get her to stand near the window and see how the reflections played on her skin. Maybe today she'd take her clothes off.

"Well, sometime I'll have to." She walked over to the window and looked onto the street. The snow has a power of its own, she thought, the way it locks the traffic up in its soft hands.

"Okay, just stand there." He glanced at her from the tripod, his head slanting to one side, calculating a line of perspective. "This light is fantastic." He could feel his throat drying, tightening. And if she took her clothes off, then what?

Sandra dug through her hair again and walked in a tiny circle in front of the window. After a minute she could feel the camera working for her, dissolving the rest of the room, insulating her from the world. Only the small clicking noise of the shutter seemed to exist outside her. That and David. And even he became a shadow — hiding behind the lens, turning it slowly, one eye tunneling through the metal casing, the other shut tight.

"You're right." She felt the intensity of the reflection on her arms and the sun warming the air. Soon the snow would be melting. "The light is fantastic."

David didn't say anything. He looked at her through the lens, clicked through the f-stops and tried three or four settings to test the variations. He never knew what worked until he finished developing the film in the darkroom, but in the last year his ability to guess and improvise had improved. The Canon had become another eye, completely attuned to him.

"What do you want to get today?" She spun around in the light again. More than anything she felt weightless, effervescent. But it was better not to identify her feelings — it might kill them.

Her skin, he thought. He looked through the lens. Her bare arms caught two little rivers of light that travelled from her wrists up her elbows. Her face was a shining pool. He depressed the shutter. Click. Her skin, he wanted her skin. Click, click.

Sandra turned her head, pulled her hair tight behind her and swung her chin into the air until she could feel the sun melting across the length of her neck. Then she stretched higher, tauter, so that the tendons in her throat rippled under her skin.

Click, click, click.

"Is that good?"

"Yes." Click. "Keep talking. Every time you say something, it bobbles your throat."

"Say something? What am I supposed to say?" she laughed and her crooked teeth showed.

Click, click, click, click.

"André Kertesz would love this!" She laughed again, then dropped her head and held a hand to her mouth. Okay, get your composure. Now turn, turn. She swung her head around and tilted it so that the light flared across her face and she had to close her eyes.

"By the way, I heard that Kertesz lives pretty close to your sister's place."

"You mean where she used to live." Click. "God, I'd love to be able to do something like he's done."

"You can." She lifted both hands to her face and washed the light over her closed eyes. He took five, six shots like that. Light as water. Light as a river. "It would be easy," she said, and with her eyes still closed she pulled her shirt over her head, unstrapped her bra and threw it onto the sofa. Then she turned her breasts towards him, her face high in the sun.

Light as the flood. He took a deep breath. Then two shots. "Twist," he said, and her belly stretched around towards the open window. He couldn't take his eye from the camera. The lens turned under his fingers and brought him closer, inches from her skin, where he could lick her nipples, the hard, dark moons. "That's great."

"Really?" She stepped out of the light and gazed at him. "Should I take the rest of my clothes off?"

He stood back a moment and unscrewed the Canon from the tripod. Then he looked at her. God. He had to think to breathe. "Yes," he said finally as he rewound the film and loaded the camera with 100 ASA film. He wanted to pace this, run the shots at a little slower speed to make everything fluid. More dreamlike. The sun would be white cream on her skin.

She pulled off her pants and one leg caught on her heel. As she hopped on the floor to free her leg, her breasts jiggled up and down. Then she slipped out of her panties and socks. She took a moment to fold her clothing neatly on the arm of the chair and then she came back into the center of the room and lay naked on the carpet, with one knee bent and her arms pulled above her head. The sun made a box of light around her, and he took her like that, with all the shadows of the room forming a black frame against the floor. Moving around her, he took seven, eight, nine shots — shooting freely whenever the mood hit him. The light remained perfect, and the only critical element was his mood. He shot everything from his feeling for her, impulses running directly from his eyes into the lens.

"You know something?" he said. He wasn't thinking. All he could see was her skin laid out like a bridge into her soul. "You know what Robert Houliman said about you?"

"Robert Houliman?" She turned her head and her breasts eased across her chest. "What about him?"

"Face the wall," he whispered and he took three shots of her back, imagining a title for the finished image: "The Ivory Wall."

She rolled over, leaning against her buttocks. The skin on her belly turned silver.

Click. Five, six more shots. "He said he wanted to sleep with you."

"Get serious." Her face turned into the shadows so he couldn't see it. Only her breasts now, just them alone, swollen in the light: "Hills of Desire."

"He said ... " He walked back in front of her, pushed the camera close to her face. "He told me that he wanted to fuck you."

"David." She turned away. "He's married to your sister."

Her hair. Take her hair. Click, click, click. Just two shots left.

"Why are you saying this?" She lay on her back now, her thighs and shoulders flat on the floor.

"I don't know." He really didn't. He meant to shut it all away. "It's just what he told me." He took another shot of her like that: supine on the carpet, her breasts lolling above her, kissing the air. "He told me that he wanted to fuck you for me."

"David. *Shit.*" She shut her eyes, forcing them away from his face.

She looks asleep like that, he thought, and he went back to the edge of the room, to the front door, and changed the lens for a wide angle to capture the entire frame of white light in the center of the apartment. In that brilliant rectangle she lay naked, completely vulnerable.

When the roll of film was finished, he stopped and leaned against the sofa, rewinding the film and thinking, now it's time to leave. He had it all on film now, so he could leave.

"So why don't you do it *yourself?*" She stood right in front of him, her shoulders reflecting two small crescents from the light of the window. "Why don't you" — she curled her arms around his neck and moved her face inches from his eyes — "do it." She shifted her breasts so that they shoved the camera away from his chest, and with the length of her body she pressed him against the sofa onto the armrest.

He looked at her face, at the way she was offering him everything he'd dreamed of for so long.

"We don't need this, do we?" She slipped the leather strap over his neck and placed the camera on the coffee table. "Or this?" she said, unbuttoning his shirt. Her breasts lolled against his skin as her hands slipped along his waist and unzipped his jeans.

Opening his lips to kiss her, he felt her fingers lifting his penis and from that moment he stopped thinking. Sandra eased him onto the sofa, then slid beside him on the blue slipcover and began to kiss his face, his hands, along his chest and arms as she immersed him in her passion. The wildness in her surprised him, and when her panting rose, he grew rigid, and she had to stop a moment to stroke his face and reassure him that she was fine, she just needed more, just a little more. He came suddenly, without warning or any sense of filling her, yet he felt consumed by her, almost smothered under the depth of her gathering heat. She propped his head on a pillow and locked him beneath her and as she regained her momentum, he turned his head to the camera. Her eyes closed tightly and her body worked in a hard, almost desperate rush, and when he finally saw the animal emerge from her and begin moaning above him, he could imagine one still shot that caught her there, churning wildly in the white light of the living room, and his eyes fixed on her clean, glossy image.

Chapter Nineteen

"Hey Daydoe." Robert climbed out of his blue Dodge and stretched in the morning air. David stood behind the townhouse door, surprised to see his brother-in-law up before noon, especially on a Saturday.

"Hi, David," Rose called from the inside of the car. She had on her sunglasses, big round ones that covered her cheeks — two black zeroes that she wore habitually now, regardless of the time of day.

"Hi." David leaned from the door and looked at the trailer attached to the back of the car. *U-HAUL* was tattooed in bold letters across the siding. He wondered how they'd hooked it up to the Dodge, but instead of going out onto the driveway to examine the trailer hitch, he walked back into the townhouse without waiting for them. He hadn't finished his breakfast, and besides, the air was already hot and very humid.

A few moments later he heard them tromping upstairs to the kitchen, the two of them and something else making a strange clawing and rubbing sound against the stair treads. They turned the corner and started laughing. Then a dog jumped onto David's lap.

"Spunky!" Rose laughed so hard that her sunglasses slipped from the bridge of her nose.

Spunky woofed and plunged her snout into David's breakfast cereal and began lapping up the milk.

"No. God no! Not the Cheerios!" Robert pulled the dog by the collar until she slipped back onto the floor. Then Rose and Robert glanced at one another, burst into more laughter and started slapping the dog across the ass. They tried to do it playfully, but the dog yelped and finally lay down.

"Meet Spunky." Rose extended a hand toward the dog and sat at the arborite table beside David. Robert sat opposite him, dumped his keys into the fruit bowl and frowned.

"Hello Spunky." David looked at the dog and then at his breakfast. He pushed the cereal bowl away with a finger. "So you got a dog."

"Yeah. Friendly old fart, huh?" Rose reached into her purse for some cigarettes. "She adopted us. Can you believe it? We were walking along First Avenue, just two blocks from our new apartment, and she adopted us. She hasn't been more than fifty yards away from us in the last two weeks."

"Three," Robert corrected as he pulled a milk bone from his shirt pocket and threw it to Spunky. The dog cracked it between her teeth and began gnawing quietly at their feet.

Rose looked around the room. She took a deep breath and her mood seemed to change. David watched her carefully. Strange, with one breath her whole attitude shifted. She was listening for something.

"Has Mom gone?" She pushed the sunglasses along the bridge of her nose.

"Yeah, down to the shore. She's staying two weeks while Dad's in Geneva."

But Rose already knew this. He'd told her on the phone last night when she'd called him at three-thirty. Another new habit she'd developed: rambling mid-night telephone calls.

"Right. They left you to study for your finals, huh?" She flicked the cigarette ash into the ashtray and grabbed Robert by the wrist. "My baby brother's going into second year at NYU!"

"Right!" Robert barked and nuzzled Spunky's nose with one foot. "We all know this to be a fact. The man's breaking out of his freshman bind. Once and for all. Freedom, Brother!" He shouted in an imitation of Martin Luther King: "FREEDOM! FREEDOM!"

David stood up and walked over to the stove. He started to prepare some instant coffee, but more than anything he just needed to move away from them. He sorted through the drawer for a teaspoon. "Want a coffee? The water's already boiled."

"Hey. Where's the girlfriend, Daydoe?" Robert twisted his head from side to side, as though he'd find her just behind the door. "When you've got the place to yourself, you're supposed to go crazy on her. What's her name? Sara?"

"Sandra," Rose corrected, "but she doesn't come around any more." She pulled her sunglasses down so they could see her eyes. "At least that's what I've heard," she added.

"What? No! You had a fight?"

"No." Rose held her cigarette in the air and examined

the tip for flaws. The tiny coal glowed perfectly, but too much heat could ruin the draw. "Not a fight. David's erotophobic."

"You mean fear of love?"

David stood there with his back to them, his shoulders tightening as he picked through the cutlery for teaspoons. Why had he told her? Why did he tell her anything?

"No, fear of sex, darling. He can only do it with his camera."

David's hands curled.

Robert stared at his back, unsure of what to say next, but certain that he should say something. "No kidding. Well, when your chick leaves, you're supposed to have a blow out. You know, a big fucking banger with all your pals."

David swung around. "Look ... " He felt the anger swirling in his belly. "Do you want a coffee? Or not?"

"Sure. Why not?" Robert leaned forward in his chair and scratched Spunky's head. The dog had eaten only half the milk bone. The rest lay in crumbs on the floor.

David brought three coffees to the table and sat down again. "So you've come for your stuff, huh?" He looked up at Rose. She planned to come home and load her bed, bureau, desk and books into the rented trailer and move everything downtown into the new apartment. She'd talked to David about how they finally had enough room for her and Robert's furniture, but she wanted to wait until her parents were away before she moved anything. That way, she could avoid any scenes, especially the possibility of their mother bursting into tears.

"Yeah. But no rush," Robert said, sipping on his coffee. It was his first meal of the day: Sanka. He drank it sparingly, in tiny sips that he rolled over his tongue. "I mean, if there is no rush, then why rush?" He glanced at Rose for confirmation. "I'm really not looking forward to moving that goddamn bed downstairs anyway. Not in this heat."

"Except David's got to study." Rose lit another cigarette and started nuzzling the dog, too.

"Screw the study. He knows it all. Besides, he's having all his pals over anyway, right?" His head pressed toward David. "Am I right?"

David could feel his shoulders tighten again. Asshole.

"Robert, don't be such a boor." Rose stood up and walked to the kitchen window. "Besides, David doesn't have any friends. Not that he'd ask over, anyway." She turned around and pressed the sunglasses against the bridge of her nose. "Right?"

"What?" David's hands curled around his coffee cup. He wanted to vanish, to fill himself with air and float away. "What are you saying?"

"I think she's saying you've got no buds." Robert tapped two fingers against his mustache. A little drumroll hitting silently.

"I'm saying ... " Rose walked back and forth in front of the window. She was digging for an exact phrase. She wanted to be accurate the first time so that he wouldn't lose the importance of it. "What I'm saying is that you're depressed." Her head nodded slightly, and she leaned forward so that he could see the tops of her eyes over the rim of the sunglasses. "You know what I mean? You've gone numb. But you're just too cosy to bother climbing out of this, this miasma." She waved her hand around the room, pointing at the arborite, the linoleum, the decorative knickknacks lining the walls. "Look. You're the last one left here. Everybody else has left this family except you."

"A lad in search of a dad in search of a pad." Robert grinned and sipped his coffee.

"Oh, why don't you shut up, Robert?" Rose slapped her fists against her thighs. "Can't you keep quiet for one minute?"

Robert slumped in his chair, curled his fingers into Spunky's loose mane of hair and rolled his fist back and forth in her fur.

"Don't you see? Jayne's in the Philippines and Mom's basically moved down to Cape May. Christ, she's the worst of all." She began pacing in front of the sink again. "And Dad's away, as usual. What's new? I really think he's got something cooking over there. Don't you?"

Was he really depressed? David wondered. Was that it? But he tried to roll the conversation away from himself. "Over where?"

"In Switzerland. How come he never takes Mom over to any of these two-week conferences that he has twice a year? He's got the money, right? I mean why is that?"

Because she's a drunk, David thought. An embarrassment. Burying her in a little house in Cape May was the perfect escape. And Rose is right, everyone else has escaped except me. There's just me alone here. He couldn't even talk to Sandra any more. Couldn't even call her.

"Huh? I mean why else wouldn't he take her, too?"

David didn't say anything. He just looked at her and wondered how long she'd keep wearing those sunglasses.

When they finished their coffee, Rose suggested that David and Robert haul everything into the trailer while she made them some sandwiches and found some beer. If they ate early enough, they could sit on the back balcony before the sun hit the west side of the townhouse and it became too late for them to cool off.

"Your sister's full of good ideas like this," Robert said once he and David had finished moving the furniture and opened the lounging chairs in the shade. He took a long sip from the beer bottle and looked across the river to the Palisades. "Got the kind of organizational skill you don't expect to find in a poetess."

"That why you married her?" David mounted a telephoto lens to the Canon and twisted the focus ring in and out, looking across the river to the New Jersey shore. With the telephoto on, sometimes he could make out people walking along the edge of the cliffs.

"Among other things, Daydoe my bro'. That and sundry other fine arts."

David swung the camera around and looked at him. Two-faced, gigantic.

Then Rose stepped onto the balcony with a plate full of sandwiches. She sat down at the foot of Robert's lounge chair and took a sip of his beer. "I put Spunky in the trailer," she said. "She's yelping like crazy."

"She is crazy." Robert ate half a sandwich and drained his first beer. Then he started another. He ate quickly, without talking, his attention focussed on the slices of spam and mayonnaise.

When they finished the sandwiches and beer, Robert cut a deep, groaning burp. He twisted his head and grinned. " 'Scuse me," he said and walked into the townhouse, closing the screen door behind him.

"Robert finishes every meal like that." Rose scratched her nose with a finger, bored by his bad manners.

"Really?" David pulled out his camera again and scanned the cliff edges. Two birds were diving below the Jersey shore.

"Yeah. By now he'll be digging through his satchel for his dessert."

"He brought a dessert along?" David had trouble envisioning Robert with a cherry pie stored in the trunk of the Dodge.

"Yeah, brownies."

The screen door slipped open, and Robert sat on the lounger exactly where he'd been before. "That's right," he said. He'd overheard Rose's last word and he grinned. He had a cowboy satchel, two saddlebags joined together with leather straps. He dropped one end into his lap and opened the clip. "But these ain't any brownies. They're smokers." He reached into the satchel and pulled open a paper bag. Inside, a half-dozen brownies had been stacked into three piles. He took one and delicately gnawed at its corner with his pinky turned up in the air. "Delicious." He smiled. He smiled all the time now.

"Try one, if you want." Rose reached into the bag and took two brownies into her hand. Both had thick, chocolate icing. "They're loaded with grass."

They ate all the brownies, two each, sitting on the loungers overlooking the Hudson. The river flowed seamlessly, and David tried to pinpoint any currents that were not simply ripples kicked up by the breeze. After twenty minutes he decided that the river might not be flowing at all. Maybe it was just a stagnating pool, mulling its fate along the rocky shore.

"Hey, did I show you my new babies?" Robert asked.

And if the river were a mere pool, David thought, Earth itself was a mere ball of mud drifting through the backwater of time.

"Uh, are you stoned yet, son?"

It took a moment for David to connect: Robert calling ... Robert's voice reaching into his ears, spinning into his brain and sticking there.

"What?" He turned around.

"My babies." Robert unclipped the second pouch of the satchel. He held it open a moment so that David could look inside. Two pistols lay together, tucked into the bottom of the bag. He lifted both guns into his lap, the muzzles pointing at his feet. "We just got them last week."

"You mean, *you* just got them," Rose whispered and turned her head away. Then she saw two bullets blaze past her and across the river. She shuddered and wrapped her arms across her chest.

"Sorry. I forgot you had an aversion." Robert rolled his eyes and handed a pistol to David. "Ninety-eight bucks for the pair. Not bad, huh?"

David looked at the gun. He'd never held a pistol before. Except the time he gave the gun to Rose. He thought of Brad Watson. Had he really touched that small German pistol, with its silver stock just like this one?

"Had to get 'em for protection." Robert turned in his chair to Rose. "You tell Daydoe what happened last month? What we saw over in the park?"

Rose watched the bullets hovering over the river. They were tiny, but so white, so blinding. Her fingers touched the arms of her sunglasses and pressed against the plastic.

"No?" Robert turned back to David. "Well, it was a goddamn mess. You wouldn't believe it. I mean I still can't believe it. " He casually tipped the nose of the gun to his chest and then away. "We were what? Fifty yards into Central Park, right off Seventy-ninth behind the museum, when ahead of us we could see this group of kids. There were about ten of them I guess, right?" He looked to Rose and then back again. "All standing around in a circle. And I could hear them talking Spanish. They were young spic kids, right?" He dropped the pistol into his lap and took another swig of beer. "Then the next thing we hear is this horrible, and I mean absolutely horrible, yelping. From a dog, as it turns out. We couldn't tell at first what it was. From where we were, just past the museum, it sounded like another kid, except much louder. And this sound of terrible pain. Then somebody else runs over to this circle of spic kids and starts screaming at them. Then the next thing we see, he drops. Just falls onto the ground. Then the kids ran like hell out of there, leaving this guy and dog sprawled out on the grass."

David held the gun in the air and sighted along the barrel. He moved his arm across the balcony over the river and pressed his finger against the outside of the trigger guard. If he wanted to, he could fire off two shots right now. Pow. Pow.

"Hey, be careful with that. You interested in this, or not?"

David felt his head floating. "Sure." He dropped his arm and let the gun rest in his lap.

"By the time we got halfway to them, the guy had pulled himself up to his knees. Then I could see he was bleeding from his arm. The kids had knifed him. Right in his bicep. It was hard to see how bad it was through his shirt, but he was bleeding all right." Robert raised the beer to his lips and finished it. "But it was the dog they'd really fucked. I mean it was bad." He stopped talking and looked around. Robert loved talking when he was high, enveloped in complete self-absorption. But he wanted them to want him to talk. Especially now that he was getting to what really happened, to what the boys did to the dog's genitals. He looked at Rose, but she sat there, motionless, the two bullets flickering above her.

David glanced across the Hudson. He saw a bird glide over the river and disappear into the water. Then his head became a bird, graceful, alert, and it glided back to Robert. "So?"

"You sure you want to hear this?"

"No," he said, "not really." David rolled his shoulders and turned back to the river. Ah, it was *two* birds. Both of them over the river now, diving. Wait, did he say that? Did he say "no"?

"Hey." Robert stood up and leaned against the metal railing. "Would you look at those two spin-heads!" His hand stretched into the air and he pointed towards the birds with the gun. "What are they? Goddamned loons?"

David stood up and focussed the telephoto lens over the water. "I dunno." His voice — a tremble — surprised him. "I don't know," he repeated, this time almost screaming.

"All right, Daydoe. You don't have to announce it to the Viet Cong, for Christ's sake." Robert started laughing, and turned toward Rose. But she sat there, mute, and pressed the sunglasses to the top of her nose with both hands.

"Maybe they are." David turned the focus ring slowly, watching the birds slam the water and then dive.

"Are what?" Robert giggled again. "Here, let me see." He pulled the Canon from David's hands and peered through the lens.

"I'm not sure." The camera strap stretched from David's neck and pulled him against his brother-in-law so that they almost touched.

"You gotta be sure." Robert shifted the eyepiece from one eye to the other. He couldn't see the birds anywhere. "An artist always has to be sure about everything. Otherwise he's no good for a damn thing."

"That's such a load of crap," Rose said from behind them. It was a whisper. She couldn't find her voice either. Then louder: "I thought everybody got over all that

Hemingway machismo in 1961. The more you admit what you don't know the better chance you have of discovering something new — instead of papering the world over with your transparent egocentric certainty and bravado."

"You don't know what you're talking about."

"Really? Then why haven't you done any worthwhile painting in the last year? Huh? Ever since you started selling out." This time her voice was clear, incisive.

"Oh, back off." Robert returned to the lounge chair and narrowed his eyes. He could hate her, his eyes said. It wouldn't take much.

David stayed at the railing and toyed with the telephoto lens. He had the birds in focus again, two of them, trying to mate in midair.

"Since, if we want to be precise about the timing of your demise," Rose's voice broke through its hard, tremulous shell, "from the day you started working for the APA and — "

The gun went off. David didn't see it, but two shots banged off behind him. He turned around. Robert sat in the lounger with his feet propped up at one end. He still held the pistol in the air, but his arm dropped slightly and he cocked his head to the left and smiled. Then he stood up and peered over the balcony. "Did I get them?"

"Get what?" David turned back to the river; he couldn't see the birds anywhere. Then he heard Rose, spun around and saw her curled into a ball on the deck. "Oh God!"

Her fingers pressed against the arms of her sunglasses. As she lay on the concrete, she tried to hold the blackness in front of her eyes. She'd seen the two bullets coming at her, streaking towards her from the river and drilling into her head. She'd shoved the sunglasses against her nose until they began to cut her skin and she heard herself screaming.

"Rose!" David dropped beside her and held his hands under her hair. He didn't want her head to touch anything. As he cradled her neck, he glared at Robert. "You bastard."

"Hey, come on. I didn't shoot her, goddammit." Robert rolled his shoulders and turned back to the railing. He cranked his head up and down looking for the birds. "I was shooting into the drink."

Rose heard the sizzling. The two bullets hovered above her, waiting for her to look directly at them before they bored through her skull. She had to look. She knew she had to look at them before she would be released. And slipping off her sunglasses, she looked into the sky, past David's head directly into the sun. Then she realized what they were. The bullets. The two bullets from the basement in Toronto. She heard two tiny popping noises, somewhere high above the river, and then they were gone. They'd followed her all this way, and now that she could finally see them, they disappeared. She sat up, hunched against the wall, and felt the past dissolving, evaporating in the heat.

"Are you all right?" David knelt on one knee and examined her face, the small bruises yellowing at the top of her nose where the sunglasses had cut her skin.

"It's taken so long," she whispered.

Robert didn't say a word. He stood with his shoulders towards them and leaned against the railing, his back flat and muscular.

"What has?"

She lifted a finger to her face and touched the small welts swelling between her eyes. "Just seeing things for what they are," she said, lifting the sunglasses with both hands. And in one motion she snapped the plastic frames under her fingers and the lenses dropped onto the concrete.

Chapter Twenty

David stood at the railing and looked over the edge. The distance from the 102nd floor observation deck of the Empire State Building to the tier below didn't produce the shock of height he'd expected. In fact he had no sense of vertigo whatsoever. In the elevator, with all the tourists, his anticipation climbed with every blip on the floor monitor, then again with the change of elevators and the final ascent to the top. He could feel it in them, the dread hope that they'd all plummet from the tower, and on the way down achieve the miraculous gift of flight. But they didn't fall, and when the building seemed to sway in the chill October wind, they giggled, delighted by their fears as they wandered around the deck and smiled whenever they spotted familiar cityscapes next to their hotels.

He lifted the Canon to his eye and scanned the horizon. Every side of the building provided an immense view of perfected decay: the factories of New Jersey, the rusty red trees fluttering in Central Park, the eternity of Long Island brownstones, the chiseled grey monoliths of Wall Street.

And beyond Battery Park, in the water, the green frown of Liberty. Here, at the top of the center of the world, he could see thousands of buildings venting their exhaust into the sky while the city rumbled and honked beneath him, as the people and cars burst through the geometry of streets and avenues that multiplied into the distance.

They're trying to hold this city together with fucking mathematics, he thought. And the camera showed it all. Whatever effect the camera produced was a function of the depth of field, the speed of the film, the shutter speed and the setting of the aperture. Pure science, and he'd learned it all at NYU from Dr. Hammersley: "You can calculate every incremental shift of any exposure. Even the light can be adjusted and filtered and exchanged for blackness. Only the human qualities, like compassion and warmth, are brought by the artist into the pictures. Something you invent, like the discovery of God."

But that means you have to believe in God before you can put Him there, doesn't it? This was a critical point, one that David was unsure of. He looked over the edge of the building. Directly below, he knew with absolute certainty, even though the tiered decks of the Empire State Building blocked the view, lay the intersection of two streets, numbered Thirty-fourth and Fifth. But nowhere was there any sign of the junction of God and humanity.

He leaned against the railing and nosed the Canon across the sky. He was here for the Chrysler Building. Why not get on with it? Give Hammersley what he wants and move on to the real stuff. He'd already taken a dozen shots of the Chrysler from the United Nations Plaza and another set from the top of the Chanin Building. He fixed the camera at an angle and depressed the shutter. Then another angle shot and another. Why not make it look like the building's falling against the horizon? He knocked off ten exposures: up, down, sideways, backwards, any perspective that caught the Chrysler Building with its art deco syringe jabbing into the ass of the northeast sky.

On the way down the elevator with his portfolio case awkwardly tucked under an arm, David thought about Hammersley and NYU. Rather, Dr. Hammersley of the Department of Photography in the Institute of Film and Television of New York University. He took two classes from him: Photographic Composition and Sensitometry. Hammersley astonished David because he never took pictures any more. At least, not in the last two decades. In the Second World War he'd been a photojournalist for the North American Newspaper Alliance, and for over twenty years since then, he'd been printing and reprinting all the exposures he'd taken overseas. He did everything in the darkroom. "That's where it all happens," he whispered through his yellow teeth. "You take your pictures outside in the streets ... or in your moldy little apartments. But you make photographs here" — he tapped the side of his head — "in the dark!"

He always whispered to the class of seventy-five students. How he managed to be heard past the second row was questionable. But David sat front row center, absorbing anything of value that Hammersley had to dispense. "You have to see in the dark!" he wheezed, and he jabbed his pipe into the side of his mouth and sucked through the stem until the bowl glowed and smoked.

An exercise in seeing. That was the key, to concentrate all his sensitivities into a vision of the world. David decided it might be possible to discipline his vision by eliminating some other form of sensation, cut off part of himself in order to strengthen his sense of sight. The only painless possibility was his voice, to immerse himself in silence. And it worked. For the past two days he hadn't spoken a word. His parents were in Washington for the week, and he didn't have to talk to anyone on the commuter train or the subway or even at NYU for that matter. Not that he knew anyone to talk to. And this silence provided the chance to transform himself into ... into what? Uncertainty. But that's the nature of experimentation, he thought, the willingness to penetrate the unknown.

Back at the university, he went straight up to the studios, opened the door to the darkroom, leaned his portfolio case against the back of the stool, locked the door and began to work in the dark. Once he'd poured the developer into the tank, the wonderful moment arrived when everything he'd seen through the lens reappeared in the negative. With the developing complete, he began to print test strips, setting the blacks up first to establish the base exposure for the print — the shadows, the corners, the smoky flavors in the air. From there he could draw out all the light he needed, the cool surface of the Chrysler Building's layered walls with the seven curved tiers of its crown glinting in the October sunlight. As he worked on the building's pinnacle he could only visualize a syringe: sterile stainless steel. But the spire had blunt imperfections. The architect, William Van Alen, had tried to create a needle-nose point (a "vertex," Van Alen called it), the philosophic pin for an infinity of dancing angels. But in spite of his intentions, Van Alen had missed the clinical possibilities that David was after.

It took another hour to find a syringe. He breezed through the library, and eventually (in his parents' old standby, *Hauser's Pictorial Guide to Family Medicine*) he found exactly what he wanted — a photo of a two-inch hypodermic needle used in the mass immunizations of the fifties.

He took the encyclopedia back to the darkroom, laid the picture on a black felt board and cranked off five exposures. The composition was beginning to explode in him. He forced himself to grip his rising excitement, to squeeze it into a hard ball as he developed the new print. Taking it through the developer very slowly, he stopped when the needle had a cold steely sheen. By bleaching the needle he could intensify the brightness and transform the tip into a brilliant dotted star. With the effect complete, he superimposed the needle of light over the Chrysler tower. He curled his fingers against his mouth and looked at it.

He lit a cigarette and stared at his original contact sheet. Thirty-six versions of the Chrysler. Thirty-six. What a damned stupid assignment. It would be very easy to despise someone like Hammersley, who gave such stupid assignments. He'd be much better off taking nudes of Sandra. Then Hammersley would see that he knew something about humanity. In fact, the only other time he'd run off a whole roll of film like this was with Sandra. God, the way her skin filled his mind, dancing there, above him. He stopped. That's it: her dancing, like the angels on a pin. He could take her and fit her on top of the Chrysler needle and perfect the vision. He snapped open his portfolio and pulled a binder from the leather case and flipped through the pages of glassine sleeves that held his negatives. He had hundreds of negatives of her, enough to fill two or three binders. But these were the portraits that he carried in the portfolio at all times — "The Crystal Session," he called them — because of the way the light had worked on her skin that day when everything became so transparent and clear. Finally, he found the shot, the one he'd taken from the apartment door looking back into the room with the sunlight all around her, the one where she lay naked on the floor.

He held the negative against the spot lamp. Then he placed the new negative of the Chrysler building with the syringe tip under Sandra's body. How to make it fit? He'd have to reduce her portrait to a scale that matched the building. Either that or enlarge the needle ... or simply, *multiply* the effect. A whole series of Chrysler towers, a bed of them, like a bed of nails. Right, then lay Sandra down on top of them, the steel tips pressing against her skin. He would show it all: the immense desire she had, the pain of her beauty pressing down on the Towers of Man.

For the next hour his silence became a bottomless well. All day he'd been aware of his own quietude, but now it formed a deep pool, and he immersed himself there. He sank down, down, letting his hands run the mechanics of the duplications, making twelve syringe-tipped spires, cutting them with a razor then gluing them into place in three-by-four rows, spaced evenly in a rectangle that filled one frame of what would result in a master negative. He watched the picture emerge as though he had nothing to do with the process, nothing to do but watch and observe the way the picture formed itself in his hands. After the buildings were laid out, he trimmed the outline of Sandra's body and eased her onto the needles. Then above the towers and her body in the right-hand corner he brushed in a small crescent moon so that it hung in the morning air, luminous and bored.

With the collage completed, he rephotographed it with the copy camera, developed the negative and printed four test strips to determine the best exposure. He always used a high-contrast number four filter, and he had to burn in and dodge around the towers to create the right balance of light among the buildings, the moon and Sandra's body. When he reached the point where he didn't know what to do next, the point where if he did anything more he might destroy whatever he'd achieved, he stopped. After he developed the print, he sat on the wooden stool next to the workbench and examined the picture under the light.

He sat thinking, drifting with the photograph in his hand, sealed in the light-tight room and wondered if he'd gone crazy somehow. How could he do this to her? But then he decided that this wasn't Sandra any more. He'd transformed her into someone else. Joan of Arc, Helen of Troy, Cleopatra — it didn't matter which one. They all had the same sacrificial value. She only needed to be brilliant, with full breasts and thighs and the willingness to suffer this perversion. In fact, she didn't even have to be willing. As long as she existed that was all that mattered. Eventually someone would track her down and bring her to the altar. Absurd. Demonic. Yet in this picture, at the heart of the ritual, he could feel his own despair.

Chapter Twenty-One

David sat up in his bed and pulled the stack of postcards from the night table into his lap and began reading the most recent one, written in Jayne's tiny, immaculate script:

17 April, 1969
   Dear David,
      I've finally figured out that the Philippines is made up of six different worlds. First there's the peasants: poor, barefoot, illiterate; everything to make you sick about life. Especially when you see them pulling their carts through the streets, leading their water buffalo past the Mercedes and Cadillacs. Then there's the world of the rich, the men and women dressed in silks, gold, polished leather. And there's the military, the communists, sects of faith healing fakirs — and the last group — which includes almost everyone — the Catholics. On Easter, dozens of them were crucified. They carried crosses over their shoulders through the streets and then mounted them on a hill and had their friends nail their hands and feet to the wood. It's so they can share Jesus' pain. Incredible. I thought it was supposed be the other way around — you know, Jesus suffered in order to save us. But

here, life runs backwards. Maybe it's backwards everywhere. Think so? Anyway, now I know I'll be coming home. I don't know when, but soon. Maybe in the summer so we can all spend a week in Cape May together. I just realize that I've got to get back to present-time. I haven't been. I've been stuck in the past. Did I ever tell you about that? I will, I promise.

Love, Jayne XXOO

David flipped the card over and examined the picture: a statue of Christ crucified on the cross with filaments of blood painted on his face, tiny rivulets streaming from the crown of thorns and down his forehead. In spite of his obvious pain, something overwhelmingly crass cheapened his passion. The statue looked like it had been cast in a rough mould and cranked out with a thousand other suffering Jesuses, then quickly painted and sold in a flea market for a few dollars.

David pressed his head into the pillow and stared at Jesus' face. He was not about to believe in God again. He didn't believe in anything; he just wanted to feel everything — the bed, his skin against the sheets, the spring air slipping through the crack in the window over his face and neck. But he thought about the end of the world and all the people who prayed so patiently for it: Jehovah's Witnesses, Christadelphians, Oral Roberts and thousands, maybe millions, of evangelists waiting for the resurrection of the dead. He thought of all this, and then of what Jayne had told him years ago, that she believed in Nothing-at-All. She'd said it like that, in capital letters as though Nothing was a divinity. But David couldn't understand how anyone could believe in Nothing.

"You actually believe in Nothing?" he'd asked.

"Well, maybe it's just that I refuse to believe in

Anything," she'd said, correcting herself. "Once you believe in something, like money or your country or God, then you end up a capitalist or nationalist or evangelist, and then your whole sense of reality is screwed. And when that happens, you're no good for anything except adding to all the misery that's killing the planet." Was it really that bad? Were they all killing the planet?

As he clicked off the reading lamp, the telephone rang. Don't answer it, he thought. However, after three rings he turned the light back on, cradled the phone to his ear and just listened.

"David?"

"Yes."

"It's me."

"I know it's you. Who else could it be at four in the morning?" He looked at the bedside clock. "Make that four-thirty."

"Look, I just need to talk a minute. So don't make me feel guilty, okay? "

He rubbed a hand over his eyes and then looked up at the ceiling.

The speckled stucco shimmered in the lamplight above him. "All right. Not guilty. What's new?" He didn't really need to ask; every night for a week the same despair ran through the line: Rose sitting out the night alone. As she waited for the morning light, she needed to hear a familiar voice at the other end of the telephone.

"Robert's really zooed tonight."

"He's zooed most nights. Either zooed or pissed."

"Yeah, but tonight he's different. He's been eating mescaline all week, and now it's really taken hold." There was a pause, as though she'd pulled her head away from the phone. Then she was back, whispering:

"And he wants revenge."

"Revenge for what?" David sat up and pressed his back against the headboard of his bed. "What did he say?"

"He didn't say anything. It's just this long threatening innuendo. I don't know. Sometimes I think it's the gun."

"Whose gun?"

"Robert's gun. Who the hell do you think I'm talking about?"

David looked at the postcard again, at Jesus' sad, bleeding face.

"Besides ... listen. I'm getting these things ... these pellets coming at me. You remember that time last summer on the balcony?"

"When Robert started shooting at the loons?"

"Yeah. And also at the book launch, and before that, too." Rose took a deep breath and sighed into the phone. "It's these small bullets trying to get me. They're trying to kill me."

"You mean ... you think they're real?" He almost laughed, but he knew he couldn't. When she phoned like this, in the night, it was as close as she ever got to the truth with him.

"They're real to me!" She almost screamed it, and then quickly tucked her breath back under control. "What difference does it make — if I see them coming at me, if I can feel them? I can even smell them. I'm telling you, someone's going to kill me." Her voice rose and then dropped into a trembling moan. "So what difference does it make if they're real or not?"

"None, I guess." He looked down at the carpet, and his forehead slumped into his free hand.

A silence floated between them, and Rose sensed she

might lose his sympathy. She tried again, this time with a calm urgency to her voice.

"And the thing with Robert is that he knows all of this. I mean, he knows what's happening. He's in on it."

"What do you mean, he's in on on it?"

"I'm not sure. But he can make them stop. Sometimes, when he sees them coming at me, he can make them stop." The sound of her voice shifted, as though she'd switched the phone from one hand to the other, then back again.

"Look, I've got to go. But I was thinking maybe you'd come over." She could feel her voice out in midair, as though she'd just jumped from a cliff. "I mean, I need somebody to come over before he wakes up." She floated, waiting. "What do you think?"

David poked his index finger through the coil of telephone line. Yes, he could go, he thought. Force himself to go downtown and stay with her. "All right. But I don't know what you want me to do."

"Just ... " Rose sucked in another long draft of air. She didn't know either. She felt she was dropping through the sky and only her words were able to fly, somewhere up above her. "Just come by for breakfast." Then in another breath she added, "Have you heard from Mom?"

"No."

"Don't tell her any of this, okay?"

David tightened the telephone wire on his finger.

"Okay?"

"Sure. I never do."

"Never?"

He let it hang. Why did he always have to assure her of what he wasn't doing? "Bye, Rose."

She hung up without another word. David clicked off the light, rolled back onto the bed and turned from the phone so that his back pushed into the pillow and he faced the river. Then he looked at the window shade, at the small lines of moonlight penetrating the room. He saw her very clearly there, her face against the window: her long red hair, ironed into flat, straight bands along her back, the dark sunglasses, her lips pinched tight, and her voice always cracking through the husk in her throat. And now there were these bullets, ready to cut her down.

Do you really believe in that kind of curse? he asked her.

I believe what's there, I believe what I see, she said from the window.

Ah, what you see: a classic mistake. Never trust your perceptions. Ever since Einstein it's not scientific any more. Even time is an illusion. There's only the speed of light left to us now. It's the only constancy. And that's all the camera can capture. Just the light. All the people, all the buildings, are just shadows passing before a flash of light. They come and go: this man, that love, some passion and joy, eternal hope and a horror of dying — they're all shadows flying through the light.

He clicked on the lamp and Rose vanished. Sleep was impossible now. He wasn't empty enough for it. He swung his legs over the side of the bed, and rubbed his feet on the nylon carpet until they burned a little, stood up and lifted the shade from the window. A quarter moon hung over the river. He watched it a moment and then went into the bathroom and showered. When he finished, he stood in front of the mirror and wondered what he would do. He watched his penis, then toyed with it, tried to play it into an erection. Nothing. Then he shoved his genitals between his legs and took three pictures of himself like that, naked in front of the mirror, his penis hidden under a swatch of dark pubic hair.

Title: "Post-Castration." Or something in Latin, for Rose: "Homo Androgynous." He let his testicles flop free again and thought of Sandra, of the fact that he couldn't love her, and his penis wormed back into its bush of hair.

Why couldn't he stay with her? He needed to answer that question, answer while he stood naked like this with nothing but his skin and his face and eyes to look at. Because he was afraid. Terrified. He'd sooner choose nothing than risk losing her. *Choose Nothing-at-All, because there is no pain in Nothingness.*

Then it occurred to him that if he went downtown to Rose's apartment, he might have to kill Robert, and what a strange thing that would be. Maybe everyone thought of killing Robert once they knew him well enough. But how to do it? To actually kill him? With the gun, probably. Wait until he got drunk enough and then take the pistol and blast him out of everyone's misery.

He looked very closely at the mirror. He examined his eyes, the black pupil at the center of each iris where Samantha said she saw everyone she ever got to know. The soul holes, she called them. But standing two inches from his own face and looking into the center of his soul holes, he couldn't see the possibility of killing anyone. He had no impulse for it. He knew he could handle the gun, even cock the hammer and hold it up to Robert's nose. But from there he would have to wait for the impulse to fire, wait for the electric shock to run from his brain into his index finger and pinch the trigger tight. He'd seen it before (hadn't he?) when Rose had done it all without thinking. The impulse had hit her twice. Without thinking, she'd fired twice, straight ahead at Brad Watson's face.

He walked over to his dresser and pulled on some underwear, a T-shirt, his Levi's. And then, digging through the rolls of socks in the bottom drawer, his hand caught the edge of an envelope. He rubbed a finger over the embossed printing on the cover: Reich's Photography Shoppe. Inside, the three-inch square photo of Brad was perfectly preserved. He'd reshot this picture with his Canon and printed a few five-by-seven glossies of it, but nothing stood up to the original. He thought that one day he should show this to Rose. Perhaps if she examined it carefully she'd see how simple death could be, how its stillness ascended through the air like a mist rising over the river. He closed the envelope and tucked it into his pocket. Then he slipped on his socks and shoes and left the townhouse.

Chapter Twenty-Two

Rose sat in a wooden chair next to her apartment window and looked onto the corner of Seventy-eighth Street and First Avenue. Her feet rested on a small coffee table littered with newspapers and coffee cups. Fingers dangling under the open window sash, she touched the steel rods that Robert had bolted to the outside window frame. He'd installed the bars the week after the police had mistakenly smashed through the glass in pursuit of a rapist who'd broken in on Myrna next door in apartment 2C. The noise of shattering glass had scared the man who escaped down the hallway. Myrna had ended up in a psychiatric ward.

At first Rose didn't mind the idea of bars shut over her windows; they made her feel secure and she could swing them open whenever she liked. But three days later Robert lost the gate key. Now, whenever she sat by the window to gaze into the street, she had to deal with the steel bars. She was locked in. And if she was locked in, she reasoned, then she was nothing more than a prisoner. Robert had put it all in place; he installed the gate on the window, locked her inside and promptly lost the key. What a bastard. She drummed her fingernails against the bars and listened to the sound of them tapping over the noise of the First Avenue traffic rushing north past the intersection. As she listened and watched, she imagined being free.

She'd waited for David for three hours. This morning, late in April, the sunlight cut across the asphalt in a slash clipped by the tops of the buildings. Pieces of garbage lay in the gutters next to the trash cans on the road. Down on the sidewalk, Jake leaned against his magazine stall and cut the binding wire from a bundle of the *New York Post*. Then he loaded the newspapers onto a rack and lit up a Camel. Jake Garanzi. He called her Miss Rose and every day he asked, "Howza poetry going good, Miss Rose?" She'd tried to make a poem using that as the first line, but she couldn't find an ending for it. Sometimes a poem would come all at once, like a flock of sparrows landing on the wires just outside her window where they nibbled a few seeds from the sill. Other times, the words came rarely and alone, like a raven or even a hummingbird, and she had to capture them one by one and cage them together. But lately, there were no birds at all; since the gate had been locked shut, they refused to feed at her window any more.

She turned her head from one end of the street to the other, then back past Jake's stall to the corner. Suddenly a tiny flash caught her eye, and she turned away. Were they back again? She stood up and pressed her face against the curtain. Was it the birds or the bullets? Another flash. From the corner, next to the apartment building on the north side, an arc of sunlight blazed into her eyes. She blinked and held the curtain tight in one hand. Something flashed and disappeared again. This time she could see it perfectly: down on the corner, David focussing his camera on her. Snapping goddamn pictures. Each time the sun caught the edge of his lens, it flashed at her. "What the hell are you doing?" she called out to the street, but even with her mouth pressed against the bars, she held her voice back. She didn't want to wake Robert. Not now.

"Christ." She pulled the curtain closed and tied on her running shoes. Then she went down the hall to the bedroom. Robert sat propped up in the bed, leaning against the headboard with his feet spread straight along the mattress. His eyes were closed, and two paintbrushes jabbed through his fingers like stilettos. Lying at his feet, Spunky raised her head to look at Rose, then snuggled her snout against Robert's ankle. Rose poked her fingers into the ceramic jar where he kept his spare change and found three one-dollar bills. She shoved the money into her jeans pocket and went out the door and down to the street.

"Come on," she said, grabbing David's sleeve. "You can't just stand here taking pictures of my bloody window all morning."

David looked at her. Why not? he wanted to ask, but instead he said, "Are you all right?"

"Come on, I'll take you for coffee." Rose tugged on her brother's sleeve again. She pulled him around the corner onto First Avenue to the donut shop where they served bottomless-cup coffee for a dime. They sat in a booth so that she could face the window and watch the street. "Do you want coffee or not?" she asked when the waitress came.

"Sure." He laid the Canon on the seat beside him and examined her eyes. They were very bloodshot. He looked away and wondered if she'd let him take a picture of them, a close-up of her eyes.

"Here." She offered him a Marlboro, mixed a spoon of

sugar into her coffee and waited for him to light their smokes.

"You look tired," he said after his first sip of coffee. Right away he was worried about saying this, worried that anything he said about her would hurt her.

"Of course I'm tired." She leaned forward over the table and pressed her lips tightly together. "I've been up all bloody night, every night, for a week now."

"Look." David shook his head and then steadied it. "Stop getting angry all the time, okay? I'm just making a small comment about how you look, and it's as though I called you the Sunday Slut of Babylon." He felt a sudden burst of energy rising through his chest and arms when he said this. It made him feel strong. "You were the one who called me in the middle of the night — every single night last week — and asked me to come down here for breakfast to protect you." Then he looked at the coffee and cigarettes and felt cheated. Where were the bacon, eggs and hotcakes?

"I didn't ask you to protect me." She eased back from the table and sipped her coffee. Although she hadn't asked for protection (never, never), somehow it was comforting to see David stand up for himself like this. "I just wanted you to come and be with me."

"Why?"

"You're my brother, aren't you?"

"Rose ... why?"

She took a long drag from her cigarette and leaned against the vinyl upholstery. "Look, if I knew why, then I wouldn't need you, would I?"

"Come on. What does that mean, anyway?"

"Shit. I don't know." She examined her fingers. They were white-scrubbed, porcelain white. She always did a very good job keeping them free of nicotine; she held her cigarettes with the tip pointing up, so the rising smoke never touched her fingers at all. For a moment she felt like laughing over this small measure of pride.

David watched her eyes. He could tell that she might fall apart, that she might disintegrate right here, right now, but he wasn't afraid of that any longer. In fact, more and more, her disintegration seemed essential. Complete collapse was the one thing that had to happen. "So what does this have to do with Robert?"

"Nothing." Very, very clean fingers, she thought. Ten immaculate siblings. Dectuplets. Suddenly she realized that she wasn't going to laugh after all. She felt the welling at her eyelids, a tight, hard pressure building behind her eyes. They started to hurt. Why the hell did they have to hurt so much? "I mean ... everything," she confessed. "It has everything to do with Robert."

"And what about the gun? And the mescaline?"

She nodded, her head rising and falling in broken skids. "Yes. Of course. It's all got to do with Robert's gun."

"Why did you marry Robert, anyway?"

She turned her head so that a strand of hair fell over the side of her face and David couldn't see her eyes any more. "You want to know?" she whispered. "Do you really want to know?"

David looked at the side of her head, the red hair brushed out in thousands of straight threads, webbed a bit at the ends, and the cigarette moving back and forth from her mouth.

"I'll tell you." She wiped her wrist over her eyes and then turned back to him. "I've gone over and over it so many times. Not only Robert ... everything. It's like I've been crossing lost ground — searching for something that's gone forever." She looked at him steadily. "You know, you're the only person who can fit it all together. I think it's the one thing I've dreaded so long — the fact that eventually I'd have to come to you with everything."

His shoulders lifted slightly and he leaned toward her. "But — "

"Just" — she held her fingers above the table and let them drop — "just listen, okay?"

She took a deep breath and stared through the window. "I married Robert because I thought, I thought at the time, that is ... " She held her hand across her mouth and waited. *Oh Christ, this is hard to tell.* "Because I wanted to have a baby. In fact, I thought I was going to have one when we got married. It was perfect: Robert wanted a baby, and I wanted a baby. You know? Someone to make up for what happened. There would be this baby that I'd have and that would cement everything together.

"And so Robert would paint and I would write and we'd have this baby, and we were going to do everything so much better than the way our parents had screwed it all up." She glanced around the donut shop and back to the tip of her cigarette. "You know, with their inability to examine life and realize, 'This is Life,' and then actually *love* it."

He noticed that her face was wet, but he couldn't see any tears.

"And then, as it turned out, I wasn't pregnant at all. I was so sure, you know, absolutely certain of this baby growing inside me that I even named him. It was going to be 'Brad.' But that was just to myself, just for me."

David fingered the photograph in his shirt pocket, the picture he'd brought with him of Brad lying dead on the basement floor. Should he give it to her now and let her see how utterly simple death was?

"Listen, I've never told that to anybody." Her eyes were

bloodshot. She looked straight at him until he had to glance away.

Rose wiped her face and went on. "That's about the time when Robert started working commercially. Doing all this work with the APA. In advertising and making money. Then around the same time I went in for some tests and found out I was sterile. I mean, I am." She lifted the Marlboro to her lips and laughed a little as she exhaled. "That's one of the things I always have to tell myself in the present tense. That I *am* sterile. It makes better poetry that way."

"What?" David angled his head slightly.

"Never mind. I'm only half into this and I've got to say it all through for once." Her voice had lost its nervousness. Everything came out clearly and calmly, and all the brittle shells around each word fell away. "Anyway, at this point I'm not sure about the facts any more. But knowing I couldn't have Brad ... I just wanted to die."

David lit another cigarette, blew a stream of smoke between them and watched it sit there like fog.

"You see, ever since he died ... " She glanced at the window, then back at David. "Since *I shot* him ... " her voice stumbled and then continued, "I had this idea that I'd have a baby and that would make it all up somehow. But then, when I couldn't, well ... " She cut herself off, took a breath and started again. "That's when the bullets started to come at me."

She looked at him for a moment. "No, that's not exactly right. The bullets have always been there, hovering, kind of. Right after it happened, they showed up even then. But now, now they're coming to get me.

"And so ... " She cupped her hand over her mouth and looked at the wall, the vinyl upholstery, the smoke and coffee vapors rising in the air. "And so that's why I started to make Robert want to kill me."

"What?" David leaned forward again. "You wanted Robert to kill you?"

She nodded calmly and sipped at her coffee. "Yeah. I think I convinced him of it." Her eyes opened wide, as though she just now understood. A flash of panic swept over her face. "He's going to shoot me. Today."

"You mean you've actually set it up? Told him to kill you?" David could feel his voice rising in his throat. "This is goddammed crazy."

"Nobody set it up." Her lips tightened and she pressed forward. "Nothing's ever verbal like that. Everything's a tone with Robert. Just shades and nuance. Don't you understand that? But it's going to be *today*. I know it."

"How do you know?"

"Look, just believe it okay?" Her face was white, and the blue in her eyes had become steel. "I know it."

Chapter Twenty-Three

As they walked up the stairs to the apartment, David heard his lungs wheezing. He breathed in shallow notes, flats and sharps, terrified this coarse music in his chest would waken Robert and bring him out with the gun.

"Just pack everything into this suitcase." Rose threw her raincoat and umbrella onto the sofa and pulled two Samsonite bags from the hall closet. She seemed to know exactly what she must do get her clothes and books and a few other things from the bedroom. She'd decided that Robert could keep the rest. But the closer she got to the bedroom, to Robert himself, she realized how foolish it would be to try to take anything at all.

As Rose eased open the bedroom door, Spunky raised her head and yawned. Robert hadn't moved. His head still lay slumped onto his chest and the paintbrushes were still propped between his fingers. She reached past him to the far side of the bed for her watch and the small string purse that hung from the bedpost. As she moved, Spunky yawned a second time and barked. Nothing loud, just a small throaty moan. But then she barked again.

Robert's head jerked forward. "Hey, Rose." His eyes blinked bits of sleep away, and he dropped the paintbrushes onto the bed and snaked an arm around her waist. "Shit, what a buzz."

"The buzz is still on, Robert. Go back to sleep, okay." She pulled his arm away, grabbed the purse and went into the living room.

"Robert's awake," she said wheeling into the kitchen. She wanted to move very quickly now. The faster she moved, the sooner she'd be gone and she could feel clean and calm again.

Twisting the focus ring, David pointed the camera at her as she walked from room to room. He got two or three shots of her face whirling around, the red hair sweeping past her shoulders.

"Look, what the hell are you doing?" They both heard Robert flushing the toilet. "Put the goddamn camera away and help me."

But David took another picture of her like that, her face telling him to stop taking pictures, the thin lips opening and closing, pinching off the details with her teeth.

"Hey, Daydoe."

David turned and took another picture: Robert, with his hand held against the slumping side of his head.

"Jeezus. The old shutterbug out snapping pics of the in-laws just at the break of day. And what, may I ask, occasioned this little photo festival?" He dipped his arm into the fridge and snapped the cap off a bottle of Miller beer. "Want a beer, anyone?" He poked his head back into the living room, and pressed his cheek against the door frame for stability. "Holy fuck, have I ever got a buzz!"

David was about to take another shot when he smelled the dog. The thick, wet smell of dog hair was trapped in the carpet, the sofa, the curtains.

"Lucid, eh?" Rose walked into the closet and brought out two coats and a jacket. She dumped them into the open suitcase.

"Eh?" Robert mimicked. "Yes, my little Canuck cluck, I'm about as lucid as they come. Now what the hell's going on?" He shut the suitcase lid and looked down at her. A little beer spilled over his hand and Spunky licked the foam along his sleeve, her tongue flicking out in long, pink slashes.

"What does it look like, dear?" Rose turned her face to him, opened the suitcase and began to fill it with handfuls of books. "I'm leaving you." Her voice was high and tense, but she felt she had to keep it tauter than Robert's if she was going to find the power to leave him. "And I'm leaving now."

"Ah!" Robert backed away from the sofa and sat down in the easy chair next to the barred window. "And that's why Daydoe has made his appearance. To rescue his wayward sister in a moment of distress."

Rose stopped packing a moment and frowned at him. She could hear a slight whistling and wondered if he'd plugged in the kitchen kettle. "Who says it's a moment of distress?"

"Don't kid yourself." He tipped the Miller to his lips and sipped the beer without blinking. "You've got it written all over you. That the time has finally come."

"What's finally come?" David looked from Rose to Robert and then to Spunky who crouched sleepily at Robert's feet.

"The end, Daydoe." Robert swept his arms around the room and then pointed to one of his paintings on the wall.

"Yours, mine and ours." The painting was done in blues, all of it, a huge blue wheel turning slowly like a thirteenth-century mill wheel grinding wheat into flour. When he looked closer, David could see the surface of the wheel inscribed with hundreds of tiny sapphire letters: IBM, AT&T, ESSO, AMEX, APA. As it turned, the wheel tossed groups of people — all dressed in suits, ties, skirts, blouses — tumbling into the air, their faces screaming into the soft blue void.

Rose heard the whistling again. The muscles tightened in her neck as she listened. "What's that?" She held her hand up and turned her head an inch. She heard it again.

"What's what, Rosie?" Robert held his lips over the top of the Miller bottle and whistled into the glass. "Hear something inaudible?"

Rose didn't answer. She walked into the kitchen and began rattling through the drawers.

"You know she's psychotic, don't you?" Robert asked this as though he could have been asking for the time, or for directions to a bus. He rubbed a hand through his shaggy hair and sipped at the beer. "She thinks something's trying to kill her. That there's an avenging force of nature seeking retribution because she killed Brad." He started laughing, then covered his mouth with one hand. "And she thinks it comes in flashes and whistles and beeps."

"She told you about that?"

"Of course. We're intimate, Daydoe; she tells me everything. And there's no mystery to it — it's simply driven her bananas."

David didn't say anything. He sat down in the wingback chair opposite Robert and pressed his back into the cushion. He wanted to feel very small, invisible if possible. He fit the camera to his eye and twisted the focus ring without framing anything. In and out, in and out. He felt comfortable like that, just twisting the ring. Then he noticed a pile of dog turds on the floor next to the window, but he couldn't smell them. He inhaled and the room smelt like dog hair and coffee and car exhaust. He swept the camera across the floor and spotted two, three, four more piles of excrement littered around the apartment.

"Stop that!" Suddenly Rose stood at the kitchen door. "STOP doing that with the fucking camera." She strode across the living room to him. "In fact, give it to me."

David glanced at her eyes and then her hands. One hand reached toward him for the camera and in the other she held a gun.

"Give it to me."

He slipped the camera strap from his neck and passed the Canon to his sister. Her hand sank slightly, as though it weighed more than she'd expected. Then she turned to the wall, lifted the camera over her head and threw it towards the window. As it smashed into the steel bars, the lens shattered behind Robert in a spray of glass fragments. The film advance and focus ring flew free, bounced off the sill and into the street. The rest of the camera bumped against the coffee table and the back snapped open, exposing the roll of grey Kodak film.

David felt his heart driving, racing through his chest. "Why did you — "

"I did it for you, for Christ's sake!" Rose's arms hunched in front of her. She held the gun in her right hand, like a coffee cup, her index finger poking delicately through the trigger guard. "For the last ten years you've been living through that thing. Now that someone's finally had the guts to smash it for you, maybe you can see that fact for a change!"

"Looking for a change, Rose?" Robert's voice was calm, a still lake lapping the sand. "Is that what this is all about? First the idea of leaving, and now this, with a gun in your hand?"

"Yes!" She listened for the whistling, but it was all gone. There wasn't a sound anywhere. Even the traffic had died. "You're bloody right there's gonna be a change."

David could feel the blood pulsing through his ears. He pressed himself against the cushions until he was impossibly small and all he could hear was the drumbeating of his blood.

"So this time you're going to plan it all out, hmm? I thought with Brad it was an accident."

"It was an accident!" Her eyes widened, and the skin in her face stretched over the hardened tendons and bones. "Of course it was an accident."

"But not this time, huh?" Moving the Miller bottle just enough to tip it into his mouth, he took a sip of beer. "It was *two* shots with Brad, wasn't it?"

"Yes, it was two." Rose's fingers were perspiring. David could see the dampness glistening on her hands as they squeezed against the gunstock. "What does that prove, anyway?"

Robert whistled over the top of the Miller bottle again. One slow note resonated there.

"I said, what the fuck does it prove?" She held the gun up now, pointing at the ceiling.

Robert tilted his head toward her. "Do you remember what Nietzsche said, Rose? 'When you look into the abyss, the abyss looks into you.'"

"Don't start that on me!" She walked along the carpet and stood beside David, as far away from Robert as possible. Then she leveled the pistol at him. Tiny dots of perspiration splayed along her forehead.

"Rose, your face has gone white. I think you should sit down." Robert spoke with calm deliberation, with a certainty that made David think he could save them, save all of them, even Rose. Then Spunky climbed into the chair with Robert and cradled her snout in his lap. He lifted one hand and pulled his fingers through the dog's matted hair.

"Rose." David could feel his voice vibrating inside his chest. He felt very small sitting there, but he thought he could talk to her now. "Rose, I think you should put the gun down and let's just leave."

She stood with the gun pointing at Robert's face, at the soft bulb at the tip of his nose. She tried to think about how she felt. She wanted a feeling for all of this, but she detected nothing except the lonely sensation of leaking, of water pouring out of her body and leaving only the worms behind.

If Robert was going to save them from this he should do it now, David thought, and he could hear his heart beating under his chest. "Rose —"

"SHUT UP!" She clamped the pistol in both hands. She was leaking so badly that the gun was beginning to slip in the moisture of her fingers. She looked at Robert, but it was very difficult to see him through the water. The perspiration dripped into her eyes and she closed them to blink the salt away and she felt —

CRAAACK. The pistol snapped back in her hands. She opened her eyes and realized the gun had fired.

"Rose!" David pulled himself up from the chair.

She looked at Robert and then at the gun. Her mouth dropped open and hung limply. Then she raised the gun again, cocked the hammer and pressed the barrel to her temple.

"No!" David's hand banged across her arm and knocked the pistol free. When it hit the floor, it fired again.

Rose's hands folded over her ears and she dropped to her knees. Her eyes squeezed shut and she began to wail in a taut, high voice.

"Rose?" David looked at her hands clasping her ears. At first he thought the sound of the gun discharging had frightened her, but now he realized that she was pulling her hair, balling it in her fists and tugging so violently that her head shook from side to side between the tension of her hands. "Christ, stop it!"

"She will." Robert pulled himself from the sofa and walked over to the gun. He picked it up, rolled his head slightly and with a flick of his wrist popped the bullets from the pistol into his palm. "That was bloody close," he said after a moment. He turned his head and looked at David as though studying something in him.

David glanced at his sister. She'd curled into a ball on the floor and her crying had diminished into dry sobs. "Give her a hand, all right?"

"I just did." Robert slumped onto the sofa and wrapped his arms across his stomach.

"What?" David stood up. "What the hell do you mean by that?"

"Just what I said." Robert dropped his face into his hands and David could see that he was badly shaken. "The last six years I've been helping her." He brushed his fingers through his hair and glanced around the room. He saw a bottle of scotch on the floor and picked it up and took a swig.

"Like hell you have."

"Look, Daydoe." Robert stepped toward him with the bottle locked in his hand. "I just sat here while your sister played out the family fucking curse. If you think anyone else can take her that far down the line, then go get him." He took another shot of scotch and walked back to the sofa. He pulled his saddlebag from under the pillows and dropped the pistol into one of the pouches. "And now it's up to you to figure the next move. You're supposed to get your camera now, aren't you?"

David looked at him and stepped backwards.

"Isn't that what happens next?" Robert sat down and tugged on the scruff of Spunky's long hair. "You're supposed to run out and get the camera and start shooting pics of the place. That right? Isn't that what happens?"

David felt the wall behind him. He glanced at the camera pieces strewn across the floor.

"Well, whatever you decide bro', it's your play." Robert stood up again and brushed past him into the bedroom.

For a moment David felt the urge to run out of the apartment, but he stood next to the wall, frozen in place.

After a few minutes Robert walked back along the hallway with a suitcase in one hand and the saddlebags draped over a shoulder. He whistled once for Spunky and lifted a key ring into his fingers. The dog sauntered off the sofa and followed him to the door. Robert turned once more to David. He was about to say something, but he closed his mouth. He frowned, then went out the door and banged it shut.

At first David concentrated on Rose's breathing. That was all he cared about, the fact that she could still breathe. Then for a while he focussed on the window. As the grey light streamed through the steel gates into the room, it split into six rectangular bands that cut across the wooden floor and over Rose's legs. He imagined that as the afternoon passed, the light would shift and eventually slip past her body and onto him, then across the door and finally it would narrow into one bright sliver before it disappeared. God, he thought, he couldn't wait that long. He couldn't wait at all. He walked to the window and looked outside. Then he heard his voice calling into the street below. He saw a news vendor beneath the window and he called as loud as he could. "Help." He held onto the bars and pressed his lips through the steel gates. "Help. Help me!" he yelled. The vendor looked up at him and David waved his hand through the grate. "Up here!" he screamed. "I'm here!"

Chapter Twenty-Four

When the news vendor, Jake Garanzi, saw Rose lying on the floor, he lifted her head in his hands and examined her eyes. "Come on," he said to David, "we have to get her to the hospital."

Together they carried her down to the street, and within twenty minutes a taxi had dropped them off at New York Hospital. Jake shook David's hand and tipped his leather hat to Rose as he left, but Rose didn't acknowledge him. She stared at the far wall of the emergency waiting room. David sat beside her and wrapped an arm around her shoulder. From time to time he tried to talk with her, but when she wouldn't reply, he thought it just as well. Instead, he examined the people around him: a black teenager bleeding from his arm, two children crying, a pregnant woman clutching at her stomach. For a moment, he compared each one to his sister. None of you have it as bad as Rose, he concluded. Not even close.

Eventually David had to complete a sheaf of admission forms and then describe what had happened in the apartment that morning. The admitting nurse called a psychiatrist and David found himself explaining everything once more. The doctor nodded quietly, and after inspecting Rose's eyes and feeling her pulse, he whispered privately with the nurse. Finally he signed the bottom of Rose's admission papers, and two interns led her down the corridor and into an elevator.

Standing outside the hospital on Seventieth Street, David could feel his knees shaking. Now what? he wondered. Now what the hell was he supposed to do? He reached to his shirt pocket for a cigarette, but instead he found the photo of Brad. What a mistake. What a bloody mistake, he thought. For a moment he wanted to rip the picture in half. The last thing she needed would be to see Brad's face again.

He walked south along First Avenue, made his way down to Grand Central Station and caught the next train to Hastings-on-Hudson. As the train slipped under the city, he examined his face in the window. Was he supposed to look different now, now that he'd dropped his sister off and left her sealed in some looney bin? When the train emerged from the tunnel, he turned his eyes from the window and thought of Sandra lying naked on the floor, of how beautifully he had captured her skin in his best photos of her. That was the place, the one good place, where he could lie down with her and never let the world in. As the train crossed the Harlem River, he closed his eyes, and in the comfort of his mind, he lay beside her on the floor and slid his hands between her breasts, into their warm, soft protection.

When he arrived home, no one was at the townhouse to meet him. As he pulled the key from the lock, he called up the stairs. "Mom? Dad?" He listened for their voices.

What had Rose told him about the family? She'd been so insistent that day when Robert brought the U-HAUL to move her out of the house. Everyone has left this family, she'd said, everyone except you.

Yes, he thought, everyone except me. With the key digging into the palm of his hand, he wandered through the house, up and down the stairs, into each room and back down into the basement. He was searching for signs of life. He began poking through drawers, dressers, the closets and cupboards, like a soldier rifling a house evacuated by unseen enemies. He had the idea that everyone had disappeared and left him alone to sift through the remains. It was up to him to find what had to be found. But what was it? What was lost and how could he find it?

After a futile search he sat in one of the wicker chairs in the den and watched the sunset fading behind the Palisades. He felt a wave of exhaustion roll through him. "Face it, you're wiped," he said and laughed a little, aware that he was talking to himself. "Yeah, bleached right out." He rubbed his face with his hands and then looked around the room. "I give up. There's nothing here," he called out. "I've been looking for the past hour and there's nothing here any more!" The words felt good rising through his chest, and he walked over to the hallway and screamed as loud as he could: "Goddammit, you're not going to leave me alone here!"

The sound of his voice filling the house energized him, and he ran up the stairs to his bedroom and packed his clothes into a suitcase. Then he collected his portfolios, binders and all his photography equipment together. He carefully loaded everything into three reinforced boxes to ensure that nothing would be damaged in the move. He would need some money, but he had the two hundred dollars he'd held back from his spring tuition. And there was the money Granny had given him. All of it in the bank. He could get that tomorrow. Yes, tomorrow everything would be different.

The apartment was on the top floor of a five-story walkup on the lower end of Avenue of the Americas. The apartment had one open room and a bathroom. Next to the entrance, a kitchen area had been constructed around a sink and countertop. Beside the sink, a twin-element stove top had been installed above a half-height refrigerator. Above these were two cupboards and four open shelves which held some glassware, plates and cooking utensils. In a small plastic drawer, a collection of mismatched cutlery had been bundled together with an elastic band. The bathroom had an open tub with purple plywood framed around the exterior and a toilet with a flush box mounted on the wall just below the ceiling. When he pulled the flush chain, David noticed five drops of water slip across the bottom of the box and onto the green wallpaper. He flushed again, and another five droplets beaded across the box to the wall. The bathroom sink was broad and deep, mounted in a linoleum countertop which ran six feet, the length of the bathroom. After measuring the room dimensions, he decided that he could build a makeshift darkroom here.

He walked across the apartment to the window, opened it wide and leaned on the rusty platform of the steel fire escape. The room looked west across an alley and faced another apartment building that rose eight stories. At most he'd get two hours of direct sunlight a day. But the apartment would likely be quiet, he thought, and silence would be an asset. He closed the window and tried the furniture.

He lay on the bed, sprawled across the sofa, positioned the wooden table beside the window and sat in one of the two chairs. He gazed into the alley. From here, he tried to imagine what living in this room would be like. He would spend hours in this chair, looking back and forth from his photographs into the ravine below. It had to work. There had to be some connection to make living here worthwhile.

When he stood, he noticed a small tabby cat walking along a window ledge of the apartment building opposite him. It would make a lovely picture, a study in textural contrast: the striped cat hair brushing against the uniformity of the stone facing. But without his camera, he could only compose the photograph mentally. He could try that for a while, the way crazy old Hammersley worked, with the art form reduced to an internal experience. Rose had forced this on him when she'd smashed his Canon — smashed it like she was doing him some kind of favor.

He watched as the cat brushed its back over the grey stone exterior and began to mew and rub its claws against a glass windowpane on the third story. Then the window opened and two hands lifted the cat off the ledge into a room. Through the window David could see a man and a woman, both of them naked. They cuddled the cat between them and rubbed its fur over their skin. For twenty minutes he stood with his face pressed to the window sill and looked down at a sharp angle into their apartment. Their heads were cut out of his view, and only their arms and chests and legs were exposed to him. Fascinated by the clipped vision he had of them, he watched how the breasts and hands cupped together and the way the legs brushed and interlocked. Finally a pair of hands reached over and shut the curtains. David eased away from the wall and paced around the room. He stood at the window again and waited to see if the curtains would be pulled open.

After ten minutes he walked down the five flights of stairs to the manager's apartment and paid his first month's rent.

Two months after David moved into his new apartment, Jayne returned from the Philippines. When he first saw her, she smiled and wrapped an arm around his waist and rubbed her hand along his ribs.

"I'm back!" she said, unable to stop smiling. "See, I told you I'd be back." She swept a hand through her hair. The sun had bleached it a silvery blonde, and her lean face and arms were deeply tanned. She led him to a window table in Small Libertys and looked into his eyes. "Are you all right?"

"Of course." He glanced about the room. "I live just three or flour blocks from here."

"You have to invite me for dinner, you know." She waved two fingers at the waitress and called out "coffee" and grinned at him. "God, I'm so excited to be back in the city." She eased into the chair and exhaled a long plume of cigarette smoke. "But tell me about you."

The waitress brought their order, and he felt happy sitting with his favorite sister again, drinking coffee in the restaurant as it filled with the morning light. He told her about getting a picture printed in France, on the back page of the surrealist magazine, *L'ARCHIBRAS*. None of the American magazines would touch it, he explained, but the French loved it, although they changed his title from "Martyr to the Towers of Man" to simply, "Towers of Man." A mild improvement, he granted. He showed her the spring 1969 issue and she seemed genuinely struck by the twelve Chrysler buildings with their needle-nose tips pressing under Sandra's skin. She said that sometimes that was exactly how she felt — impaled by all the perverse obsessions of the world.

"So you must be doing well at NYU?" she said once he put the magazine away.

"It's not as inspiring as it could be," he said, glancing past her at two couples strolling into the restaurant from Washington Square. "And really — this is going to sound like bragging — some of the profs can't teach me a damn thing." As he talked, he thought of trying to explain why he'd dropped out. But he hadn't even rationalized it to himself. And he hadn't told anyone. The idea of leading everyone on about his successes at NYU seemed very attractive. He'd even thought of announcing scholarships and prizes he'd won for the work he'd published. He knew that losing his college status meant he'd be eligible for the draft and that meant soldiering off to the war in Vietnam.

"What about Sandra?" Jayne turned her head and examined his pale, dry face. The thin brown hair that he brushed back and forth with one hand made him look fragile, almost delicate. "I bumped into Samantha the first day I was back in town. She said Sandra hadn't seen you in a long time. Is that right? For over a year, she said."

He narrowed his eyes slightly and stared at the arch in Washington Square. It looked so French in this brash, Afro-Anglo atmosphere.

"Do you want to hear what she said about Sandra?" Jayne sat up and held her fingers against the edge of the table top.

He screwed his eyes shut. "No. Not really." Not knowing is best, he thought. Besides, he knew Rose was right: being in love — the vulnerability of it — terrified him.

"She still wants to see you, you know."

He shook his head slightly and sipped the dregs of coffee from the bottom of his cup. "You want another? Here, I'll buy." Rather than wait, he walked over to the cash register, tapped the waitress on the shoulder and asked for the coffee. As he sat down at his table again, he began to prod Jayne about the Philippines. "What was it like?"

"Another world," she said without smiling.

"Yeah? What about the mission? And the people?" He tried to be enthusiastic, but more than anything he just wanted her to talk. He wanted to watch her face, the familiar movements of her mouth as she spoke and unravelled the mystery of her world.

She kept her eyes on him as she explained how everything had seemed when she'd arrived. "You can't imagine it, the people are so poor. At least in the country, where I had to go. I just couldn't stay in the cities. They're disgusting; everything about Manila is completely corrupt." She sat back in the chair and stared across the room. "So after my first three days there, I went straight up to the mission and began working. Even though I'd never been to one before, the mission seemed like the one place I could relate to."

David nodded and lit a cigarette.

"The missionaries really push their religion. They wanted me to convert to Catholicism — to get me up in front of the cross. But they want to help the people too. They're the only ones really working for the peasants." She described Sister Mary and Sister Ruth, two nuns who labored in the fields with the people every day. Then she described their daily life and how the missionaries added prayer to the routine so there was a sense of hope that helped everyone whenever the communists raided the village, or the army retaliated, or the police began a new round of interrogations.

As she spoke, David realized she'd been in the Philippines for almost three years. It had changed her, made her more optimistic. "Do you believe in God now?"

She drank some more coffee and looked at him carefully. "No. But I do believe in *life*."

"You mean you didn't believe in life before?"

"Oh Christ, I don't know. Look, I went there thinking" — she shook her head a moment, then turned back to him — "I guess I thought I'd find some kind of redemption, that somehow I could save everything I'd lost, save myself from the fact I'd lost my baby."

David blinked. Of course, her baby.

"I was supposed to help the peasants dig wells and irrigate their crops, to teach the kids to read and write and add. Very simple stuff, but to these people it was the world. After a few months I got to know some of them pretty well. Better than most people I've known all my life. And that's when I realized how they lived. There were so many young women there, David. So many of them with babies, and I realized that most of them weren't married. Hardly any had a man around because most of the men went into the cities to hustle for money or into the bush to fight the regime. It was always one or the other. And when they did come back, for a day or two at a time, some of the girls would get pregnant, and then their parents and uncles and grandmothers took them in, and they'd all raise their babies together. The babies belonged to all of them, you see. The whole community, all these poor, poor people, would take the babies in, and nobody would even think twice about it."

She dug through her purse for a handkerchief.

David sat up and reached across the table for her hand. "Are you all right?"

"Yeah ... I'm fine." She squeezed his fingers and pulled her hand free. "Do you see what I'm saying? Against all the horror and pain and misery, there's life itself. My little girl's out there with life itself. And she's okay. I really believe that."

Yes. He wanted to say yes, but instead he simply nodded.

Jayne put the handkerchief back into her purse and lifted a small plastic envelope in her hand and held it out to him. "Did I ever show you this? They gave it to me when I left the hospital," she said evenly.

"What is it?" He rolled his face toward her, relieved to hear the calmness in her voice.

"From the baby." She smiled. This small packet that she'd kept for the last eight years was proof of everything she'd endured. "It's a lock of her hair." She handed him the clear envelope. "I stole one of your photograph envelopes for it," she added. "Do you mind?"

He frowned at first, then his mouth turned in a wry smile. "Yeah, I forgive you." He pinched the glassine envelope between his thumb and index finger and examined the lock of hair in the light from the window. Was her hair still this fine, he wondered, still such a soft, light yellow? Could this little girl be outside right now? What if she were standing outside the door or running through Washington Square with her flag of blonde hair flying in the breeze? He stared through the window and gazed into the street at the hundreds of people crossing back and forth in front of him. He tried to contain an image of them all in his mind, a wide-angle freeze-frame which held everyone in place.

Chapter Twenty-Five

In mid-July David took the bus to Cape May to visit his parents. Jayne had arrived a day earlier, and as David unpacked his suitcase she told him the news: "Rose is being discharged tomorrow. She's coming down in three days."

"But I just visited her in the hospital last week." David placed a handful of socks into the drawer and stared at his sister. "She didn't tell me anything about getting out."

"Me neither. Anyway, looks like we'll have a family reunion after all." Jayne rolled her eyes and smiled. "At least Mom and Dad will be happy."

"Yeah, happy forever." But David doubted it. Especially when he considered the new domestic order his parents had established in Cape May now that he'd moved into his apartment. His mother sat for hours on the porch and watched TV game shows every weekday afternoon. She'd relegated most of the household chores to Harris, who vacuumed the floors, washed the laundry and cooked all the light meals. Occasionally he left part of the dinners for Catrina to prepare. It seemed an odd division of his mother's labor, and David wondered how she managed when Harris departed on his overseas trips.

Three days later on the way to pick up Rose at the bus depot, David told Jayne that he'd never seen their mother "so flat."

"You can't worry about her," Jayne said. "She's living her life. You've got your own to worry about."

He eased the Buick into a parking slot next to the terminal and glanced at her. "You think I've got worries?"

Jayne turned her head towards the depot doorway. "You said it, not me. Hey, there she is!" She reached in front of David and beeped the horn. "Over here!"

David watched Rose step through the entrance from the terminal and walk toward him. When she leaned into the car window, he laughed, uncertain what he should say now that she was free again.

"You must be the welcome committee," she said, slipping onto the front seat beside her sister. Rose's hair was cut very short. In a brisk phantom movement, she tried to brush it over a shoulder with her hand, just as she'd done for as long as David could remember.

"You bet we are." Jayne kissed her softly and then lifted her small suitcase over the seat and dumped it onto the back floor.

As he started the engine, David turned to Rose. "You want to take a drive around or just go straight home?"

"Drive," Rose said. "Drive and bloody thrive!"

They all laughed. David drove the car onto the Garden State Parkway, then into Wildwood and along the beach front. The traffic slowed for the tourists ambling across the roads, and he had to dodge several kids who ran off the sidewalk as they chased a frisbee. As the car idled at a crosswalk, David could feel himself waiting, waiting for Rose to tell him something, to explain what had happened in the hospital, or what had become of Robert. None of it had come out during his visits with her over the past three months.

"Hey, let's hit the beach," Rose said when a car at the curb pulled away from a parking space. "It seems like years since I've been down here."

Jayne bought some egg sandwiches, bananas and Coke, and they walked down to the shore. David felt the urge to hug both of them, to wrap his sisters in his arms and stroll along the water the way he'd seen it in a hundred TV clips. But the commercial image stopped him, and instead he listened to them talking about the color of the water, the heat, the smell of cocoa butter.

They sat on a log facing the sea and ate the sandwiches and watched a group of children running in and out of the surf.

"So when did you find out about being discharged from the hospital?" David finally asked. "You didn't know about it two weeks ago, did you?"

"Yeah, Dr. Minton had been talking about it for a while." Rose pulled a few tufts of her hair through her fingers and toyed with an unlit cigarette in her free hand. Then she lit the cigarette and flicked the wooden match toward the surf. "I just didn't want to get anyone's expectations up."

David glanced at Jayne. Behind her he saw a couple amble past them, then veer away towards the lifeguard station. A few yards along the high-tide line, some kids threw a wet tennis ball back and forth. "Well, it's good you're out," he said when no one else offered anything.

"If you spent one night in that place," Rose said as a

cloud of smoke rolled from her mouth, "you'd know what I mean."

Jayne buried her bare feet in the sand and carefully raised her toes so that only her toenails were visible. "You mean they didn't tell you when you could start planning to come home?" she asked, cupping some sand in her hands.

"Planning?" Rose crunched the sandwich bag between her fingers and shoved it against the log. "Every person in there — every single one — has enough trouble *just being*, let alone planning!" She stomped over to the shore and stood bristling, her back to them, but still within earshot.

David rolled his arms together in the folds of his shirt sleeves. He looked at Jayne, who was sifting sand through her hands. She whispered, "I'm sorry, Rose." The last grains of sand drifted to the beach and she dusted her hands against her jeans. "Look," she said in a louder voice, "I was just trying to — "

"No." Rose swung from the water back to her sister. "It's okay. I mean, thanks." She took a few steps toward them and cocked her head to one side. "I just ... I'm just finding it hard to believe that I'm here, that's all. That I'm 'out.' Can you understand that?"

Jayne nodded and stared at the waves slamming onto the beach.

Rose rubbed her hands together and walked back to the log. After a moment she sat down again and drank from her Coke can.

"Come on." Jayne stood up and balanced on the edge of the log. "What d'you say we head back."

"In a minute, okay?" Rose lifted her purse onto her lap and folded her arms around it. "I've got something I want to show you."

Jayne walked around the log and eased herself down next to David.

Rose opened the bag and pulled out an envelope. "It's from Robert." She held out a handwritten letter for her brother to see. "He's in New Mexico now."

"He wrote you?" David hoped that somehow Robert had disappeared forever.

"Uh-huh. It's a typical Robert letter. Here, why don't you read it?" David looked at her eyes; suddenly her face seemed so clear. She lit another cigarette from the ember of her first and passed the letter to him.

He cradled the sheet of paper in the shade below his chest and began to read:

Rose,

I had a telepathic dialogue with Dr. Shrinkwrap, your renowned chief medicating officer who informs me that the traffic of your whirling spectral vision has been reduced to zero and that you've been cleared to land. This after what? Three months of calibrating the dimensions of the yellow walls of Bellevue? Well, I dare say you needed it. It was time. Once you fired that gun off I figured it was time we all needed it. So I came down here to where D. H. Lawrence tried to straighten out and then I discovered some things that I thought you should know about:

One, it's definite that when you shot Brad it was an accident. I realize this because you missed when you shot at me. You hated me and you missed. I went back to the apartment and I saw where the bullet hit the wall. It was six feet off. You wanted to kill me — but not Brad. Didn't you say that in the basement in Toronto it was dark, and he was in some kind of cellar? And you had your eyes closed. See? You hated me; and you missed. You're a shit of a shot, kid, and you can thank God for it. (But then if you want to take up loving

God you might as well stay right where you are until they completely medicate all your spunk and vaporize anything resembling your soul.)

Two, that you never really loved me and therefore any remorse about us is a mockery. I was a ticket out of your life and you should recognize that. Maybe you do already — I don't know. You were a way out for me, too. Somehow you let me believe that I could do whatever I wanted. But it wasn't true was it? Neither of us could do what we really wanted. Let's face it, without the truth there can never be love, just the deception of desire. Doesn't sound much like me, I know, but for the first time I've come to face all the bullshit about myself. I'm just alone now and thinking. No booze, no drugs. Just me alone.

I found the two shells from the bullets you fired and send them along. You need to look at them carefully. Please notice: they're empty now. Emptiness is a universal quality — if you can find it. I took Spunky, too. She misses you at night, she told me so yesterday before she went to sleep. New lesson for me: even dogs have souls.

Get clear and stay there,
Robert

David folded the letter into the envelope and passed it to Jayne. Once she began reading, he slumped onto the beach, pulled off his sandals and rested his neck against the log. He listened to the soft roll of the waves as the tide dropped away from them.

"And he sent these along, like he said." Rose held the two bullet shells in her fingers. They rolled together, making a tiny clinking sound as they touched.

David took the shells into his hand and examined them. He put his lips to one and whistled into it. "What a shitty thing to do."

"No, it's not. He's trying to show me that it's all over.

That I don't have to ... " She opened her hands in front of her face, moving them away from her head.

Jayne dropped the letter in her lap and looked at Rose, at the pain lingering in her eyes. "Hey, you don't have to do anything," she whispered.

David lifted himself back onto the log beside her. "Look, are you all right now, Rose? I mean really okay?"

She curled her lip and stared into the waves. She would never be sure. The worst part was the fear that the bullets would come back to haunt her. What would she do then? "Well, I guess the medication worked. But I won't need it anymore now that I'm out." Dr. Minton had said she'd need her "meds" until Christmas, but Rose had stopped taking them the day of her discharge. She thought that if she got off the drugs, the fog lingering in her mind might dissipate and perhaps her poetry would come back. That was the essential thing, that the doves of poetry return home. Certainly she'd be okay then.

"Yeah?" Jayne reached past David to touch Rose's hand.

Rose smiled and nodded her head as if to say, don't ask any more questions about sanity. Nobody knows. Nobody.

She glanced at David and Jayne and turned her face away. "You know, I really think he did love me. Don't you think so?" She curled her fingers tightly together and pressed them under her chin. "Just the fact that he sent me that letter. If he didn't care — if he didn't care at all — he wouldn't have sent anything, right?" She rolled her face towards them again, and David could see her eyes welling slightly. "And the fact that he said we never loved each other, that was just to make the end easier. Christ, I know it's over. But he did love me, once."

David noticed that her voice was very soft, that all the roughness had disappeared.

Healing the Dead

Jayne passed the letter back to her sister, but David held onto the shells. He guessed that it didn't matter if he kept them. What mattered was that he could finally take the bullets away from her. "Christ, what a screwup," he said after a while. "Who the hell ever let everything get so screwed up?"

"That's the one thing I've figured out," Jayne said. "It's not anyone's fault. It's the world. But if you can keep on living, if you can just survive, you can let the damned, crazy world go on its own."

The world. He thought about the world while Jayne lit another Marlboro. It struck him that both Jayne and Rose had almost been ruined by "the world." One because she'd had a baby and the other because she could not.

He squeezed the shells in his palm and jumped up from the log and ran along the edge of the water. His legs pumped against the earth. When he passed the tide line the sand was compact and hard, and he could feel his feet cutting into the surf. He lifted his arm into the air and pitched the bullet casings out as far as he could. He watched the empty metal hulls drop into the ocean — somewhere out of sight, somewhere far into the past.

As he drove the Buick around the corner and up to the clapboard house, David could see Catrina sitting in her rattan rocker on the porch, screened off from the flies and mosquitoes that she hated. In the kitchen he saw Harris inching his neck closer to the double-sash window as the Buick rolled into the driveway. Then as David pulled Rose's suitcase from the car, he could hear his father open the front door.

"They're home!" Harris called towards the side porch where Catrina sat. "Everybody's home!"

"Hi, Rosie!" He wrapped his daughter in his arms and drew her into the hallway. "I'm so glad you're back with us."

Rose could smell him, smell the father-smell oozing from his pores as he cradled her and pressed her head against his shoulder. Suddenly she felt too bound up in his arms and she pulled herself away.

"Do you like my hair?" She needed something to say, something to distract him from hugging her again.

"Why, yes." He cocked his head slightly in amazement. "Of course I do."

They stared at one another until David dropped her suitcase on the foyer carpet.

"Why don't you both take that up to the bedroom and then come on down and see Mom." Harris nudged David towards the stairwell. "And hey, what do you think of those astronauts? The three of them up on the moon!"

"It's really something, Daddy," Rose said dutifully.

"Isn't it?"

As they climbed the staircase, David bumped the suitcase against the carpeted nose of each step and felt the old emptiness pooling in his stomach. He left the suitcase at the door with Rose, turned the corner and leaned against the wall to settle himself. They'd become a hotel now, all of them checking into separate rooms. He felt like the porter, running their bags in and out, up and down, past and through. He took a breath and slipped down the stairs, pausing at the kitchen door to watch his father chopping some onions and mushrooms at the counter. After a moment he walked down the hall and opened the porch door, rattling it against the outer wall as the hinges wobbled in the door frame.

Halfway down the veranda Catrina sat with a stack of corn at her feet. She held one ear of corn in her hands and rubbed the green stalk with her fingers. She felt the grooved skins and the tufts of fibre that grew from the tip like a beard. In the open kettle at her feet she'd placed one cob of corn. It was immaculate, all the green skin stripped away without any fibrous hair left clinging to the kernels. From the doorway he examined her carefully. She looked like a museum exhibit, he thought, an artifact of her own life. He imagined the whole family sitting in wicker chairs, living in their own shadow, and he composed a picture of them posing on the porch in the evening, the twilight just dark enough to blur any distinguishing features.

Later, as they sat in the veranda eating their hamburgers and corn-on-the-cob, his father mentioned David's photo publication. "Congratulations," he said, wiping his chin with a paper napkin. "I know I said it before, but I just wanted everyone in the family to hear it all at once."

"Thanks. I may even win a scholarship for it." It came out before he could think. "Just a small bursary," he added, trying to diminish the lie. "You know, fifty bucks or so."

"You mean from NYU?" Jayne asked.

"Yeah, well, just because the picture was printed in *L'ARCHIBRAS*." He tried to laugh. "Or maybe just because the magazine's from France."

Rose put her plate on the floor and looked at him.

"Anyway," his father said, chewing his corn, "it's great."

"But you're not enrolled at NYU any more, David." Rose stared at him from across the coffee table. "How could you win a bursary, or anything, from there?"

David tried to swallow. He looked at the floor and across their feet. How could she know he'd quit?

"Rose, of course he's enrolled at NYU." Harris forced his voice to a calm, even tone. "He just got his grades. Straight A's, Rosie. And one B, right David?"

David looked at his father, then out into the yard.

Rose stood up, walked over to Jayne's pack of Marlboros and lit a cigarette. "I was trying to reach you two weeks ago," she said turning towards him. "I called the NYU records office for your new address, and they told me you'd withdrawn."

Finally he looked at her. "All right. So what? I got the picture published in the magazine didn't I?"

"But you've been lying to us." Jayne put her plate on the coffee table and shook her head. "Why did you lie about it?"

"Because he's got to lie to himself." Rose wrapped her arms across her chest and walked back to her chair.

"Come on, girls." Harris looked at his wife. Her head wobbled slightly, almost imperceptibly, but he saw her neck tighten and lock. "Just go easy."

"Go easy? Don't you see it?" Rose stood again. "His whole life has become some kind of fantasy that he lives through his camera."

"That's not true." David's throat loosened and he could feel his heart thudding. "You smashed my camera months ago. I haven't used one since. Not once."

"David, what I don't understand," Jayne said, "is what's happened with Sandra. You make hundreds of photographs with her, but you won't go see her. You haven't even told her what's wrong — "

"Stop it!" David slammed the table with his open palm. "There's nothing wrong!"

"Another lie." Rose moved a step closer to him. "You're living alone, you've quit school, you can't bear to see Sandra, let alone hear about her."

"So what?"

"You spend all your time making prints of her don't you?" She dragged on her cigarette waiting for him to answer. "David you told me so yourself less than a month ago!"

"Look I don't need any damn prints of her to live the way I want!" He reached over to the issue of *L'ARCHIBRAS* tore off the back page and ripped his picture in two. "I don't need any of it!"

He ran from the porch into the living room. Next to the sofa he found his portfolio, grabbed it in one hand and strode back into the veranda. "I'll show you." He zipped open the portfolio and dozens of glossy prints and negatives slid onto the floor. "You see!" His breathing came quickly as he started ripping up print after print tearing them four and five times. "I don't need any of them!"

Jayne leaned over and picked out a three-by-three inch picture from all the other enlargements. It was a black-and-white photograph of a boy's head. But there was something wrong with his face. "What's this?"

She showed the picture to David then held it up to Rose and Harris. "Is this a picture of Brad?"

Rose examined the snapshot, then Harris took the photograph in his hands and turned away. "Good Lord," he whispered.

Rose's face suddenly hardened, and she leaned toward her brother with a look that frightened him. "That's what you've been doing isn't it? For thirteen years you've been keeping that thing." She pointed at the picture. "Nursing it. Feeding it. While the whole time I'm trying to let it go." Her voice was an iron wedge hammering into him with every word. "Well stop it! Stop trying to heal the dead!"

"Rose. Please." Harris touched her shoulders and she spun around to face him.

"No! I can't stand it any more!" she screamed. "Every time we get this close to the truth you make us back off! David runs away to his camera and you — you fly off to *fucking* Switzerland!"

From the far end of the coffee table, Catrina braced her arms across her shoulders and let out a low wail that rose from the bottom of her chest. She began rocking back and forth in slow grinding motions that wobbled the wicker chair frame. She covered her face with both hands and when Harris tried to comfort her she shook him away. After a few minutes, she let him fold her into his arms. Yet even as he held her, the sound of her crying broke so harshly that David knew it would last long into the night.

Chapter Twenty-Six

As David lay on his mattress that night, he gripped the bed frame with both hands and listened to the silence that had descended on his family. He wanted to shout at them, to scream in their faces. He wanted to rake his nails along the wooden flooring until his father, Jayne — anyone — finally grabbed him, sat him down in a chair and said: Listen, this is what happened, *this is how we got here*.

But what had happened, especially to his mother? Her crying had frightened him, and even after Harris led her up to their bedroom, David could hear her wailing. Later, as he lay in bed, he finally guessed that Catrina knew everything about Harris's trips to Switzerland, and that Rose's suspicion about their father's infidelity was true. David felt a kind of relief, the satisfaction of fitting the last piece of a jigsaw puzzle into place.

A little after three-thirty he pulled on his clothes, packed his suitcase, and walked quietly down the stairs and out the back door. He left his portfolio and all his prints, even those he hadn't destroyed — just to show them, he thought, that everything they'd said about him was a lie. He started walking, anywhere at first, then over the Cape May harbor bridge, where he stopped to watch the fishing boats slapping against the rubber bumpers on the wharves, and along the coast road past the estuaries and over the four bridges that led into Wildwood. He made his way to the bus station and laughed when he considered that he could have caught the same bus a few blocks from home. Doesn't matter, he thought. Besides, it's not home any more.

He sat in the back seat on the right side, knowing that as the bus pulled closer to New York, he'd see the towers of the city, the way they nosed into the sky, and he imagined Sandra floating above them, massive in her desire. He could feel his hands embracing her luminous skin, the great pleasure he had in the perfection of her nakedness. But as the bus approached Manhattan, he noticed that low clouds bunching above the skyscrapers had cropped the tops of the tallest shafts, an effect he'd never seen before. He considered how he could print his negatives of the city skyscape to duplicate this strange truncation that joined the sky to the land through the hard, flat concrete walls. He could do it all without a camera, process everything in the darkroom with composite images so that the final print would be a picture he'd made, not taken.

Walking up the five flights of stairs to his apartment, he felt a heightened sensitivity to details he'd passed over before: the curl in the linoleum tiles, the splintered wood on the handrail, the frayed fire extinguisher hoses, the smoky odor of butter burning on a stove top. When he opened the door to his room, he stood for a moment to examine what was inside — his unmade bed, some back issues of *Look* magazine, a small pile of laundry, a plate on the table next to the window. All were traces, he told himself, evidence of his existence.

He pulled the key from the lock and shut the door. He stood still for a moment and examined the walls to ensure his photographs were still taped to the plaster. Everything seemed undisturbed: his self-portraits, Rose's hand holes, the Chrysler building, Sandra naked, Sandra pressed on top of the towers, and, as always, an enlargement of Brad alone on the basement floor. Over the last few months he'd blown up all the best pictures to eight-by-tens. Since Rose had smashed his camera, he'd begun to rework his negatives again and again, trying to perfect the prints, to capture the present moment in every one so that each subject could stand alone outside time. He finally understood why Hammersley had done nothing but reprint his war negatives for the past twenty years. He was drawing them out of time, all the casualties, the mutilated and dismembered; he was calling them up from the dead, and the feeling of power this resurrection engendered was too marvelous, too sweet, to leave for more than a day or two at a time.

He dropped his suitcase on the bed and leaned against the window frame and looked into the alley. The clouds were still packed thickly above the city. There was no sign of the tabby cat on the window ledges across the way. The curtains to the third-floor lovers were drawn shut.

He'd named the lovers "The Headless Exhibit." Almost every day he spent some time watching them as they passed the open window in the nude. Because of the downward view he had of their apartment, he'd never seen their faces, only the heavy breasts, the flat stomachs, the hair swirling over the man's back and chest. It was like any exhibit he might see at a zoo: the daily routine of animals captured in the satisfaction of their simple needs.

The next morning David buttered some toast and sat at the table to eat. He tried not to think of his family and decided that he should get to work in the darkroom. He walked into the bathroom and opened the binder which held his negatives of the Manhattan skyline. Yes, he had all the negatives he'd need to show what he'd seen. The clouds would be a challenge. Did he have anything on file — any tight, billowing clouds stacked against the horizon? He remembered the first picture he'd taken of Sandra, in Washington Square on his birthday. There were good clouds that day, clouds he'd shot with the new filter Jayne had given him. He flipped through the binders which held his negatives of Sandra. He could feel the sense of absorption which always swept through him in a wave whenever he was building a print that would really come alive. The wave was fast and deep, a rolling surf of intensity that dragged him down into the work — a place where he couldn't think. He could only react to the pressure as it squeezed him across the bottom and filled him with the fear that he might never come up for air. Then he saw a picture of Sandra next to the window in Samantha's apartment. She'd stripped off her top and flashed her breasts to the street. He wondered, what could this have looked like from Seventh Avenue? Was it possible that someone across the street had watched her posing naked on the floor as he shot picture after picture?

He closed the binder and walked back to his window. Across the alley, the curtains to "The Headless Exhibit" had been drawn open. He sat in the chair and pressed his chin to the window ledge. Someone walked past, then back again. No, he thought, there's no chance. But as he stared across the way, he felt a quiet dread building. Was it possible that Sandra herself lived below him? That almost every day for the past three months he'd been watching her without even guessing the truth?

He swung away. No. Absolutely not, he told himself. Besides, Jayne had said Sandra still lived with Samantha. But the possibility gnawed at him, and finally he walked down the stairs and through the basement into the alley. He stood with his back pressed to the wall of his own building for a few minutes and hoped she'd pass the window. But even from ground level, he couldn't see more than the ceiling and light fixtures in "The Headless Exhibit." When three black teenagers wandered up the far end of the alley, he turned away and walked to the opposite end, around the corner and up the west side of the block.

It took just a few minutes for him to reach the front steps of the neighboring building. He paused at the stair rail and then forced himself up to the front door. Go on, he implored himself, just go in the front entrance and scan the tenants' buzzers. He opened the door and stood next to the mail drop and read every name on the third-floor index. No Sandra Keppke. Not one. He walked back down the entry steps and leaned against the lamppost.

As he watched the traffic cruise past him, he felt empty, gutted by loneliness. Rose had been so right. He hated her for it, but she knew that he couldn't touch anyone. God, how he wanted to scream his pain at her.

All right, he thought, you watch. Samantha's apartment was about six blocks up on Seventh. He pushed himself along the sidewalk, and his chest tightened as he thought of what he would say to Sandra. And what he would tell Rose and Jayne when he saw them again. They were wrong. Completely wrong about him. The photographs didn't matter any more. The prints, the negatives, they could take the whole damned mass of it and burn them. Rip them to shreds. He would get to Sandra and tell her he wanted to see her again. She had to believe that he didn't mean to hurt her. And now he hurt too. God, the emptiness hurt.

Then he remembered last night — how the water rippled lightly as he flicked the surface with a finger. Normally he washed each print for about twenty minutes before he clipped it to dry on the line that ran from corner to corner across his bathroom ceiling. But last evening he had felt no sense of urgency. In fact the late hours had held a pleasant anticipation for him, for the moment when another negative had come into its perfection. He had spread all his best negatives of Sandra before him in two open binders. He'd been able to take his time with her, wash her carefully, bring her skin to its full luster. When he had finished, he had printed another series of photographs with just a shade of variation. And with each shift and change, he thought, he'd discovered something new in her — a small detail in her hand, or a gesture of her mouth that even Sandra had never noticed. There was something inviting about her face, something full of promise.

When he came to her block David crossed the street and looked above the parked cars into her window. For a moment he examined the surrounding buildings. Any number of people could have watched them that day. It was the first day of snow, he remembered, when the light had been so perfect as it came into the room. He looked at her window again and decided it would be best just to watch from the far side of the street, maybe wait for her to come down to him. Then he would walk over to her and greet her with a smile. He would tell her what he'd seen in the photographs, how he had come to understand. Hammersley. Himself. Her. Once he started to explain everything she'd have to listen to him.

The front door opened. It swung into the lobby and at first he couldn't see who was holding the door. Two older women eased down the stairway holding each other's arms. He paced along the sidewalk with his hands bunched in his pockets. Then the door opened again, and Sandra stepped onto the landing. She wore jeans and a red T-shirt and her hair was shorter but still very dark. She began walking down the steps to the sidewalk. Her face turned slightly and he saw the smooth glossy texture of her skin and her narrow lips lifting slightly in a kind of amused distraction.

He took a deep breath and began to cross the street. When she reached the sidewalk, would she move in his direction or away? He stepped between two parked cars and realized she was coming towards him. But still she hadn't seen him yet, an advantage, he thought, as he stepped up to the curb. He knew he would smile when she reached him and then he would say her name.

She glanced at him. At first she shifted her head away but in a small gesture of recognition, her face brightened slightly and without breaking stride she swept past him towards the corner.

He turned as she brushed by him. She seemed so beautiful from this angle, easy and confident. He remembered her desire for him. He could feel his voice coming up through his chest. *Sandra.* If she looked back at him — when she turned — he would smile and call her name.

He drew another breath, shallow, and said her name like a question. "Sandra?"

She turned, thought a moment. And when she spoke it sounded like an answer. "Yes."

More by D.F. Bailey

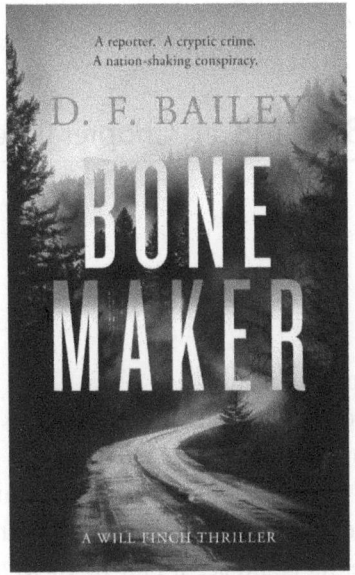

vinci-books.com/bonemaker

A relentless reporter. A cryptic crime scene. A conspiracy that could shake the nation.

Will Finch, a tenacious San Francisco crime reporter haunted by tragedy, stumbles upon a chilling mystery in the Oregon wilderness. A deserted car, a wounded bear, and a town gripped by a ruthless cop – all connected to the murder of a senator's daughter's fiancé. As Finch investigates the multimillion-dollar bitcoin scam behind it all, he uncovers a sinister conspiracy that threatens to consume him.

Turn the page for a free preview…

Bone Maker: Chapter One

A whiff of blood in the air.

The bear rose on his back feet, turned his head upwind, and flared his moist nostrils. He needed food — anything to slake the deep hunger that clawed through his empty belly. The forest, thick with fir and cedar trees, surrounded him. In the distance, he could see a blur of rocks on the hillside. His ears filled with the sounds of the spring melt rushing down the creek beds and the heavy tree limbs pulling in the wind. He listened for the sound of more gunshots and car engines but they had passed now. Still, he felt a lingering danger. He set his forepaws on the ground and made his way up the slope to the gravel road. He paused and looked along the muddy track and then walked with purpose toward his prey. As he approached, he could make out the scent of several men and their machines. He hesitated and moved forward again — a force of nature.

Hungry, willful, unrelenting.

When Ethan Argyle first caught sight of the bear he assumed it was a boulder that had fallen from somewhere above the ridge onto the gravel road. The bear stood motionless, hunched forward, about fifty yards up the track from the Mercedes GLK. But since something was obviously amiss with the car — the driver's window wide open, despite the late morning drizzle — neither Ethan nor his son Ben focused on the animal. Until it began to move.

"Look at that, Dad." Ben pointed toward the bear with his gloved hand. He dug through his pocket for his binoculars. "It's big enough, but it *can't* be a grizzly. Not here." He pressed the glasses to his eyes, then gasped at the size of the animal gnawing away at something on the roadside. "Have a look," he whispered and passed the binoculars to his father.

"It's not a grizzly." Ethan focused the lens with the nose screw. "It's a black bear. He's feeding on something," he added but he couldn't make out what it might be. "No wonder we haven't come across any deer all day."

The father and son worked their way down the hill onto the switchback. There were dozens of dirt roads like this that cut through the forest above the coast, gravel tracks barely wide enough for two cars to squeeze past one another. But today no cars were visible and no trucks could be heard struggling up the long ravine. Nothing except the Mercedes, Ethan whispered to himself. The car looked abandoned; its engine was silent. A spray of mud caked the exterior, a dusty-gray paste that had hardened in the sun and then smudged under the light rain. He figured it had been parked here at least a day, since Saturday, when it had been sunny through the entire afternoon.

"There's just something wrong about that open window," Ben said as they approached the vehicle from the rear and then stopped about five feet away. He eased his rifle into the crook of his elbow and studied the car.

"Yeah." Ethan kept an eye on the bear, who seemed oblivious to them as it nuzzled a carcass on the roadside. They stood downwind from the animal and as Ethan sniffed the air he caught a whiff of fresh kill. "He can't smell us," he whispered to his son, "but he might hear us. Keep 'er quiet." He made a downward motion with his left hand and then brought his rifle from his shoulder into his arm. "Let's look at that window."

They walked silently beside the big SUV and peered into the black interior. It took a moment for his eyes to adjust to the lack of light, and only a few seconds longer for Ethan to make out the pool of blood that soaked the driver's seat. "Good lord!" he moaned, much louder than he wanted. He looked toward the bear to see if he'd startled.

"Dad ... I think that bear took him." Ben's voice was breathless. He wiped a hand over his mouth and angled the barrel of his gun towards the bear. A defensive move, nothing more. He kept his eyes on the bear, sure that it was more important than whatever might remain in the Mercedes.

"Doesn't make any sense," Ethan said and drew a long breath before he forced his head back through the top of the window. He could see the key fob lying in the CD tray. An opened pack of cigarettes, Marlboros, lay above the dash. A half-empty bottle of water stood uncapped in the drink caddy and beyond it a discarded Starbucks cup had spilled across the passenger seat. A rain jacket had been tossed onto the back seat and a duffle bag tucked in the rear footwell. He tried to imagine what could have transpired: a lone driver crossing the switchbacks is confronted by a rogue bear who refuses to yield an inch of the road ahead.

"He's starting to move, Dad. He might be onto us."

Ethan turned his attention to the scene up the road. The bear now stood upright over his kill with his eyes fixed on Ethan and Ben. Must be six hundred pounds, Ethan murmured to himself. The bear stole a step toward them and paused as if to consider his next move.

"I might have to take him out, Ben." His voice sounded apologetic but firm.

"Yes sir." Ben stood behind his father and readied his gun. They'd done this a dozen times before when they were after deer. They hunted the old-fashioned way, with bolt-action Winchester Model 70 rifles. If one missed his shot, the second fired the insurance round. But Ben never had to make a shot like this. Not with his fingers this damp, his heart pounding.

The bear lurched another step forward, then charged. Ethan had to shoot before he was fully prepared. Still, when he fired, he thought he'd hit squarely in the bear's torso. The bear bobbed and weaved, paused to sneer with a look of puzzlement, and then staggered forward again. A second later Ben fired his rifle. The bear roared and wheeled away as its front paw dissolved into a red pulp. It clambered into the scrub brush at the edge of the road, moaning loud wails that filled the depth of the ravine below.

"Damn. Now we have to go after it," Ethan murmured and fixed his jaw with a weary determination. "It's my fault, son," he said to dispel any misgivings the boy might have. He set their pace toward the bloody, abandoned carcass sprawled next to the weed-infested shrubs beside the road.

As they neared the corpse they staggered backward in an uneven motion that forced Ben to miss a step and move behind his father. The cadaver lay on its back, the chest cavity ripped open. Nothing of the man's throat — or his face — remained. Already the corpse was abuzz with flies.

"Oh no," Ben whimpered. He sunk to his knees and began to vomit onto the gravel.

"Give me your phone," Ethan said as he turned away from the mess that lay at their feet. "We've got to call the sheriff." As he punched 911 into the keypad, he prayed for a miracle. But he knew they were off the cellphone grid and they had little hope of connecting with anyone. They'd have to hike over to the switchback above the Lewis and Clark River where he'd parked the four-by-four, then drive down toward Astoria before they could make a cellphone connection.

He pulled his son by the forearm and braced him against his side. "Come on, it won't take us more than an hour," he said with forced certainty as he directed them back toward the ridge under Saddle Mountain.

Above them he saw two hawks surfing the aerial drafts in wide, easy circles. Somewhere below he could hear the bear crash through the bush, dashing loose rocks down the ravine into the rushing creek. Jesus, he moaned to himself and set his jaw once more. What kind of mess have we stumbled into this time?

Bone Maker: Chapter Two

"Well, well, well. Will Finch — welcome back!" Wally Gimbel's wide face emerged from his office doorway when he saw Finch walk toward his cubicle at the far end of the writers' pool. Gimbel held his landline phone in one hand, the mouthpiece covered with a thumb.

"Good to see you," Will replied with a nod. Gimbel's face looked puffy and more inflamed than Finch remembered, but the voice retained the same edge of authority.

"Take a minute to dust off your keyboard," Wally whispered with a hint of fondness, an affection that he hoped the other reporters would not hear. "Then get back here in ten minutes." He winked and for a moment Finch imagined Wally was glad to see him again. "And bring Fiona Page with you," he added and turned his attention back to his phone call.

Finch continued down the aisle through the narrow labyrinth of walled pods known as "the bog" by the staff writers who complained that despite their urbane surroundings, they worked in a swamp seething with leeches and snakes. Most of them ticked away solemnly at their keyboards, a few others spoke in low tones to the digital images on their screens. The reporters had quickly learned the optimal volume to employ during Skype calls: a narrow spectrum between barely audible, and a murmur which could not be heard in the adjacent pods.

No one made eye contact with Finch until he reached Fiona Page's station. "Will!" Surprised, she pulled the earbuds from under her hair and leaned back in her chair. "Welcome back," she said and wheeled her chair to one side and waved Finch toward the guest chair.

"Thanks." He forced a smile and dropped onto the padded seat. Settled below the five-foot wall baffle, he was now invisible to everyone else in the bog. Hiding in the trenches, he thought. A good place to spend his first few minutes back on the front line.

"I didn't realize you were coming back this week." She pulled a length of hair over her shoulder and tipped her head to one side. "Sorry to hear the news." She frowned and looked away. Then she smiled a genuine good-to-see-you grin that flecked the dimples in her cheeks.

"Back at it," he said halting a little, unsure how much she knew about his situation. About Bethany and Buddy. And everything that happened after that. He forced himself to focus on the job. "So did you pick up the threads on the Whitelaw trial?"

"You bet." She opened a file on her screen and tilted it in case he wanted to have a look at her notes. "Not much to report over the last month, but I can send this to you if you want." Her tone was back-to-business.

He was silently thankful to her for immediately forcing him back into the game. Into the chase where they hunted and pecked out their daily nourishment from the world of politics, fame, sex, money, and crime — and the attempt to make sense of it all.

"Sure. Forward it, but only if Wally wants me back on the story." Finch nodded toward the managing editor's office. "By the way, he wants to see us both in five minutes in the boardroom."

The boardroom doubled as the staff meeting room at the *SF eXpress*, the internet division of the *San Francisco Post*. Willie Parson, the *Post's* CEO (and with his brother, co-owner of Parson Media) explained that the "e" denoted "electronic" and the "X" meant there would be no press machines cranking out actual papers. And no more press union, machine operators, typesetters, bundlers, truckers or paper carriers.

Like everyone else at the *eXpress*, Finch had quickly accepted Wally Gimbel's invitation to help him establish the digital version of the *Post*. If Finch had rejected Wally's offer he would have enjoyed a direct exit onto the street with a week's pay for every year of service in the old newsroom. Six years in his case. Three for Fiona. Dozens of reporters, many with more seniority, weren't offered any opportunities within the paper — print or internet. And when the cuts hit they came fast and hard. No good-bye parties, no chance to see the old news hounds off to another, better life. As far as management was concerned, the shame of teetering bankruptcy outweighed any loyalty to dismissed veterans.

"He'll want you back on the story," she said with certainty. "Did you hear what happened this weekend?"

He nodded no.

Before she could fill him in, her phone buzzed. She picked up her handset, listened a moment and said, "Okay, Wally."

"That was less than ten minutes," Finch grumbled as he

followed her toward the boardroom. He hadn't even seen his old pod, let alone dusted off the keyboard.

From the look in Gimbel's eyes, Finch figured a new crisis had hit. Something lower on the Richter scale than presidential assassination or global financial collapse, more likely another horrible mass shooting, or perhaps the long-anticipated closure of the newspaper.

"What's up?" he asked and leaned against the doorframe as Gimbel eased into a swivel chair at the head of the massive oak table. If needed, the boardroom could accommodate the entire digital-edition staff, stringers and freelancers. Roughly twenty people, ten sitting around the table (snatched by Gimbel from his old editorial office downstairs), with latecomers allotted to standing room only. Fiona stood beside Finch and then sat next to her boss.

"Close the door." Gimbel rolled his lower lip under his teeth and tapped a finger on his tablet screen. "You read the news feed this morning?"

Fiona shrugged with a sense of resignation. "Yeah ... it's hard to believe."

Finch raised his hands. "No time, Wally. Haven't even set eyes on my desk yet." He shrugged, a plea for a time out, and then realized he wasn't part of the game. *I need to suit up and join the team*, he told himself and walked behind Gimbel and sat on his left. They hunched together in the windowless room and stared at the list of links on the tablet screen.

Gimbel looked into Finch's eyes. He wanted to test the reaction, witness the surprise voltage on his face. "Ray Toeplitz is dead."

"Ray Toeplitz?" Finch glanced away. "Dead?"

Healing the Dead

Gimbel tapped his finger on the computer screen. A window popped open revealing the headline: *Key Witness Dies Tragically*. Below the text stood a picture of Toeplitz's worried face as he exited the front doors of the Hall of Justice two months earlier.

"It gets weirder than you think," Fiona said and let this idea sink in before continuing. "Did you hear that crazy story on Sunday? About a black bear dragging some guy from his Mercedes in the backwoods in Oregon — and eating him alive?" She paused to see if this registered, examined Finch with a hint of absolution, knowing that if he'd skipped the news over the past month it was understandable. Everyone understood.

In fact, Finch had purposely ignored all the news — TV, radio, papers, the web. He ignored her questions and set his eyes on Gimbel. "So what's the connection?"

Wally clicked on another link and the article about the rogue bear flashed onto the screen. "Toeplitz."

"What?" Finch brushed a hand over his mouth and quickly scanned the story. When he finished, he tipped back in his chair and gazed at the ceiling. Toeplitz: the genius with a PhD in Finance Mathematics. In his early twenties he'd made his mark on Wall Street, engineering complex hedge fund strategies that funneled millions into traders' bank accounts. Ten years ago he'd been hired by Whitelaw, Whitelaw & Joss and then promoted to the position of Chief Financial Officer.

But was Toeplitz a player in the Mt. Gox Bitcoin scam in Japan? Maybe. And was he part of the financial manipulations that defrauded investors of over four hundred and fifty million dollars? Possibly. Although he vehemently protested his innocence, as a member of his company's Board of Directors, Toeplitz was arrested and accused of fraud in a trial which everyone assumed would last at least six months. The tabloids called it "The Battle for Bitcoin."

But recently Toeplitz experienced a moral epiphany, or more likely, Finch assumed, he'd negotiated a compelling plea bargain with the District Attorney. Whatever his motivation, Toeplitz said he possessed records pointing to a massive fraud perpetrated by the senator's half-brother, Dean Whitelaw. And so Toeplitz decided to take the stand as a prosecution witness against Senator Franklin Whitelaw's investment house.

The senator himself claimed prosecutorial immunity because all his business affairs were held in a blind-trust, which he referred to as a "Chinese Wall." Another racist gaffe from the politician who'd built a populist reputation on similar foot-in-mouth blunders. Republicans loved him. Democrats laughed. Five times he'd been elected and sent to Washington.

And now came this latest episode in the most bizarre corporate saga that Finch had ever covered. Somewhere in a remote coastal forest, Raymond Toeplitz had been devoured by a bear.

Finch turned his attention back to Wally. "So there is a natural justice, after all."

"Mmm." Wally pressed his lips together and shrugged doubtfully. "I hope not, especially if we can squeeze new juice from this story. With the executive team in Parson Media threatening to roll the print edition of the *Post* back to three days a week, it would be helpful if your tale of Toeplitz and the bear could draw in a few more readers. Just to keep their office doors open another week or two." He pointed toward the floor, to the offices one story below.

They all smiled at this, at the fantasy that the digital division might save the print edition from insolvency. In any

Healing the Dead

case, Finch felt relieved to have the story pitched in his direction. Something substantial to chew on instead of the bitter fruit of Bethany's guilt and depression. And the tragedy with Buddy.

"All right." Finch sat up in his chair. A jolt of energy radiated through his chest. In his gut he could feel the story coming back to life. He never expected the fraud trial to reach a satisfying conclusion. Now a new chapter opened before them. Everything had changed. "So. Fly to where? Portland? Interview the local sheriff, the coroner, and whoever bagged the bear. Right?"

"No." Gimbel smiled with a miser's grimace. "*Drive* to Astoria, the county seat of Clatsop County. Check the map. It's on the rear end of the back of beyond. Take the company car," he added after he remembered the photo of Finch's destroyed Toyota. A total write-off. "And so far, no one has found the bear, dead or alive. But don't let that stop you. Everyone loves to talk about the one that got away. I'm sure if anyone can pick up the story from there, you can." He turned to Fiona. "Meanwhile, I want you to develop the human angle. For the first time, Toeplitz appears as a victim in this sorry tale. Did he have a wife? Kids?"

"No." Finch shook his head. "No family at all. He was a childless orphan." An interesting combination, he thought and then realized it was a circumstance he and Toeplitz now shared: no parents, no siblings, no spouse, no children.

Gimbel paused. "Then get Dean and Franklin Whitelaw's reaction to Toeplitz's demise. If he stonewalls you try Senator Whitelaw's sons. They're twins. The two boys were brought into the firm in the last few years. They probably knew Toeplitz, too. Or his daughters, there's two or three of them. Remember, both of you, we don't work at a news*paper* anymore. We're looking for the human dimension here — opinions, rumors, innuendo — not *just* the facts." This was Gimbel's new mantra based on his theory that print delivered news while the internet delivered opinion. Overall, Finch had to agree.

"You got it." Fiona pulled her notes together and rose from her seat. "I'll email you the files I gathered over the last month," she said to Finch and pursed her lips, a sign that read: buckle up, we're both in for a long ride.

Finch stood, ready to follow her when Wally raised a hand and said, "Hold up a minute, Will. I've got a few questions for you."

Wally seemed nervous. A rare moment of hesitation gripped him. "I didn't have time to check in with you." His head wavered from side to side. "I mean about what kind of workload you can handle right now. Do you think you're ready for this?"

Finch shrugged. Good of you to ask, he thought, but what I need more than anything is to slide into the old groove. More than that, to get back into my life. "I'm ready. Hell, I'm here a week earlier than anyone expected," he said with a curt nod, and when he realized Gimbel needed more assurance he added, "Look, this new angle on Toeplitz might ease me back into the routine. After a day's drive through the Redwoods, maybe I can step into the Whitelaw story through the back door."

"Good." Gimbel raised his eyes from the oak table and studied Finch's face, unsure if he could carry the load so soon. "You know, normally we wouldn't send anyone up to Oregon to dig through this mess with Toeplitz. A few phone calls would reel in the details. But since you're back a week early and still technically on medical leave, it might prove a good way to bring you in." Gimbel raised his eyebrows as if to add, so don't treat it as a vacation.

When Finch sensed that his reliability was the issue he leaned forward and stared into his editor's eyes. "Wally, look ... it's over. It's been thirty-three days." To lighten the mood he faked a smile, checked his watch and said, "Make that thirty-four."

Gimbel gazed at Finch with an expression that softened his face. Not with pity, but with an air of empathy.

Finch could understand his concern. Gimbel had assembled the *eXpress* team only ten months ago. And eight months in, just as the Whitelaw trial began to gather a national following, Finch's calamity hit. Wally had to assign Fiona to cover the trial while Finch checked out of the bog and into Eden Veil Center for Recovery. The bucolic retreat provided the space Will needed to come to terms with the black pit into which he'd stumbled, and then been shattered.

"I'm okay now. The time off did me some good. Really. It's over, I've picked myself up and I know I have to move on," he said and swept his hand toward the wall. "It's all about my job now. That's what I do." The palm of his hand hit the table. "*This* is who I am now."

Gimbel tipped his head to one side. "All right," he whispered and set his fist against his mouth. He shifted his weight, a signal the meeting might soon be over, but then he settled again and angled his wide face toward his reporter. "And what about Bethany?"

Finch leaned back in his chair, a bit startled. This was getting personal. Six months ago Wally had mentioned Bethany's drinking. Said he knew where it could lead, that he'd lived through something similar himself. Will realized that his boss needed some assurance that this part of Finch's world wouldn't blow up again. "I haven't seen her in thirty-five days. She's...." He looked into his open hands, at the emptiness they held. "Look ... she's completely broken." He narrowed his eyes. "You want the honest truth?"

Gimbel nodded.

"With luck, I'll never see her again."

Gimbel pressed his lips together and drew a long breath. "I know you think this is none of my business, but I need to know if you can stick this thing."

Stick this thing? What did that mean? Could Finch stick with the job — or stick a knife into the part of his life destroyed by Bethany and surgically remove the diseased tissue? He fixed his eyes on the far wall. "Okay. Here's the bare essentials, for your ears only: she's been suspended from her job, with pay, pending the medical examiner's report and criminal investigation. Likely there'll be a trial for criminal negligence, maybe manslaughter. I hope so. If that sounds like revenge, then so be it. I'll take my slice served cold." His eyes narrowed. "As for me, I've moved into a one-bedroom place on South Van Ness while I'm looking for something better." He felt as though he'd just climbed a steep flight of stairs. If nothing else, at least he still held a grip on the facts of his life.

Will had a sense that his managing editor wanted more, that he wanted to hear something about Buddy. But he felt that if either of them uttered Buddy's name, some kind of emotional disaster could follow.

"South Van Ness?" Wally Gimbel shook his head doubtfully, then smiled, happy to divert their attention.

"Do you know how hard it is to find a place in San Francisco for two thousand dollars?" Will tried to fix a grin on his lips but instead looked away.

"All right," Wally said and exhaled another long breath,

a sigh of relief that they'd both survived this conversation — a topic that they had to resolve before they could move forward. "I'm going to give you a week," he concluded. "Then you tell me if you can stick it."

**Grab your copy...
vinci-books.com/bonemaker**

About the Author

In 2015, D. F. (Don) Bailey published The Finch Trilogy — *Bone Maker*, *Stone Eater*, *Lone Hunter* — three novels narrated from the point of view of a crime reporter in contemporary San Francisco. Following the trilogy's success, *Second Life* (2017) launched a new saga based on the characters introduced in the first three books. The series prequel, *Five Knives*, came out in 2018. The Finch chronicle continues with *Open Chains* (2019), *Run Time* (2020), *White Sphere* (2022), and *Burnt Embers* (2023).

His first psychological thriller, *Fire Eyes*, was a W.H. Smith First Novel Award finalist. His second novel, *Healing the Dead*, was translated into German as *Tödliche Ahnungen*. The *Good Lie* (2008) is set in his adopted hometown, Victoria. His fourth novel, *Exit from America*, appeared in 2013.

After his birth in Montreal, Don's family moved around North America from rural Ontario to New York City, Mississippi, and New Jersey. "After years of seeking the ideal place to live", he says, "I finally landed on my feet on Vancouver Island — where I live next to the Salish Sea in the city of Victoria".

For twenty-two years, he worked at the University of Victoria, teaching creative writing and journalism and coordinating the Professional Writing Cooperative Education Program — which he co-founded. From time to time, he also freelanced as a business writer and journalist. In the fall of 2010, Don left the university so that "I could turn my preoccupation with writing into a full-blown obsession".

An Amazon bestselling author, he's also a ManyBooks.com Book of the Month Award winner and a Whistler Independent Book Award finalist.

www.ingramcontent.com/pod-product-compliance
Ingram Content Group UK Ltd.
Pitfield, Milton Keynes, MK11 3LW, UK
UKHW041112260226
468438UK00002B/61